THE

TASTE

OF

HUNGER

THE
TASTE
OF
HUNGER

BARBARA JOAN SCOTT

© BARBARA JOAN SCOTT 2022

All rights reserved. No part of this publication may be reproduced, stored in a retrieval system, or transmitted in any form or by any means, graphic, electronic, or mechanical — including photocopying, recording, taping, or through the use of information storage and retrieval systems — without prior written permission of the publisher or, in the case of photocopying or other reprographic copying, a licence from the Canadian Copyright Licensing Agency (Access Copyright), One Yonge Street, Suite 800, Toronto, Ontario, Canada, M5E 1E5.

Freehand Books acknowledges the financial support for its publishing program provided by the Canada Council for the Arts and the Alberta Media Fund, and by the Government of Canada through the Canada Book Fund.

Freehand Books
515 – 815 1st Street SW Calgary, Alberta T2P 1N3
www.freehand-books.com

Book orders: UTP Distribution
5201 Dufferin Street Toronto, Ontario M3H 5T8
Telephone: 1-800-565-9523 Fax: 1-800-221-9985
utpbooks@utpress.utoronto.ca utpdistribution.com

Library and Archives Canada Cataloguing in Publication
Title: The taste of hunger : a novel / Barbara Joan Scott.
Names: Scott, Barbara, author.
Identifiers: Canadiana (print) 20220231834 | Canadiana (ebook) 20220231842 | ISBN 9781990601187 (softcover) | ISBN 9781990601194 (EPUB) | ISBN 9781990601200 (PDF)
Classification: LCC PS8587.C619 T37 2022 | DDC C813/.6 — DC23

Edited by Deborah Willis
Copyedited by Suzanne Skagen
Book design by Natalie Olsen, Kisscut Design
Author photo by Jazhart Studios
Printed on FSC® recycled paper and bound in Canada by Friesens

This is a work of fiction. Names, characters, places, and incidents are the products of the author's imagination or are used fictitiously. Any resemblance to actual events, locales, or persons, living or dead, is entirely coincidental.

For Keith

because I prayed

this word:

I want

Sappho, "If Not, Winter" (trans. Anne Carson)

PROLOGUE

YOU LIE IN THE ditch at the edge of what was once the largest slough in the district, ribs grassy and waiting, empty sockets taking in the sky. Mice nest in your pelvis, once the site of such disturbance; ants and spiders war along femur and tibia. The ditch holds all your secrets, left behind with rotting flesh and sinew in soil several layers down. Whatever fires lit your belly, flamed from your eyes, ignited your dreams, have long been banked. You have lain hidden here through years, damp soil clogging nostrils and mouth and weighing on chest, above you the whispering of faraway winds, beneath you the frost heaves and spring floods that lifted you even as they wore you away. Raised you finally to the surface, exposed you to the sky. Eased you out of the earth the way living flesh eases out a splinter. Your jaw hangs open, tongueless and silent, waiting for the winds to teach you to sing.

WANT

I know
You won't
believe me,
but
it sings,
salt sings, the skin
of the salt mines
sings
with a mouth smothered
by the earth.

Pablo Neruda, "Ode to Salt" (trans. Margaret Sayers Peden)

· 1926 ·

HE FIRST SAW HER standing in a hen house, lit up by a shaft of sunlight that sundered the murky dimness of the rough shack. She seemed suspended in light, along with motes of dust and down and chicken shit lifting from the dirt floor with the slightest movement of foot or air. He had to stoop to speak to her, the low roof putting a crick in his neck and the stench of the place pushing his breath into his throat. The defiant set of her chin under his gaze pressed on his lungs like a heavy and familiar hand.

His first job in this country, a fresh-off-the-boat immigrant from Ukraine fleeing the aftermath of the Great War, had taken him deep into the Ontario mines where he'd pitted animal strength and pickaxe against a rock face deep under the soil of the gentler surface. One day he pried loose a rock that fell on his hand and smashed against his index finger. Blood darkened the nail, a dull throbbing spread from his finger to encompass his

whole body, becoming the focal point of all his concentration, his effort to stay at his task. At the end of his shift, in too much pain to eat, he buried his hand in a bowl of ice and staggered to bed, and still the pain wrenched his arm to the shoulder. Two precious dollars later and he was in the doctor's hut. The doctor took one look at the taut and shiny-black skin and reached for a drill, steadied it against the blackened nail. "Don't move," he said, and it took every muscle to obey him. The drill ground down, churning up bits of fingernail like wood shavings, tearing his nerves from finger to skull, he could hear himself grunting from somewhere far away, and just when he couldn't stand it, he had to pull away or smash that bastard doctor's face in, the drill bit through the nail and blood spurted two feet in the air. The relief was immediate, the blood bright and red; he felt strong just looking at it.

When the girl lifted her chin like that, resisting the weight of his gaze, Taras felt again that pressure, the relentless turning of the drill.

By the time he was twenty-eight he had had it with the mines. The lousy pay, the eighteen-hour work days, never seeing sunlight even in summer, what meagre life he had played out in darkness or twilight only. So he left the mines and worked his way across the country as a railway labourer, paying a dollar for the privilege of wielding a pickaxe under the open sky. Every step he had taken in this country seemed accompanied by a wedge of rusty metal piercing dull earth, one or the other shrieking in protest. Before long he'd had it with the railway too. One night in Estevan, drinking long and deeply in the hotel bar, he fell into conversation with a man sodden with booze. Wasyl, a fellow Ukrainian.

"I'm getting out." Wasyl's nose drooped over the pint of beer into which he'd poured two shots of rye. "Godforsaken country. I bought my ticket to Toronto and then it's back home to Ukraine. Fuck this place, fuck my land. I thought I'd bring my wife over, make a go of it, be a landowner. Ha!" He took a long pull at his drink, wiped the foam and spittle from his mouth. "Call that land?"

"Did you sell it?"

"Who'd be fool enough to buy it? It isn't broken yet, or at least, not more than a few acres. I sold off my plough to my neighbour, but even he didn't want more land to break than he could manage. Let the fucking mosquitoes and black fly have it, I say."

"How much you want for it?" Taras had been saving what he could, probably not enough, but it didn't hurt to ask.

"Take it." A magnanimous wave almost brushed Taras's nose. "It's yours."

"No, no," Taras said, checking to be sure he was considerably more sober than this man. "We'd have to do it right. Write up a bill of sale." Hope was sparking in him and he banked it down so this man would not sniff it out.

"Here, bartender!" Wasyl yelled. "Bring us a pen and paper." When it arrived he scrawled something onto two sheets of paper, signed both pages with a flourish then shoved them toward Taras. "You fill in your name."

The script was barely legible but Taras made out on each one: Received from _____ the sum of One Dollar for Quarter Section NE55-15-4-W2.

"You sure?"

"Much good may it do you. And that nag and decrepit wagon out front, take them too. Free gift." He let out a bitter crack of laughter. "Like the land. Curses on the government of this godforsaken country who told us we could make a living out here. Begged us to come. Fuckers. What better to dangle in front of peasants than land, eh? You have two years to cultivate, mind, or they take it back." He drank another beer with another two shots while he sketched out a map to show Taras where to find the section, his head nodding ever lower, his words slurring, the pen slipping from his grasp. Taras snatched up the map and the papers, filled in his name and signed, then stuffed one of the pages, along with a crumpled dollar bill, into the man's vest pocket, and slipped out before Wasyl could come to.

The horse and wagon were out front as Wasyl had said. Taras was trembling at the stroke of luck but also with a quiver of fear. What did he know of breaking land, or farming for that matter? He'd been raised on a farm, but his father had died when he was a child, and his mother had been unable to cope. Their tiny strip of land had barely made enough to pay the rent to the landlord, let alone the tithe to the church. But what the hell. He was young and strong. He hadn't known anything about mining or the railroad and he had managed. He stole a pickaxe from the CPR locker, threw it into the back of the wagon, and headed north.

The property was at least a week's journey away. Not wanting to spend his meagre savings until he got near enough to buy supplies, he slept in the fields or the wagon, caught fish in the streams and cooked them over an open fire, accompanied by hard tack biscuits soaked in creek water. Worked along the way at farms, sometimes for money, sometimes just for food to get him a few miles farther down the road. He was still several days from his destination when he stopped to ask for water at a weathered shanty.

There was no one by the well, but he heard a commotion coming from a chicken coop, a hut only slightly smaller than the house. He ducked his head down low to get through the doorway. Cautious. Could always be a coyote, and they got nasty when cornered. But it was a girl, fifteen maybe. If she was nervous at the sight of a strange man blocking the doorway she gave no sign. She was holding a tiny chick upside down, where it fluttered furiously. When she saw him she righted it and put it back near its mother, the hen that had been making all the noise.

She said nothing, so he had to speak first, in halting, accented English.

"Hallo? I have come to ask for vater."

"I can give you that." She spoke in Ukrainian, the sound of it as much a joy to him as her brief smile at his accent. "But I have to finish with these first." Grasping another chick firmly by the legs, she upended it. It dangled at the end of her hand as though dead.

"What are you doing?"

She didn't glance up from her task. "Seeing if they will be cocks or pullets." She placed the chick in a small slatted box in which several other yellow balls cheeped forlornly, then took up another. This one fluttered its stubby wings and tried to right itself, its small and frantic movements looking ludicrous at the end of that tanned and muscular arm, until she tucked it safely back with the hen.

"How do you tell?" As she reached for the next fluffy ball, her worn dress pulled across her breasts, the faint light from the doorway caught the curve of her arm, the glint of her dark hair. Her feet were bare and flecked with chicken droppings and their tiniest movement raised dust motes that danced around her.

She upended another chick, held it out for his inspection. It hung limp in her grasp. "Which do you think? Cock or pullet?"

"I don't know — pullet?"

She put the chick in the crate and dusted off her hands on her thighs. "Cock. It's the female that fights back."

"Why do you need to know?"

"Too many cocks in a yard cause trouble." She spoke with mild contempt. He didn't remember his mother sorting chicks on the farm in Ukraine. He hadn't paid attention to women's work. Dimly, however, he remembered the priest coming for the tithe and rejecting contemptuously the box of chicks his mother had proffered instead of money. Maybe the priest also knew the secret of sex detection and saw the trick Taras's mother was trying to pull. Or maybe he'd been just another greedy bastard.

The girl pushed past him into the daylight and fresh air. "Just one minute more and I'll give you well water. There's some up at the house." Plunging the dipper deep into the rain barrel, she rinsed her feet sparingly, returned the leftover water to the barrel, then led him up a worn track, their footsteps kicking up small eddies of dust.

"My name is Taras," he said, to her back. She walked with short, brisk strides, her whole body involved in the concentrated movement, her shoulders pulling against the faded cotton dress that was too small for her, showing more of her calves than was proper, and outlining more of her rear too.

"Like the poet," he said, wanting to impress her somehow, make her turn toward him. "My mother named me for Ukraine's greatest poet. Taras Shevchenko." He didn't know if this was true. Probably not. His mother, like most peasants, especially women, had been illiterate. He had read Shevchenko's poems as a young man fired with nationalistic fervour, thrilling to the poet's calls for Ukraine to claim her rightful place in history.

> Await no good,
> Expected freedom don't await —
> It is asleep: Tsar Nicholas
> Lulled it to sleep. But if you'd wake
> This sickly freedom, all the folk
> Must in their hands sledge-hammers take
> And axes sharp — and then all go
> That sleeping freedom to awake.

But that had been before Taras embraced communism and learned that the nation state was dead. As, of course, was land ownership. He smiled wryly, thinking of his homestead, and thankful, over all, that the girl didn't press him further on questions of poetry.

The house was larger than it had seemed from the chicken coop, but its sagging porch and loose and weathered boards, one in particular dangling from a final stubborn nail, confirmed his first impression that, whatever its actual size or number of rooms, this was a shack.

An old man in threadbare coveralls stepped onto the porch, followed closely by a crone dressed in black.

"Who's this?" the man barked.

"He's here for water," the girl barked back.

The crone spat in the dust, almost at Taras's feet, perhaps by accident. When he glanced up at her, startled, he realized she was probably no more than fifty, but her face was so deeply lined and stained with sun and labour she looked more like seventy. The man was as lined and leathered as the woman. Not an ounce of spare flesh to soften the wrinkles, his face ground into a permanent scowl. Taras resisted the urge to reach for his own face, to probe beneath the scrape of stubble for lines drawn by his own years of labour. Would he look as worn down as they in — what? — twenty years? Surely not. And this girl with her taut and glowing skin — it didn't bear thinking about.

"Well," the old man said, "I suppose we could give you a cup of tea." The woman spun on her heel and ducked into the house, banging pots in what Taras assumed was a protest.

"Olena, you finished with those chickens?"

"Yes, Papa."

"Go help your aunt." So, not her mother. Olena. A supple name, like the pull of her dress across those breasts, those thighs, as she moved to obey her father. Taras felt a stirring in his jeans and looked away, strode up the steps behind her to shake her father's hand.

"My name is Taras Zalesky."

The old man motioned Taras towards a chair. "Metro. Metro Kulyk. And that," he jerked a thumb toward the doorway, "is Varvara, my sister."

Varvara propped a rigid back against the door frame, staring at Taras, malevolently it seemed to him. But perhaps weather and age had simply sculpted her face into a constant glare. Her nose hooked down, her chin hooked up, even, by God, a wart in the middle of her leathery forehead, for all the world like the Baba Yaga from his childhood stories.

Olena emerged carrying a tray of tea things. Taras had to hide a smile. And here was the little Vasilisa, awaiting rescue.

"Sit," his host said, and Taras sat in a rickety willow chair that teetered under his weight. "Where you headed?"

"Homestead," Taras answered with some pride. "Another fifty miles or so, north. Near Quesnel Lake." He smiled up at Olena as she handed him a steaming tin cup but she did not meet his gaze.

"Bush country," Metro grunted. "Lots of clearing left to do. Best land went before the war."

"I'm not afraid of hard work." Taras opened his hands to show his calloused palms. "I've been in the mines, on the railroad. I can use an axe and spade as well as anyone."

Metro smiled. "Can you, by God. Olena," he called over his shoulder, "bring the vodka." He tossed his tea over the edge of the porch. "And fetch the man's horse and wagon up to the barn."

Several hours later the jug Olena had brought was empty, and Taras and Metro were roaring with laughter.

"So then," Taras brought his hand down on the arm of the chair, which rocked wildly beneath him, "I ran him off the place. Black skirts flapping and his cross swinging. Like an old crow!" He glanced sideways to see what Olena thought of this tale, but her face was expressionless.

"Damn priests." Metro spat over the porch railing. "Take your last egg."

"Damn right." Taras almost launched into an impassioned speech about how communism would wipe those greedy crows from the face of the earth, but reined himself in. He was drunk and talking to a stranger. Better to be cautious. His mouth was dry and empty. He tried to moisten it with his tongue. He had been glad of the liquor but what he needed now was food, and it looked like the last thing on the old man's mind.

"Brave men, in talk anyway," Varvara's harsh voice broke across his thoughts. "Olena. Go kill one of those hens since it appears we have company for dinner."

"Stay! Stay!" Metro was delighted, expansive, waving his hand as though inviting Taras into a mansion. "Maybe you'll stay a few days, eh? Help with the chores? I have only one girl now," his words weighted with sorrow. "All my other girls, three of them, gone. Married. Left. They all leave." His nose dripped with emotion, his eyes reddened. "Only Olena is still here." He peered slyly at Taras. "And who knows, she may be leaving soon too."

Taras felt the pull of his homestead, the land he hadn't seen. But even stronger he felt the pull in his pants, strengthened by the white lightning. A few days, a chance to strain those breasts and hips against him, feel the squash of flesh and the thrust of bone, crush those lips like honeyed blossoms. He heard the long squawk of the dying chicken and smiled.

"Which way is your outhouse?" And went, staggering only slightly, in the direction Varvara pointed.

They ate the chicken in a kitchen dimly lit by an oil lamp. As far as he could see it was the only room not affected by the general decrepitude of the place. The floor swept clean and not one board creaking, the wood stove polished a gleaming black, the fire flickering, and a kettle simmering over the hot water reservoir. The whole kitchen redolent of garlic, which he hadn't smelled in a long, long time, the Angliki preferring their food bland on the nose and tongue. It smelled of home, and Taras tore into his meal. Varvara snorted with what he hoped was satisfaction at his appreciation of good food. The flesh was a bit stringy, but sweet with fat. He sucked the bones and his fingers to prolong the pleasure of good meat. The old potatoes and carrots, taken from barrels of sand where they had wintered, were a bit withered but still tasted fine when boiled then tossed with butter.

All of it washed down with more of the fiery liquid that seemed in inexhaustible supply.

"Delicious." Taras stretched back in his chair and glanced once more at Olena. She too had given all her attention to her food, barely speaking a word all evening. He had told his best tales, of deserting from the Polish army and escaping into Germany, heart in mouth as he scrambled underneath barbed wire, waiting for the shouts of discovery, the shots that could end his life. Of Germany in shambles after the war and his coming to Canada in another of what was beginning to feel like a long line of escapes. She had barely looked up from her plate. Taras was puzzled. He had not lived to be thirty without realizing he was attractive to women. Not handsome, but he had something, an energy that drew women to him. They liked to touch him, trace the raised veins on his wiry arms, the bumps of spine down his back, and usually they liked to listen to him. But this one? She was polite, but mere politeness was not what Taras was used to. He found himself in the ludicrous position of having seduced the father, who, pouring steady streams of vodka into his glass, appeared ready to adore him in his daughter's stead.

He stayed the next four days, ploughing, picking rocks, and dragging stumps from the fields, doing his best to shore up outbuildings that sagged under the weight of Metro's neglect. Wasting time that would have been precious to his own homestead, attempting to woo the daughter through the father by reciting what scraps of Shevchenko's poetry he could remember, or recounting adventures of Ukraine's mythic revolutionary, Taras Bulba, all while Metro sucked up liquor and let the words whistle past him like the prairie wind.

Metro seemed to regard the situation as a huge joke. "Like Jacob and Rachel, eh?" he chuckled. "Lucky for you the others are all married, but I could still play a trick, eh? Put Varvara in your bed." Then off he'd go in shouts of laughter.

Taras couldn't puzzle out what drew him so strongly to Olena. She was no beauty, hadn't the height for it for one thing. Short, almost stocky. And he so tall, almost a foot more than she. But those muscles, their power, their precision. He could watch her carry the milk pails across the whole yard just to see the strain of her arms, the scissor step of her legs. Her lips thin with determination not to spill one drop. Every day she went for a walk, when Taras and Metro were sitting on the porch with their vodka, their boots unlaced, the leather tongues lolling away from their sweaty socks. Out across the flat fields into the sunset, then circling the house, a speck on the horizon, as though she were tethered. He ached for her to invite him on one of her rambles, even hinted, but could only assume she didn't get the hint. For a while he hoped that she walked for his benefit, giving him the opportunity to appreciate her hips, her shoulders pulled back and chest inhaling, but she ranged too far afield for this to be her motive. Yet his desire followed her, stretched thin across the fields, glinting in the evening light. Surely with the right tug at the right time it would draw her to him. He watched the circle of her arms as she swept the porch, flung grain to the chickens, the sudden swirl when one day she chased the barn cats away from the milk pans, a tornado of dust and feline hissing and girlish laughter. Watched and was helpless. He tried every seductive wile that had never failed him before, brushing her hand when she offered him bread at the noon meal, breathing on her neck ever so slightly when they passed in a room or on the porch. She appeared not to notice. It was driving him wild. He had never thought to marry before, but why not? He was about to settle on land of his own, he would need someone to work alongside him, and certainly he would rather have a Ukrainian girl than any other. Ukrainian girls knew how to work, take the place of an ox at the plough if need be. English girls were all right for a bit of fun, but not for marriage, with their need for fine houses and clothes and furnishings, their wrinkled noses when they came across the smell of honest sweat.

He found himself bending toward Olena whenever she returned from her walk, to inhale the mix of earth and sweat and open air. Once he watched a trickle of perspiration travel slowly from her neck to where her breasts rubbed together and was half crazed with desire to bury his tongue there, to lick the pure salt taste of her.

He decided to speak to her. Her father liked him. He had land, good prospects. When he caught himself thinking like this he almost blushed. She was the daughter of a destitute peasant, a drunkard old before his time, whose farm was crumbling beneath him thanks to his late-night drinking and late-morning rising. She should be glad of the offer, of the chance to get away. What was she that she could reduce him to a self-conscious schoolboy?

For two days now Metro had made a great show of following Varvara into the kitchen after dinner to help with the washing up, instructing Olena to keep Taras company on the porch. In the dusk her hair became a dark blur that blended into the night; he half expected to see stars come out in it. She sat so self-contained, so easy in her silence that he was tongue-tied the first night. The second night, when he moved his chair close to hers and she raised eyes that held no question in them, he was again thrown off balance, realizing he should have prepared something fine, articulate man that he was. Instead he blurted, "Marry me."

She turned her eyes away but not before he saw a flash of something — anger? Surely not. "But," she pushed back her chair and stumbled to her feet, for once clumsy, "you're ... old." And then, worst insult of all, she smoothed out her expression and tone and said, as though remembering her manners to one so much her elder, "I'm sorry." And left.

A few moments later Metro emerged with the vodka bottle and shrugged as he filled two glasses. Taras grunted his thanks and tossed back the shot, eyes burning. He kept them lowered, afraid to see Metro's disdain for a man who was rendered speechless by a girl, hell, a child. Anger rose in him like bile. Who was she to turn him down? So there were grey smudges at his temples, crow's feet at the edges of his eyes. He was her superior in every way. Older, yes, but wiser, more experienced, more educated, with land. He held out his glass for a refill, tossed it back this time in search of the slow burn at the back of his throat.

"She says she wants to go to school." Metro spread his hands to show his own confusion at this turn of events. "High school of all things. I tell her we have no money for that, not just school but room and board in Norfolk. Craziness. Back when Olena was small and her older sister Katya was still here to help out, the inspector came, said Olena must go to school, so she went. But when Katya left there was too much work and then the school closed so that was the end of it. I told Olena, what more learning does she need just to work a farm and have babies?

She reads and writes some, knows her numbers. Already she has more than her mother ever had — she could barely write her name. But Olena, she's stubborn. The youngest, you know. Only fifteen. Her sisters were almost grown when she was born. Her mother lived only a few weeks after the birth. I did my best..." he waved ineffectually at the air, "but without a mother's care..." His moist eyes pleaded blurrily for sympathy.

"I could have seduced her," Taras spoke between stiff lips. "I could have taken her, and made her pregnant, and then you'd never have gotten her off your hands."

"Here, now," Metro sputtered, half rising from his chair, the bottle clutched in one hand, his glass spilling vodka over the other. Taras stopped him with a gesture.

"But I didn't," he said. "I behaved with honour. Like a fool." An invisible fool, some old crony of her father's.

"Women." Metro filled their glasses again. "Who understands them? They do what they want in spite of all good sense."

Each draught of vodka spread Taras's chest wider, wider. He had worked so hard, fought so long to get here, to the Canadian steppes. For what? He understood being treated like a bohunk by the ignorant English, hated it, writhed under the jokes, the insults, but understood they could not know the land he came from, her history of Cossacks and resistance to the nations that had ridden roughshod over her for four centuries. From the time he was sixteen and running from the Polish army he had dreamed of these new steppes, this new land, where he could live the way the Cossacks had lived, with freedom and dignity. And now, here among his own kind, the same ignorance, the same invisibility. The tears rising from the hole in his chest to sear his eyes had nothing to do with Metro's vodka.

Metro slammed him on his back. "I'll talk to her. She's old enough to understand this world was not made for her. Fifteen! Her mother already had our oldest by then. I'll talk to her."

Here was the moment for pride, the moment to say he'd have nothing to do with a girl who didn't want him. But his tongue was still, swollen inside his drunken mouth. Taras nodded with what he hoped looked like dignity, as he held out his glass.

The next day he woke dry-mouthed and throbbing, hanging half out of the narrow, makeshift bed Olena had put together in the narrow storage room off the kitchen that first night. Varvara was standing over him, rock-faced. Taras scrambled to pull the bedclothes over himself.

"She will marry you." Varvara's voice was as rigid as her face, her back. She gazed appraisingly up and down his body, while he resisted the urge to cover with his hands the blanket bumping up over his morning erection, then left.

From the blaze of sun at the small window, Taras could see the family had let him sleep late. He dressed hurriedly, then entered the kitchen. Olena sat at the rough table, her face turned toward the window, away from her father who sat opposite her, her hand absently gathering invisible crumbs, sweeping them into her lap. Varvara stood behind her, a funereal presence. Taras peered across the room. Was that a bruise on Olena's cheek or only deep shadow? Varvara poked Olena's back with one bony finger. Olena pulled her gaze from the window and stared in the direction of Taras's feet.

"Thank you for your offer. I will try to be a good wife." Her gaze returned to the window and its small patch of sky. Varvara nodded dourly.

"She is a good girl," Metro said. "She will work hard for you."

Varvara poked Olena again. "Much to do for a wedding." Turning her back, she dismissed the men from the kitchen.

The next couple of days went by in a blur, with few of the usual preparations for a wedding. Taras didn't know anyone in the area who could represent him, bring presents of bread and vodka to the bride's family, or negotiate a dowry on his behalf. What use asking for a dowry anyway, when the thing was already decided? It was a hangover from the old ways, and Taras had no use for those. "What has it done for us, all that tradition?" he mumbled at Metro during another vodka-soaked night on the porch. "Nothing but kept us in chains of poverty and ignorance. Bah!" He spat into the dust and Metro spat with him, snorting with laughter. Taras suspected in many of these conversations that Metro liked the bombast, but missed the underlying argument. Varvara, however, sitting off to the side in her willow rocker, her small glass of vodka at her feet, and some task or other in her hands, gave a small, stern nod.

"Look at her, the old crone." Metro waved a wobbly finger in her direction. "No one would have her in the old country, so she came here. And still no one would have her." He banged a hand on his knee and snorted again.

"Except you, brother," Varvara snapped. "And a good thing for you I had the nerve to emigrate, for you surely never would have."

"Do you mean you came alone?" Taras felt surprise, even a stirring of respect. An almost unheard of thing for a woman twenty years ago, to travel by herself to a strange country. Not so common now, for that matter.

"There was no living with her in the old country." Metro looked mildly ashamed. "I would have gone, I was only waiting for a proper wife."

"Hard to find a wife in the public house," Varvara said to her knitting as Metro buried his nose in his glass. "You and the others practically pushed me onto the boat. Why I sponsored you to come out here I'll ask myself until the day I die." Varvara swept up her knitting, and her vodka, and stomped into the kitchen where Olena was weaving a wreath for her wedding day.

Metro waited until Varvara was well and truly gone before continuing in more subdued tones, "She had a fiancé in the old country but he died of the influenza. She never speaks of it. I came out with my wife but then she died and the older girls left. They all leave," he sniffled. "And Varvara and I," he spread his fingers wide in a helpless gesture, "we just carry on."

"You mean I push you on," a harsh voice rang from the window over their heads.

Metro brushed some wetness from his eyes. "Oh go to bed, you old harpy."

TWO DAYS LATER, with Varvara and Metro as their only witnesses, Olena and Taras were married in a clerk's office, a bare wooden space with the wrong kind of cross hung on the wall and an English service Taras heeded only partly and Olena not at all, judging from the way her eyes drifted from floor to ceiling to window. She wore a simple print cotton dress and the wreath of wolf willow that, in a nod to custom, Varvara had placed on her head before they entered the meagre building. Taras had barely had a chance to speak with Olena over those two days, only to say good morning and good night, for Varvara kept her busy cooking the wedding supper and packing up her trunk with items for their new home. This silence between them did not change, apart from the few words they spoke during the ceremony, even when they were seated at the head of the wedding table. Their guests had preceded them and had obviously been dipping heavily into the vodka before the happy couple's arrival. Metro went out to the still for another jug before the welcome toasts could take place and his return was met with a roar of approval. There were no women, Taras noticed with some surprise. Varvara had told him it was too far for Olena's sisters to travel on such short notice, but he had expected at least some neighbours, and here were only half a dozen men, all about Metro's age or older, all with the telltale red nose. When Varvara cut into the korovai, the braided wedding bread with its ornaments of grain and flowers crafted from dough, the men barely waited for the first slices to go to the newlyweds before tearing into it with their hands. Olena nibbled at hers before setting it aside. Taras chewed but tasted nothing of the bread or the other dishes placed before him. The scent of her wolf willow headdress, the warmth of her body radiating in that enclosed space, raised the hairs on his arms with desire. Whenever the men hoisted their vodka glasses and yelled the traditional wedding toast — "Hirko!" — he pressed his lips to Olena's. She submitted to, but did not return, the pressure, and he felt a twinge of superstitious anxiety. "Bitter!" An odd toast for a wedding day, even if it was followed by the sweetness of a kiss. As if reading his thoughts, Varvara, who had been presiding grimly over the proceedings, matching the men drink for drink, stood and sang a traditional song about the sorrows of marriage for a young maiden. But when one of the men made a joke about what smells like fish but tastes like chicken, and Metro opened his fly and starting dancing around with his finger jutting out of it like a tiny cock, Varvara clapped her hands — "Enough!" — and released Taras and Olena from the festivities.

She led them to Metro's room, which he had offered for the wedding night. In the light from the doorway Taras could see the bed had been freshly made, the sheets folded down, another spray of wolf willow on the pillow. Varvara closed the door behind her and the room fell into darkness, save for faint moonlight trickling through the window. In the kitchen the men were still hollering "Hirko!" and banging the vodka jug on the table, as if they hadn't noticed that Taras and Olena had left. Taras reached out blindly, not waiting for his eyes to accustom themselves to the gloom, but Olena flinched from his groping hand. He wanted to be her teacher, to instruct her in the singing of the flesh, the slow sweetness of breathing, the meaning of crescendo. He wanted to be gentle, considerate, tender. To win, if not her heart's devotion this first night, then at least her body's. He was not a clumsy man. He had had many women, not all of them prostitutes, who were expected to moan and tell you how crazy you made them. But others who had blushed in the daylight to think where he had led them.

He wanted to undress her, to unwrap her as the greatest prize he had ever won for himself. But she sloughed off her dress, slip and bra, as though she were shucking corn. Throwing back the covers, she laid herself out on the bed. He undressed himself with clumsy fingers, already rigid, feeling as though he had been erect forever, in readiness for this moment. When he slid beside her, the touch of her cool skin made him draw his breath, his desire pure pain in his groin. His hands, then his mouth, to her breasts, sucking and biting, and she totally still, not resisting, but not yielding, not melting into him as he'd hoped, imagined. He was wild with greed, tasting every place on her body, his hands still at her breasts while his mouth travelled lower, lower, his tongue tangling in the wiry hairs, and probing the opening hiding in the tangle, and then she moved, fractionally, and a sudden breath flared her nostrils, but whether it was passion or disgust or shock he couldn't tell, and couldn't wait to find out. He rose over her, parted her thighs and he could hear himself saying, "gently, gently," but the fire between his thighs was past caring, past listening, just seeking, seeking its way, and he thrust into her with a cry that rose from so far within him he thought surely she would have to answer. She didn't make a sound, but her body betrayed her, for she was slick and hot inside, however cool and unyielding on the surface. He came immediately, pouring himself into her, one hot pool into another, sperm and tears and saliva in one mighty outrush.

Then all was still. He wiped the spittle from her breast. She lay inert beneath him, while he shifted his weight to withdraw from her. Even then her vulva betrayed her, closing tight around him for an instant before releasing him.

He moved to hold her close but she was wiping between her legs with the sheet.

"It will be better, next time," he said, feeling his total inadequacy, hoping he was not lying, and realizing that depended entirely on her.

She turned away from him and slept almost immediately. But he stayed awake beside her, straining to hear her faint intake of breath, to see the slight rise and fall of her chest. He held his hand over her naked shoulder and felt the space between them as a magnetic charge, marvelling that she did not shift toward him even in sleep, so powerful was his desire. He ran his hand above her body's dim outline, not touching her, exulting in the knowledge that she was his. If he wanted, he could wake her, but he desisted. Still, that knowledge, and her scent rising from her body and his fingers, made him almost groan, and he slowly, stealthily, brought himself to climax again, straining not to wake her, her stillness next to his turmoil part of the intensity of his pleasure.

HE WOKE the next morning to a clatter he thought at first was the party still going on. When he reached across to his wife's (his wife's!) side of the bed, to hold her, talk to her about the night just passed, make love again more tenderly, slowly, his hand felt only the cold and wrinkled sheet. He opened his eyes to find the room empty. The noises coming from the kitchen were the clanging of pots and dishes, as though the cook were reminding him there was a long day ahead and breakfast still to be eaten. Throwing back the sheet he roughly scrubbed his crusted privates with water from a chipped jug on the washstand, dressed in his stiff wedding suit, and entered the kitchen. Olena and Varvara were at the black stove frying eggs and bread. Neither looked at Taras. Metro, who sat at the table, stinking of stale rye and sweat, glanced up briefly, then dropped his head in his hands with a sour belch. The old hag Varvara startled at the sound and Taras smiled to note that she too looked a little the worse for wear. So even witch's blood couldn't stave off a hangover.

Olena wore her everyday cotton dress. Her cheek and the back of her neck were flushed and Taras hoped the cause was her memories of last night, not the heat from the oven or the spit of fat from the frying pan. He wanted to give her a kiss and a hug but Varvara was between him and the stove. So he sat opposite Metro and waited for his breakfast.

Olena brought the frying pan to the table, about to serve Metro his eggs, when Varvara poked her in the back, and jerked her head toward Taras. Taras tried to brush her wrist as she scraped eggs onto his plate, but she stepped back, as though to make room for Varvara, who plunked a platter of fried bread in the centre of the table, then poured strong coffee into their mugs. The women sat, and they all ate in silence.

HOMESTEAD NE 55-15-4-W2

Nothing

will do but

to taste the bitter

taste. No life

other, apart from.

Denise Levertov, "At the Justice Department November 15, 1969"

OLENA STOOD by the wagon in her coat and hat. Taras's eyes tried to engage her, but Olena stared straight ahead — if he crossed her vision's path she stared at the horizon, the horse, the wagon, her feet. All with impassivity. Taras embraced Olena's father stiffly, thanked him for the plough and a pot-bellied stove, which they had just wrestled into the back of the wagon, trying not to show his surprise, since he had not held much hope of a dowry. The old man must like him better than he'd realized, though when they'd hauled both items out of the back of an old shed, Taras had had his doubts that either implement would be worth the effort to scrape off the rust. And with his horse looking to be on its last legs, Taras could only pray it would stand up to the extra weight and last the trip.

Olena allowed her father's brief hug but did not glance at him either. Only Varvara could make Olena raise her eyes. Varvara, holding a plate covered with an embroidered cloth, and a small sack. She handed the plate to Olena, who lifted the cloth to reveal a round, fragrant bread. The first gift to any married couple. The second, which Varvara placed in Olena's hands after she put the bread on the wagon's seat, was a sack of salt. Olena tucked the sack among the other provisions in the back of the wagon then turned to go.

"Wait." Varvara handed her a small dish made of blood-red cut glass. "From the old country," she muttered gruffly. "Because life must also contain some beauty." Olena opened her small valise and wrapped the dish carefully in her nightdress, then, ignoring Taras's outstretched hand, swung herself up onto the seat, and waited with hands folded until he climbed up beside her and the wagon lurched forward.

SWAYING WITH the movement of the wagon, Olena refused to look back as her home vanished behind her, lest she lose her balance and accidentally brush against her husband. He made several attempts at conversation: the weather, the landscape, the dryness. But after her monosyllabic replies he drifted off into silence, leaving her to her thoughts. And her anger, which she was holding back just as she was holding back her body. This man who had ruined everything, and she hadn't even seen it coming. He had watched her walking, he told her in one of their brief conversations. Watched and thought it was for him, when all the time it was just the urge to get out and away, to move beyond the circle of that small, dusty farm. To get to a town, a school, a city. Somewhere else. She smiled sourly at the irony. For she was going away, but not to any new life, just the same old life filled with the same old chores, and now with the added duty of what had happened last night.

She wrenched her mind away. Varvara. How could Varvara have betrayed her as she did? Varvara who'd come to her bedroom the night Taras proposed and said, "You must. I know you say you want to go to school, learn enough to be a teacher some day, work in a town. But this is a pipe dream and not only because there is no money for foolishness. For women there is no choice but to marry."

"You didn't." Olena shrugged herself upright and pulled the worn blankets to her chin, shivering even though the night was warm.

"Make no mistake, my girl. I am tied to a man nonetheless, and look at what a man! Your father. If ever he was a man he's long since forgotten it. While your mother was alive he worked, never hard, but enough. But after she died . . ." She plunked down on the bed beside Olena, the light from the candle on the tiny bedside table flickering in the gust of her passing, throwing ghoulish shadows onto the splintering walls. "Well, you know what he is. I do what I can but in another few years he will have driven this farm, all we've worked for, into the ground. Your sisters were lucky. They married while there was still money for a dowry, however small. But now. There is no life for you here, no money for you to go where you wish. You are not the first to be unhappy with what fate has served up. But in life you learn to eat what has been put in front of you."

Olena knew Varvara spoke the truth. Her father was a drunk and a fool. Their only visitors were the men who showed up to buy or beg the vodka he mixed up in his still, then stayed to carouse into the small hours, staggering home far past milking time. There was little chance of anyone respectable in the area offering for his daughter. Olena knew this, and Varvara knew she knew it.

"The man is no better or worse than other men."

"But *old*," Olena protested.

"Old!" Varvara snorted. "Old is seventy, sixty. Talk to your cousin Maryska, saddled with a fifty-year-old lecher when she was only fourteen! Bitter, her name means, and she certainly is. Ten years married and she looks older than he does."

Olena nodded slowly. The last time she'd seen Maryska she'd hardly recognized her, the lines in her face rigid and deep, and such emptiness staring out of her eyes, as though she'd been starved so long she no longer knew what hunger was. Olena shuddered, dragged her mind back to what Varvara was saying. "This one at least can work and isn't afraid to do it. I've been watching. He wants you badly, didn't even think to ask for a dowry. Your father is very pleased. I had my work cut out to talk him into giving you that old wood stove and plough. They are rusty but with a bit of elbow grease they'll work fine. At least until you can afford better."

Olena set her lips, but Varvara grabbed her by her bruised chin and forced her to look up. "This Taras, he has land, and a bit of money so you won't starve. You think this is nothing, but I tell you it is everything." Her eyes flared eerily in the candle's dancing flame. "There is less than nothing for you here. Even your sisters and their families don't visit any more. You must go. The homestead isn't far, but far enough."

Under the force of those eyes, Olena nodded.

This morning Olena had slipped from her marriage bed and quietly dressed, hoping for a few moments alone on the porch, watching the sunrise, settling her mind and body. Only to find Varvara, skinny frame ramrod straight, sitting at a kitchen table cleared of all traces of the night's debauch.

Varvara gave her a shrewd look and seemed satisfied with whatever it was she'd seen, then said before Olena could sit, "Come," and led her to the cabinet in the corner. "I have seeds to give you, healing plants, plants for eating, all kinds. All you need to start your own garden." With gnarled, arthritic fingers she took pinches from various small drawers and dropped them onto squares of paper which she folded tightly into tiny packages, labelled with her tortuous handwriting, and presented to Olena: beets, carrots, onion, cabbage, cauliflower, pansy, peony, tansy, bergamot. Women in the area used to call on Varvara for herbal remedies, and to help deliver their babies, but that was a long time ago. She had just started to teach Olena about the uses of various herbs and Olena had hoped to follow in her footsteps.

Now even that opportunity for a wider life had been closed off. She would be stuck on a homestead, even more than Varvara had been, all her life.

Olena blinked rapidly and concentrated on the landscape slowly clopping by, letting its vast flatness flatten her thoughts, watching the light thicken over the horizon as the heat buffeted her in waves. Taras's voice became a drone to which she murmured absent responses, her eyes on the hypnotic skyline, and he did not press her for more. Perhaps this was what he thought conversation was. Late in the afternoon he pulled the horse to a halt. "We'll stop here, I think. There's a stream, some shade. I can make a fire and we'll sleep in the wagon rather than pitch the tent. We should make an early start tomorrow."

Olena started to rise. Taras stretched out his hand to stroke her hair and she tried to evade him, but he grabbed a strand of hair and tugged, softly at first, then harder, until she winced and looked into his eyes. He seemed to pull her to him both by her hair and her eyes, until she lowered her lids just before their lips met, their kiss infused with the pain of her scalp and her anger at being mastered. Then, to her surprise, her body stirred. As though it were a thing unto itself and didn't care that she disliked this man, that with her mind she never wanted him to touch her again. Her body rose to meet his lips, harder now on hers, it arched her back, bent her will, parted her lips, softened her thighs.

"It will be better this time," Taras whispered into the hair he had released. Olena nodded, her resentment and desire so twisted together, pressing on her so heavily she couldn't speak, didn't want to speak.

Later they took the bread Varvara had given them and some dried sausage from the back of the wagon to make their first meal. But when Taras reached for the salt there was only a pool of burlap snagged on a nail. The white crystals had been draining behind them like Hansel and Gretel's trail of bread crumbs. All that was left was a small pile beneath the wagon, glinting white in the fading sunlight. Taras glanced suspiciously at Olena, then looked away when she returned only a steady gaze. She trod on the salt as she followed him to their small fire. Let him wonder.

THEY ARRIVED at their homestead three days later. Olena's lips tightened at the sight of how little the former owner had cleared, how much of what he had cleared was studded with rocks, and how much bush they'd have to attack with just the grub hoe Taras had bought along with basic supplies at their last stop, the town of Norfolk, a long day's drive back. The man hadn't even built the most rudimentary of shelters, must have lived in a tent. But as Taras and Olena walked the land together in the honeyed evening light, dry grasses crunching beneath their feet and pulling at their clothes, they discovered at least the fool had managed to dig a well. "It's good," Taras said, after he hauled up a bucket of sweet water and they each took a long, cold swallow. "And here, a stream, just like on the map. Good fishing." They washed the dust off their feet in the cold stream, grateful for the cool of the willows' shade and the air off the water that Olena splashed on her face, her wrists, the back of her neck. Her bones felt loose in their sockets from the constant jarring of the wagon, her skin taut from the beating of the sun. Taras sluiced his head in the creek, turned to look back at her, laughing and shaking droplets from his hair in a wide spraying arc, like a dog, then took her hand.

"We'll put the house here, near the stream. It's a good spot."

Olena shrugged off his hand. "Better get fishing. I'll build a fire so we can eat while there's still light." She moved back into the relentless glare of the sun and began gathering deadfall.

TARAS STRODE to the wagon and rooted through their supplies for his fishing tackle, fighting down his irritation. Give her time, he thought. Just give her time. She is young. She has never been so far from family before. But his hunger for her gnawed at his guts. A yearning not only for her body, but for warmth from her eyes, her lips, her arms. Their time on the wagon had been better, sounds coming from her throat, strangled and surprised, her hips urgent against him, her head thrown back. Still, he couldn't escape the feeling that they were more animal than human in their love play. No. More than that. It was as if all the human emotions of desire and yearning were on his side, and on hers none at all. Taras banged his fist painfully against the rough wood of the wagon. Time. Bang. Time. She was younger than he by fifteen years. She could outwait him, outlive him.

That evening as they sat by the fire eating the last of the trout Taras had caught and Olena had cooked up in a cast iron skillet over the embers, Taras told her more of his life. How he'd lost his faith in governments at about the same time he lost his faith in the church, watching his mother hand over, uncomplaining, their last coins to a landlord or priest. How he hated her for her subservience, couldn't wait to see the back of her and their hovel and that wasted little village. How the sight of a priest's black skirts swishing over his legs even today made the acid rise in his throat, such was his urgency to spit. How in Germany after the Great War you would work the day and spend your money that night because the next day it would be worth half, one quarter what it had been. It was true, wheelbarrows of money to buy bread, one week's wages to buy a shirt. You lived in the moment, working till nightfall, drinking till daylight. At seventeen it wasn't so bad. But by the time he reached his twenties, he wanted more. So he travelled to France, then on to Canada. He reached out his hand to her, to show that he was happy the long search was over.

Somehow without his noticing she had crawled into the tent while he was caught up in his stories. She was fast asleep.

The next day Taras set snares along the creek for rabbit, built a fish trap out of willow branches and set it under a small waterfall. There would be no time for fishing once they began work on the house. Metro might be a drunkard but he'd given good advice on how to make the most of what the prairie and bush offered in the way of construction materials. Taras cut down the straightest poplar poles, and he and Olena dragged them from the creek to level ground, notching and stacking to make four outer walls. They wrestled the pot-bellied stove into the centre, their muscles straining together, their breath rasping in time. He was proud of the way she could work, and laughed inwardly at the jokes Ukrainian men told of the Angliki women, too dainty to lift a finger unless to point out where their Ukrainian maid had missed a spot of dust. He watched the sweat spread under Olena's armpits and inhaled deeply whenever he got near her. By God, she was tough.

After several days, when the shell of the house stood like a skeleton awaiting flesh, they carved out slabs of sod and Olena lugged them up the ladder to Taras, her hair a tangle of grass and dirt clumps, her face runnelled with soil and sweat, her dress thick with prairie.

That night they washed in well water heated over the fire, and for the first time Olena turned to him, her body feverish with fatigue and the desire for oblivion. He thought his tongue would never tire of the taste of salt and dust, as though he were making love to his land as well as his wife.

Once the roof was finished, Taras dug a pit deep into the topsoil down to the clay beneath. Olena hauled buckets of water from the well, pouring them into the hole, then mashed up clay and water and dried grass with her feet. Together they slathered the mess all over the inside and outside of the house, smoothing it by hand, then letting it harden in the sun. Taras built a door from smaller logs, and they tied canvas over the windows. He would get glass on his next trip into town.

Two weeks after their arrival, they moved into the house. Olena swept the dirt floor until it was hard and bare and they set up a straw mattress in one corner. Taras made them each a willow chair, determined to prove he could turn his hand to anything this country demanded of him. They were a bit rickety, and his skill hadn't stretched to making them rockers, but they would do until he could buy store-made furniture. The house was too dark to sit in while the weather was good anyway. Though they needed a smudge burning constantly to ward off the mosquitoes, the evenings were cool and fragrant. The land was alive with gophers and hare and deer, the stream with trout and small pickerel. Olena checked the snares along the creek and that night they ate rabbit stewed in a black cast iron pot, washed down with some of Metro's homemade vodka.

Once the question of shelter was settled, they turned their attention to the land, starting with the grassland near the house, tearing up chunks of sod, and breaking up the soil so Olena could plant potatoes, cabbage, carrots, an herb garden just outside the door.

BY MID-SUMMER they had gone through Taras's savings, spent on window glass, some chickens, a plough to replace the rust-eaten gift from Metro which had fallen to pieces within a week. Olena had gone at the stove with a will, scrubbing with salt and vinegar until it was free of rust. It would do for now as a source of heat and simple meals. When Taras got back from harvesting for hire, with any luck he would have enough money to buy not only winter supplies but a real wood stove, maybe even a cow. In his absence Olena could get on with attacking the bush with the grub hoe, picking stones from what they had cleared so far. She nodded curtly as he ran these thoughts by her, saying she would be fine when he asked if she would be nervous living alone, especially since he would have to take the horse and wagon. As usual, Taras talked into her silence: yes, he was sure she would be fine. She had a small but solid house, a well that gave plenty of sweet water, snares to set, the stream for fish, a full sack of flour, eggs from the chickens, and the garden was beginning to produce chard, lettuce, spring onions. He worried they had no dog, but Olena brushed off his concerns. "Just one more mouth to feed." That was all she needed, one more creature demanding her attention. "I have the shotgun."

"Yes." Taras was watching her closely. "And if you are in any trouble, you can always go to the Masiuks."

Earlier that day they'd had a visit from their new neighbour, Alexey Masiuk, who would be homesteading with his wife a mile or so away. He hadn't brought her on the visit because she was in the family way and didn't want to be jolted over those hellish roads. He was younger than Taras and winked at Olena when she served him his tea, and when she laughed, Taras stood abruptly, urging Alexey to bring his tea outside where they could talk about what crops he would be planting, whether he'd need help putting up his house.

"You'll be fine," Taras said again. Olena nodded, wishing him gone. Her desire to get away from the snare of domestic duties had been frustrated, but at least having only herself to care for would be a kind of freedom.

Taras brushed her cheek. "Will you miss me?"

She flinched and rose from the table.

"Tell me," he urged, grasping her wrist and holding her fast.

She tried to pull free, irritated with him for always wanting from her what she didn't have to give, for pretending that theirs wasn't an arrangement, for trying to make it a romance. She resented his weakness, his need, his obtuseness. He yanked harder to draw her to him, hurting her wrist, and saying in a grating voice, "Tell me you'll miss me!"

In a sudden spasm of rage, she swept their dinner dishes to the floor, thrilling to the tinny crash, and straining against his hold.

"No, I will not miss you," she spat at him. "What is there to miss but extra work? One less to cook for, clean up after. None of your stupid stories of how brave you were before I ever knew you! Of the old country I've never seen or want to see. None of your nagging at me for kisses. What do you want me to say? That I will miss you in bed? Fine. I'll miss you here, between my legs. You fuck good, is that what you want to hear? But you act like what you do between my legs should give you a place in my heart. What did you think you were getting when you married me? What we do in there," she stabbed a finger toward the bedroom, "is what farm animals do, and that is the pleasure I get from it. Why do you want more from me?"

He had gone white and utterly still, his hand on her wrist like iron, and she too became still, nervous. She opened her mouth to say something to ease the tension when suddenly, mechanically, he hit her with his free hand. Over and over, open-handed but hard, one side of her head, then the other, the smacks ringing through her ears.

"Stop it! Stop it!" she screamed, swinging wildly with her own free hand, connecting with his jaw, his chest, pinching and scratching the arm that held her.

He was saying something beneath his breath, a kind of sobbing, blood spraying from his nose and still he kept hitting and hitting. Her head was throbbing. She kicked at his legs to jar him back into himself.

"Taras!" She shouted as though across a great distance, and realized she had never spoken his name before. "Taras! Stop it this instant!" She landed a crashing blow on the side of his head.

He blinked rapidly and pulled her to his chest, groaning. They slumped against one another, exhausted but still raging, their breath gusting, and then, unbelievably, his cock hardened against her, her hips pressed against his. She hit him again, but with less force, and when he pressed his face against her neck, she moaned aloud. Not all his blows had made her cry, but now she was sobbing, sobbing for the home she had wanted to leave but not for this, never for this, sobbing for a life that beat against her harder and more implacably than any of Taras's blows, sobbing while she tore at his trousers and her skirts, as they fell onto the dirt floor and fucked like animals. No. Not like animals, for surely animals would never feel this rage, this pain.

THE NEXT MORNING Taras left early, not bothering to discover if Olena really was still sleeping or only counterfeiting, throwing the few things he needed into the back of the wagon and hurtling down the road at a foolhardy speed, lashing his horse unmercifully. He was still angry — at Olena, at himself, at this broken-down excuse for an animal that he despised himself for whipping. As he despised himself for hitting his wife. But another side of him wanted to turn the nag around so he could go back and hit her again. Of course he'd hit her! He'd have done better to hit himself, a thirty-year-old idiot married to a fifteen-year-old girl who'd never wanted him and had told him so.

He'd always thought of himself as a self-taught intellect, a communist, a talker, a thinker. But Olena held a mirror to his face that said nothing but "Fool."

A fragment from one of Shevchenko's poems, about a young virgin pining for love, rose unbidden to mock him further: "What use is all my grace to me, if none I have whom I may love, with whom my soul may meet? My heart, my heart, how hard it is for you alone to beat." It should have been simple. He'd seen someone who called to a hidden place in him, laid bare a hunger he had never felt in all his thirty years. Then she starved him. She fired in him a desire when lovemaking to dissolve the flesh between them like so much air, to move so deeply into her he could touch her soul. And then she refused him entry. He could force his way into her flesh, could even, as he had last night, make her betray her anger so that she eventually joined him, biting and nipping and driving him to frenzy, but it was more a hate-making than a love-making, with an orgasm that hit like shrapnel. He groaned in frustration to feel himself harden again at the memory, for this was not what he wanted, this bitter parody of love. He wanted to be wanted, to see the same yearning in her that drummed so relentlessly through him. And she. She treated his great desire like an annoyance, a trifle, threw it back in his face like chaff.

AFTER TARAS HAD LEFT Olena rose and made herself tea, which she drank in luxurious solitude, even though her swollen lips winced when she pursed them to blow on the hot liquid. Two whole months of days all her own. Not that her chores would be any different than when Taras was here, but it would be hers to say, now I will set the snares, now I will wrestle with the sod and willow bushes, now I will bathe in the creek. For the first time in her life, she had only her own will to consult. She took her tea to the door and surveyed her garden, the potatoes sprouting deep green in spite of their late start. The carrots needing to be thinned. She chuckled softly, bowing to the demands of the day: best to break up the sod in the morning, when it was cooler, do the lighter gardening work mid-day, then check and set the snares and fish trap along the creek in the evening cool. So. Not hers to decide after all. She rinsed out her tin mug with water in the bucket by the door, plunked it down on the porch step and set off to work.

That night, by the creek, after rinsing off the day's dirt, in the fading light she wandered through the grasses, snapping off bright yellow buttons of tansy, searching the roadside ditches for the leafier pennyroyal, face set, eyes hard. Back at the house she steeped the plants in boiling water, strained the liquid into the teapot and drank several cups of the bitter stuff. Then she went to bed and waited for the tea to take effect.

‹1929›

OLENA STOOD on the porch watching the puff of dust that was the wagon coming up the road. She didn't bother to wave, knowing Taras and Varvara would never see her through that cloud. This would be the first time she'd seen Varvara since her wedding three years ago. There had been little money and less time to travel the several days' journey to her father's derelict farm. In the early days, Olena's resentment had been strong. Later she'd grown more resigned. After all, what did she really miss? Her father's drunken moods and sodden friends? Varvara's waspish remarks? Work on a farm was the same work anywhere. In the end, Olena had grown very used to living apart from her family, even to the solitude of this remote homestead. Still, Varvara's help would be welcome now.

As if in agreement, the creature inside her kicked hard when the wagon pulled up beside the porch. Olena pressed her hands against the tight drum her belly had become. Taras was so anxious about this pregnancy he'd insisted on fetching a doctor for the birth. "Bah," Olena snorted. "It's too far. By the time he got here it would be over, for good or ill. Even if he made it, think of the cost! Bring me Varvara." And he had done so, even though he had never liked Varvara. Olena wasn't sure how she felt about this approaching visit herself. She moved toward her aunt, who was shrugging off Taras's offers of help and clambering down from the wagon.

"Well, niece." Varvara ran a professional eye over Olena's bulging body. "You seem to be in good health."

Olena hugged her, startled at her body's response of pure happiness to be holding one of her family again. She kissed Varvara on both cheeks, saw her own surprise mirrored on Varvara's face.

"Come inside." She ushered Varvara into the kitchen. "I've made tea."

"Save tea for later." Varvara hauled a jug from under her cloak and banged it on the table. "A present from your father. I've dust in my throat from the trip no tea will cut."

Taras brought in Varvara's bag and sat with them for a glass of vodka, then left to check on the cows.

"You've done well." Varvara's gaze took in the gleaming wood stove and tidy day bed, the pounded and polished dirt floor as she poured another glass of vodka for Olena and herself. "Cows, chickens, garden looks good, hay's up. And the land is yours, that is most important of all."

"Yes." Olena's mouth twisted at the thought of all they had done to get to this point. They had barely met the deadline for breaking the land. Taras taking every day he could spare from the farm to work other men's fields for money to buy supplies. Olena wrestling with tree roots and stones in his absence, struggling to get her garden planted, tended, harvested, and stored so they could see the winter through. The soil was poor, more suited to hay than wheat. Small wonder there were so few homesteaders in the area. Still, they could graze their cows, enough for their own use and later to sell. Eventually they'd managed to replace the one room hut they'd built that first year with a properly roofed three-room house, along with a barn and chicken coop. Wood siding for the house as they could afford it. Glass for the windows. A long, hard time. Almost, almost she'd felt she could breathe and then this — her hand tightened over her belly.

Varvara tossed back another glass but Olena sipped her vodka slowly. She rarely drank liquor as the baby gave her vicious heartburn whenever she tried. But the vodka tasted of home. Her old home, she corrected herself, the bile rising.

"Ah," said Varvara, "I see you have started your own chest." She hauled herself up out of her chair and began opening the small drawers of the chest Taras had bought second-hand for Olena their second year on the homestead. Varvara poked her fingers into the various herbs, her eyes sharpening at the large supply of dried tansy and pennyroyal. She eased the drawers shut and returned to Olena and, tilting her chin, peered into her eyes, pulling down on the lower lid with her thumb and turning Olena's head this way and that.

"What's this I hear about miscarriages?" Her voice harsh.

"Oh, I just had a bit of trouble," Olena hedged. "It happens, after all."

"Yes," Varvara scowled. "Especially if it's helped along. Have you been drinking tansy tea? Bergamot? Tell me! You don't know as much as you think you do of herbal remedies, my girl! How often have you been taking these?"

"Quite a few times, if you must know. I tried with this one too, only it didn't work."

"How many miscarriages? Taras told me of three, but he wouldn't always know, would he." Varvara's lips clamped into a tight line.

"I'm not sure." Under Varvara's glare Olena's defiance fizzled into a whisper. "More than three. I don't always wait until I know I'm pregnant."

"Ach!" Varvara rapped the table so hard it shook.

Olena winced. "You don't understand. I don't want children, not his children, not *any* children."

Varvara snorted. "A bit late for that." She ran a hand over Olena's belly, her face darkening. "How many times did you try to get rid of this one?"

"Three, but I stopped because it made me so sick. I told Taras it was the flu." Olena was beginning to feel frightened. "What's wrong? Why are you looking at me like that? It's only what I heard you tell other girls who came to you for help."

"True enough, but those girls weren't married and they weren't coming to me every year. You foolish thing, don't you know these herbs can harm you? Nothing comes without cost, and your body will pay the price of your stubbornness. And not only *your* body, but maybe the body of this little one too." Varvara pressed her ear to Olena's stomach. "These remedies aren't something you play at. They eat at your insides. They can turn this little one into a monster. All because you want to defy your fate as a woman? Bah!" Varvara spat as she moved to the sink. "Hike up your skirts and stretch back," she ordered over one shoulder, as she washed her hands, and then a hand was moving in Olena's vagina, pressing up to the entrance to her womb. Her cheeks scorched to feel someone probing where only Taras had been before, but the examination took only a few minutes and then Varvara was back at the basin, washing her hands once more and saying, "Well, we'll know soon enough what you've done. We can only pray."

She strode up to Olena and grabbed her chin hard. "This has to stop. If I hear about any more 'miscarriages,' I'll tell Taras what you've been up to. And don't give me any nonsense about loyalty. I'm not fool enough to risk your life even if you are. If you keep this up you'll be dead in a matter of years." Her voice softened. "An unhappy marriage is not the end of the world, you know. The sun still shines, honey still tastes sweet. I know what I'm talking of."

Olena nodded, too scared to be resentful. "You will stay, yes? To help me birth it?"

"But of course! You are stupid, perhaps, but you are still my niece!"

Olena went into labour five nights later, a hard and ravaging labour she could almost believe was God's revenge for all those miscarriages. It lasted two full days, and Varvara said ordinarily she'd have given her a tisane to bring her on, but Olena had already had too many herbal remedies for one lifetime. Taras appeared ravaged also, poking his head in every so often to ask if they should send for the doctor after all.

"Go away." Varvara closed the door on him. "This is no place for men, not even doctors. I've seen many worse than this. We shall come around, no fear." She bathed Olena's face and changed the towel between her teeth when it got soaked with spit and blood. Olena grunted and hated the child that had brought her down to the level of a sow, the child she knew in her bones would kill her if need be, just to get a chance at the world. "That bastard," she whispered when one of the thunderous pains had passed.

"You want to get even with him?" Varvara gave a grim wink. "Forget the towel and start to holler when your pains come. That will make him squirm. And it will help you a lot more than being a martyr."

Another wave bore down on Olena and she roared her way through it.

"That's it," Varvara purred. "Now, push!"

Olena and Varvara pushed and roared together, and eventually, out of the haze of pain and noise, the largest wave swept out a mass of blood and slime.

"Good girl." Varvara held up the infant, examining it intently. "A girl, and healthy, thank God — *no* thanks to her mother."

Olena closed her eyes. "Take her to her father."

"No such luck, my girl." Varvara clipped the cord and laid the slippery body on Olena's chest. "Let her rest here a minute, and feed, and then I'll tidy her up. *Then* she can see her father, who will be sorry she's a girl, but that's as it always was. What is her name to be?"

"I don't know. He said he wanted an English name, that it would make a little one's life easier in this country. He probably made some suggestions but I don't know. I wasn't really paying attention." Olena opened her eyes. The tiny body rose and fell with her breath, its own a mere flutter. It latched on to her breast, its crumpled face forming a tiny frown, as though already it knew life to be a disappointment. Surely Olena should feel something more than exhaustion? Some flicker of affection even beasts feel? Dully she watched the baby suckle, but when Varvara moved to pick it up she said, "Wait." Why should Taras control this too? "It's Cherven, yes? The month of June?"

Varvara paused mid-reach and her eyes narrowed, but before she could say anything Olena's eyes drifted shut again as she murmured, "Tell Taras her name is June. Now clean her up and take her to him, and let me sleep."

TARAS WAITED at the kitchen table. Every time a scream erupted from behind the bedroom door he sprang up from the chair and shoved another stick into the stove. It was sweltering in the room already, but he couldn't help himself. He was tempted to go outside for some cooler air but was afraid his fear might so take hold of him that he would keep on walking, through the fields he'd laboured over these past years, and off into the tangled brush that went for miles beyond their borders. Three years he had waited for this moment, and now he was terrified he'd be left with a baby and no wife, or worse, with neither. He shoved another stick into the inferno and wiped the salt from his eyes. Over the years he had tried to console Olena. Three miscarriages in three years, she must be sad and feeling as though she'd failed him. But she didn't show any emotion about it, not to him anyway. She seemed invariably placid, resigned to fate.

Another scream ripped through the rough wooden door and he slumped at the table, face in his hands, stomach churning. He had other worries too, ones he hadn't discussed with Olena, worries so close to superstition he was ashamed to acknowledge them, atheist that he insisted he was. But after the third miscarriage he'd begun to fear he was being punished by God. His first trip away from home, when he'd left so angry with Olena and himself, he had gone into town, to look for work, yes, but also to find a bar and the company of men. He was sick of the impenetrability of womankind. He wanted the straightforward dealings of men, the rawness of drink and argument, of working and swearing and playing together. The thoughts of beer and store-bought whiskey, of a bar where no decent woman was allowed, sustained him on the long drive into Norfolk.

And the beer was good, the rye even better, the one cooling, the other firing his throat. He joined some men at a table and fell into conversation. Within an hour he had a job as a field hand, bunk and meals included. Shit pay, compared with the mines, but the mines were far away, and the work the very devil. He was feeling better than he had in a long time, especially once the farmer who'd hired him left and the rest of them, several of whom had been miners, could talk freely about the problems for workers, now that wages had fallen so badly and jobs were so few, about how a communist government would give them the power they needed to improve their lot. It had been a long time since he'd had this kind of debate. He was as fired up by it as by the whiskey. Olena, in spite of all her supposed desire for an education, seldom read, and refused his invitation to improve their English skills together by reading the newspapers he brought back from his trips. She would talk about crops and his plans for the homestead when he broached these topics — she certainly knew about farming, despite her youth — but when he brought up politics, or communism, the need to rein in the capitalist system that ground people into paupers, her eyes grew distant and she would find some chore to take her from the room. Some of these men had read the communist circulars and could tell him about the attempts to form unions across the country, in the mining towns especially. His old enthusiasms surged and he almost forgot to eat, finally stuffing several pickled eggs down his gullet to soak up the booze.

It was late in the evening and the crowd had thinned somewhat when he noticed a woman perched awkwardly but somehow defiantly on a stool at the bar. Her stockings were snagged, her shoes badly scuffed, and her hair dishevelled, but she was attractive in an untidy sort of way, and she kept glancing over toward his table. Most of his companions had staggered out the door, with promises to be back early for the morning drive out to the farm. He had planned to sleep in the wagon, but casting an experienced eye over her, thought he might as well spring for a room. He signalled to the bartender to pour her a drink and as she smiled her thanks over her raised glass it wobbled a bit in her grasp. The town was too small to have open prostitution. He could probably have her for the price of a couple of shots at the bar, and a bottle in the room. He rose and crossed the floor to her side. He felt strong, he felt defiant, and if she looked a little like Olena, so much the better. This one would be grateful, and it would make a pleasant change.

The next morning he'd woken disgusted at the sour smell of stale whiskey coming off both of them, at her smell coming off him. He hustled her out of the room, splashed as much of her off himself as he could before running to the pickup point, stomach churning from too much booze and no breakfast, glad he'd be staying at the farm and wouldn't have to run into her again.

When he returned home after the summer's work, with a second-hand radio as a present for Olena along with enough supplies to last the winter, he was certain she'd know what he'd done. But she made no sign. His appetite for her was stronger than ever. Her scent, her sounds, the texture of her skin. Her murmurs, not of endearment but at least of pleasure, her sharp cry as he brought her to climax, told him that what she'd spoken to him in anger the night before he left was true: she had missed him between her legs.

But that knowledge was enough for only a short while, then the gnawing for signs of affection would start, and eat at him until he had to push her to anger, sometimes to violence. So on almost every trip he made out of town, when he met women who were willing, he had other adventures, always following the pattern he'd set that first time. Heavy drinking, whiskey-soaked self-pity, the desire for revenge against one woman and for the admiration, however brief, however feigned, of another. Followed by a morning of guilt and revulsion and, as Olena's belly grew, fear. He cursed the priests who had instilled in him such blindly irrational beliefs. But he had sent for Varvara all the same, hoping her skills as a midwife, and his concern for his wife and baby, would placate whatever grim deity might be pursuing him.

It had been silent behind the bedroom door for some time. How like that hag Varvara to keep him in the dark. These were his wife, his child. Then it struck him that the silence might be a sinister one and Varvara afraid to tell him. He strained for the slightest sound and thought if he heard another howl behind that door he would howl right along with it.

The bedroom door opened. He started up and reached for the bundle Varvara was holding.

"A girl." Varvara plunked the infant into his arms and helped settle her there, roughly but efficiently.

"Olena?" His voice rattled in his throat, strangled by worry for Olena and awe at the tiny face filling his gaze.

"She's come through very well. She's tired, though. Doesn't want to see you until she's rested. You can have a bit of time with your daughter, and then I'll take her back in."

The small bundle drew a deep breath that pressed her sides against him. He marvelled at the strength of such a fragile being, felt one moment of regret that he didn't have a son, but then the tiny creature raised her crusty eyelids and gazed at him with empty eyes. She had something of Olena about her, crumpled and red as she was. And she had Olena's ability to stop his heart, to swell it to the bursting point of pain and sweetness in equal measure. But here the similarity to her mother ended. This little one came to him open, untouched. He could shape her, could fill those eyes with adoration, with love. She would be his, as her mother would never be.

Varvara broke in wryly on his reverie. "She said to tell you the baby's name is June."

Taras barely heard Varvara's voice. He held the baby close to his chest, so she could feel his heart beat. With his pinky he smoothed out the funny little frown between her almost invisible eyebrows. "Fine," he said, with eyes only for his daughter, "tell her I said fine."

·1937·

OLENA STOOD IN thick smoke, thick enough to discourage the mosquitoes that lifted in clouds from the grasses at every footstep, thick enough to sear her eyes and lungs, but not thick enough to filter her daughters' squabbling, or to keep the occasional determined black fly, deer fly, or horse fly from zooming in, tearing a chunk of her flesh, then zooming away. Out for blood. Any blood. A person mattered no more than a horse or a dog, except perhaps that human flesh took less effort to tear. Black flies could drive a team of oxen to madness, those sluggish, lazy, godforsaken brutes suddenly plunging and rearing like unbroken ponies. If this was so for beasts with hides as tough as horn, what chance did a human have?

So she lit another smudge. Damped the straw, a muddy gold, and touched the blazing sage brush to it till it caught smoky light.

She was bucking logs, then chopping them up for firewood.

Her hands blistered and reddened, grew clumsy with pain. Usually Taras split the wood, but he had gone into town to sound out possible work for the harvest. He must have found something because he'd been gone for over a week. Knowing him, whenever he finally did return, he'd be with one of his bar friends looking for a meal they could ill afford to offer and a bed to fall into once he was stinking drunk. She coughed and spat black phlegm, then straightened and rubbed a fist against her spine. Her back ached with bending and lifting, with the burden of this place, this life. And now perhaps the added burden of another life on the way, in spite of the recipe for a contraceptive pessary Varvara had given her after May's birth five years ago. Olena could hear the old woman's voice as clearly as the horse fly whine: "One pound cocoa butter, one ounce common boric acid, one half tannic acid. Melt it over hot water, then pour half an inch thick to cool. Cut in half-inch squares, like fudge. Don't let the children at it, it smells like candy too. Before each time put one high up there and wait for a minute or so for the heat from your body to melt it." Olena, morosely suckling May, hadn't liked to tell Varvara that her sex life was not so orderly, that often her body drove her to Taras when she was most resisting him, hating him even. It was something that baffled and shamed her. Besides, they couldn't always afford the ingredients, especially the cocoa butter. Still, she had managed to keep from getting pregnant for five years. But now here she was, drinking tansy tea nightly in spite of Varvara's warnings, and splitting logs long past her point of exhaustion, hoping that if there was a creature attempting to take root inside her, this exertion would break its hold. The thought of another mouth tugging at her, more hands grabbing at her, pushed her back to the wood pile.

Olena steadied the round fat log that she was using for a chopping block, bent down and grabbed another log, stood it upright. She raised the axe, hoping the pull in her side was the fetus loosening its grip.

"Mama?"

"June! Get back! You know not to come near me when I'm using this axe! Stay with your sister."

"But my eyes hurt," and it seemed that whine was part of the weave of her life, threaded in so tight it chafed her chest. "And May is crying because she got bit *again*. And it's *too hot*."

"I'm not telling you again. You go mind your sister!" She smacked the shadowy head beside her, her flat hand glancing off an ear, and the whining faded to snivelling and disappeared into the smoke.

Another fly droned by her left ear, hovering, menacing. She swatted at it blindly, eyes streaming so profusely she couldn't see to hit it. Sure enough the damn thing bit clear through her worn cotton dress. She clawed at her back with one hand and swung around as though she could take aim at the fly with the axe, chop it cleanly in two. Stopped only when, with a trick of the mind, she stood off from herself, outside the smudge, and watched a woman in a faded cotton dress whirling in the smoke, chopping at air. Taking aim at the prairie. She gave one sharp, hard burst of laughter, rubbed at her shoulder to work out the stinging, turned back to the log, steadied it once more.

She raised the axe. It felt heavier than before, when she'd felt she could barely lift it. She hefted it high above her head, struck down on the log with all that was in her. Fuelling the thwack of the axe, the crack of the split log was her rage at this country, this land. Her dry crack of laughter echoed the split of the log. This land. This free gift. Promised by the government to people who hungered for earth the way others hungered for food. Land that could be theirs for nothing. Nothing but the dollar Taras was fool enough to pay to a stranger in a bar, and years of heartbreaking labour, bending their backs to tangled brush and logs and root systems that thwarted their every move. Her father, her aunt, and now she herself, caught in the trap of that gift. She reached for another log, biting her lip against the pain of a blister stabbed by splinters. Steadied it. Thwack. Remembered the Sorskys who lived across the way when she was a girl. How the bailiff took their oxen as payment on their debt to the store. Without oxen they couldn't finish the last few acres by the deadline. The whole quarter taken back. Taken and sold to dainty-fisted English, too finicky to sit down with bohunk peasants, but not to take advantage of their effort. The family on the next quarter almost going the same way, except that their twelve-year-old daughter spoke enough English to convince the bailiff please to leave them one horse so they could still use the plow. Thwack. Olena supposed she should be grateful this miserable piece of land was securely theirs, had become theirs just before the crash of '29, which Olena had barely noticed until the price of grain and cattle and labour plummeted. Others, Alexey for one, had not been so fortunate. His baby son, a premature birth, continued sickly, and Alexey was always making the long trip to town for the doctor. But cows that a year before had fetched eighty dollars were now worth only five. A man would work twelve hard hours in the field and be grateful to come away with a dollar. People could not even pay for supplies through the winter, let alone the cost of a doctor's visits. The Masiuks had lasted barely a year after the crash. Thwack. But maybe they were the lucky ones after all. What the Zaleskys' secure possession meant beyond an endless horizon of hard labour, Olena could not say. And now the possibility of another mouth to feed when they were stretched to the limit as it was. Even if she'd wanted it, she couldn't have it.

She was breathing too hard, leaned on the axe and coughed out the smoke from her lungs, shook the sting and sweat from her eyes.

The notes of a violin penetrated the smudge and everything — time, heart, breath — stopped. Their neighbour, Conor Maguire, who'd bought Alexey's quarter and two sections more, must have dropped by the house on his way to the dance hall in Norfolk, where he played with a band once a month, staying overnight. His wife Shena seldom went with him, disliking the drink, he said, but not minding the money he brought back. Every so often he would stop on his way and send a tune across the fields on the chance Olena was near enough for a brief visit. Usually he played jigs or ragtime, but this time he played an old ballad, the notes soaring high and mournful. They caressed her ears and wormed their way down into her gut, her groin. Deadlier than any black fly, more stinging than any smoke, they whispered that some hungers can never be satisfied, some beauty is too terrible to gaze upon, some joys butt up against pain so close you have to take them all together or not at all.

The song set up in her a hunger for leaving. A yearning to throw down the axe, trample her children under her feet, cast off their clinging arms. To get away. Futile longing, for beyond the smudge lay open prairie. As a girl, nearly a decade ago now, she had seen the ever-receding horizon as freedom, possibility. But she had come to accept the bitter truth that endless space was a more effective enclosure than any prison wall. The limits of the prairie would always far outrun the limits of her endurance. She could strike and strike, but no matter whether she threw up her hands, or raised her axe, she would only ever be striking at air. No place for the hunger to go. It writhed inside her, riding the ragged notes of the violin, and she wanted those notes to last forever, so she could remain impaled on this longing.

"Mama?" For a split second the axe wavered in the direction of that whining presence, and the horror of that second blotted out the violin, blotted out the smoke, the flies, the prairie. Her spine crumbled with exhaustion. How easy it would be to swing just a bit to the left. It had happened before. A woman late in the day, tired after too much chopping, lets her mind slip just for an instant, and the swing of the axe glances off the log and into her own soft flesh. How much pain, she wondered, before the bite of the axe becomes the lesser of the two? Doctors too far away, she'd be gone before anyone could get help to her, her blood pulsing into the soil, moistening the dry land. A feast for the goddamn black flies. No peace even in dying.

"Mama?"

She lowered the axe, opened her eyes. Besides, she liked Conor, liked the way he watched her, slyly when Taras was around, openly when he was not. She liked how he wanted to laugh and kid around and wink with those blue eyes, how he hadn't reacted to Taras's rants about the working man and unions at their first meeting, just calmly remarked he'd be looking to hire in the fall, which had the blessed effect of shutting Taras down mid-rant. She had treated Conor coolly when she first met him, resenting Alexey's loss of his land to an Angliki, but the first time he'd stopped by when Taras was away he took her hand as she gave him a cup of tea and said, with that ready laugh, "Sure, and ye must know the English have treated the Irish like bohunks for centuries. We're not so different, you and I."

Really, she'd thought drily, then how is it you are prospering on two sections while we struggle on one quarter. But she was grateful for the work he'd offered Taras, and for his teasing, the lightness between them so different from her dealings with her husband.

The violin called again.

"Here, chickens." She walked out of the smoke towards June and May. "I think Mr. Maguire's at the house. We'll stop for lunch with him, shall we?" She fluffed her hair and straightened her dress. Nothing to be done about the smell of smoke and sweat hanging from her as though she were trailing the smudge behind her. But she undid the top button of her dress and figured Conor wouldn't mind. They could drink their tea in the shade of the porch, with luck there'd be a bit of a breeze. Who knew, maybe she could persuade the girls to lie down for a nap. Taras wouldn't be home until long after Conor had left for Norfolk, if then.

JUNE TRAILED BEHIND her mother out of the smudge, eyes stinging. She knew what that violin meant. Mr. Maguire was at the house and her mother would have to give him a cup of tea and a biscuit, tripping over her English, "Ve have no sugar for tea, Mr. Maguire, so sorry. I use it all for baking. But Taras, he bring some when he come back." Mr. Maguire smiling, and June struggling to follow the words, "Sure, a cup of tea from those hands is all the sweetness a man needs." Even though June liked tea and biscuits she did not like what would follow. Her mother would say how hard they'd all been working, even though all June and

May had done was breathe in smoke and swat flies, and then her mother would send June and May to have a nap. June did not like Mr. Maguire, even though he tried to be nice, or thought he was trying to be nice. But June did not like being tickled, or having her chin chucked and being told she was pretty. She knew she was not pretty. Once she had asked her mother that very question and her mother had answered, not looking up from shelling the peas into a pan in her lap, "You have a long chin."

May was pretty. May, with her light hair and green eyes. Her quick smile. May liked everyone, even Mr. Maguire, and would sit on his knee while he fed her half his biscuit, dunking it in his tea before giving it to her to finish. At five, May was small and lithe and nobody would say to her, as June's father said to June, "You're too big to be carried on my shoulders, sweet one."

Gawky June, scrawny and over tall for her eight years, a permanent frown etched between her brows. With her sallow skin, brown eyes and hair, she resembled the dark sisters in the book of fairy tales her father had bought second-hand and brought home for her when she was still very small. Its pages greasy with fingerprints, the cover weathered, the spine tattered and creaking, barely holding: it was her most treasured possession. Whenever he was home her father made time to read to her. She would climb into his lap, and snuggle into the crook of his arm while with his free hand he traced the words he was reading aloud, encouraging her to sound them out herself. Sometimes he would take her hand in his and guide her finger over shapes that magically began to coalesce into meaning. Even in the midst of this happiness June could not help but notice that in many of the stories things rarely turned out well for the dark sister.

Once she knew enough to read, however haltingly, on her own, June could lose herself for hours in the lives of princes and princesses, ogres and dragons, fingers tracing the lines, lips mouthing the words her father had taught her, until her mother snapped at her to get her nose out of that book and do something useful. Often adding, "And don't look at me like that. Why don't you ever smile?"

June was too scared to say the same thing to her mother, though she could have. Olena seemed always too busy to smile. Except when Mr. Maguire came by. Then she never stopped laughing and tossing her head back in a way June found disturbing without quite knowing why.

Well this time, June would refuse to go for a nap. She would stay and keep an eye on Mr. Maguire and her mother, though she didn't know what she would be keeping an eye for. She just had an uneasy feeling whenever he was there. The feeling that her father wouldn't like it. Her mother was only being neighbourly, she said, poor Mr. Maguire had a sickly wife. To which June thought, then why doesn't he stay home and look after her? June had lots of thoughts she couldn't say, not even to May, who was too young to understand. The one time June had said she didn't like Mr. Maguire, May, occupied with making a mud pie and decorating it with yellow bursts of tansy, had replied without looking up, "I think he's nice." And that had been the end of that. Still, something kept June from mentioning Mr. Maguire's visits to her father. She did not want to see his darkening face, be sent to her room with May while the voices rose in the kitchen, fists slammed the table, pots and pans and the door banged, June's heart banging with them, hard against her chest. Like the time last year when a hunter caught in a sudden autumn storm had knocked for shelter at the door and her mother made up a bed for him by the kitchen stove. He left a side of deer as thanks. When her father got back a few days later, June, excited to have such a story to share, ignored her mother's warning glance and told her father all about it. That night she had covered May's ears with her hands, huddling with her in her cot, whispering fairy tales to her until she settled. No. June would not be making that mistake again. Much better to keep quiet so that they would all be in the kitchen together, and her father would bring out of his knapsack little treasures: candy sometimes; a new book of stories; once some paper dolls, which had so enraptured May she couldn't speak, just introduced the dolls silently to one another all evening. Their mother, not laughing, but working quietly in the corner by the kitchen stove fire, perhaps knitting, or mending. There.

IN SPITE OF all her determination to refuse a nap, June woke in her narrow bed, May snoring softly in the other. The sun was dipping down in the sky, sending a strong shaft of light through the tiny bedroom window, almost blinding her. Out of the light was walking a tall figure, shimmering like a mirage in the dust it was kicking up, a knapsack dangling from one hand. June's heart and body leapt together as she jammed her feet into her shoes, startling May awake. She ran out the door, past the garden and through the grasses beyond it. "Wait for me!" May called behind her. But June couldn't wait, wouldn't wait. Her father. Home after ages away.

But as she got closer another man emerged from the light behind her father and June stumbled with disappointment. She had wanted him all to herself, would share these first minutes with May because she had to, but with this stranger? May sped past her and hurtled into her father's arms. "What did you bring, Papa?"

June's father dropped the knapsack to put both arms around his youngest daughter and June's heart contracted. "What kind of greeting is that, little hellion!" Shifting May to one arm he reached down with the other to pull June close and all there was room for was gladness. "Here, Petro," her father laughed. "These two are my daughters. Though they behave like wild animals, they are my flesh and blood."

Then he handed Petro his knapsack, set May on the ground and he and June walked hand in hand while May ran ahead to the house where their mother was standing on the porch. Though he chatted with Petro, every so often her father squeezed June's hand, their own private conversation. A weight June hadn't known was there lifted off her chest. Her father was home and Mr. Maguire was nowhere in sight. Her mother didn't look any more pleased to see Petro than June had been, but she told May to put an extra plate out for supper and June to pick more lettuce and radishes and green onions from the garden for the salad, which they ate with early potatoes cooked in cream and more green onion until the sauce was sticky and pale green and clung to every piece of potato June speared with her fork. Now that her father was here to eat it, June thought it the best meal in the world.

LATER THAT NIGHT Olena slipped out to the still in the little shed tucked into a hollow in the middle of the field to bring back a jug, for as she had predicted, Taras and Petro had gone through what there was in the house by the end of supper. She poured for herself before banging the jug down on the table beside a dish of dill pickles, then took her glass of vodka to the girls' bedroom where she sat on one of the small, hard beds, letting the fiery liquid burn all the way to her gullet. May and June, already in their nightdresses, huddled together on the other bed in the circle of light from the lone kerosene lamp, flipping through the shiny pages of the Eaton's catalogue — the softer paper inserts having long vanished into the outhouse — and looking at all the things they would never order. June had been trying to read from that old book of fairy tales, but finally yielded to May's poking and now they were giggling at women's lingerie, pointing at the more elegantly dressed women they wanted to cut into paper dolls. Olena thought of trying to read one of the English newspapers Taras had brought home, as she often did when he couldn't see and try to join her, but she didn't like to disturb the girls. The first year on the homestead Taras had bought a second-hand radio, a gift for Olena to hear more English, but the first time they turned it on there was a popping sound, smoke poured out the back, and it died. If it weren't for the papers and her conversations with Conor she'd have been in a fair way to losing the English culled from her few years at school.

Beyond the heavy curtain in the bedroom doorway came roars of laughter, glasses banging the wooden table, and once the crash of broken glass. "We should have gone, Taras," Petro moaned. "We may be homesteading now, but we both worked the mines. We should have gone to give our support."

The Estevan strike again. Did they never tire of the story, even after seven years? It always cropped up when Petro hit a particular pitch of drunkenness. They had gone, had started out anyway, half a dozen of them. Big men, all card-carrying members of the communist party, all drinking white lightning and talking bigger and wilder until somebody offered his truck and off they stormed, never mind the crops, never mind the work to be done in neighbours' fields so they could buy supplies for the winter. Big men. Off to fight for justice and the common man. Big men with big dreams, who stopped off in some drinking hole and didn't emerge until long after it was all over and the stories were filtering back from the south, of RCMP riding around with machine guns and three strikers dead. They emerged from their stupor long enough to go to Bienfait for the funeral, where they heard that one of the wounded, a man Taras had worked with in Timmins, was refused treatment in Estevan, and so was jolted over fifty miles to Weyburn where he died the next day. Taras told her this when he returned home, tears running down his face, and threw himself on her like a madman, pounding into her as though trying to hide so deep inside her he would never have to find his way back, groaning "Gryshko! Gryshko!" with every thrust. To her horror more than her tissues had softened, her heart tugged toward sympathy by the depths of his grief. Almost she reached out, but reminded herself that he'd taken on this homestead without inspecting it, the soil so poor and rocky they'd been barely making ends meet even before the prices fell, and now when he needed to be sowing as much winter wheat as possible, where was he? Off chasing his brave schemes that just like the homestead had come to nothing. Worse, there wouldn't even be any money coming in since he'd left the fields he was meant to be harvesting without telling the farmer who'd hired him. Christ, he'd probably thought of it as some heroic labour uprising. Her heart seized up like frozen earth and stayed that way long after he'd worn himself out and collapsed on her, snoring and spent. But that unguarded moment of yielding had been all it took to allow May to take root inside her.

Olena glanced at the girls, each so different, the one dark and sullen, the other fair and sunny tempered. Her heart twisted, and not for the first time she wondered if Varvara had been right, that all Olena's efforts to get rid of June in the womb had tainted the child, marked her somehow. May had snuck up on Olena. There had been none of the usual signs, no sickness, her monthly bleeding continuing well into the third month so that by the time Olena realized she was pregnant it would have been too risky to try to abort. Varvara's warnings the night of June's birth had still been harsh in her ears. But now the thought of another baby — the stinking diapers boiling on the wood stove, the midnight feedings, the mewling — had made her shut her mind to Varvara's nagging. She had managed to hide her condition from Taras, which hadn't been difficult given how often he was off working, off to his life of men.

Now one of those big men was back and crying over his hooch. Just as she curled her lip at the thought, the curtain was flung back and Petro staggered half into the room.

"What's this? Olena, come have a drink, won't you, Olena?"

"Go away, Petro. Go talk your big talk with Taras."

June closed the Eaton's catalogue but the man grabbed it and took June by the hand. "Here, come out here with Petro and your daddy, little one, eh? Come show us what you've been doing with your mother here in the dark."

"Go to bed," Olena ordered May, waiting only long enough to see her order obeyed before going out to the kitchen where Petro had pulled June onto his lap and was opening up the catalogue. June pointed to a pair of black patent shoes with ankle straps.

"These are called Mary Janes."

"Mmm, she smells good, Taras." Petro buried his nose in June's tousled brown hair. "Young. Free." He sighed so hard he blew June's hair out over her eyes, and when she brushed it back, he hugged her close to him, swaying her back and forth like a pendulum. June clutched at the catalogue.

"What it is to be so young."

Taras stared stupidly into his drink. "Not for long, Petro," he sighed. "Not for long."

"She should be in bed, Taras," Olena snapped.

Petro's arms tightened and a tear trickled into the ragged beard jammed up against the side of June's face. Her nightgown was hiking up her legs from all the swaying and Petro, still holding her tightly with one hand, tried clumsily with the other to pull the skirt down, then gave up, resting his hand on June's thigh.

Pig! Olena thought. Go on, Taras, see your pig friend, pawing your daughter. June wasn't even looking to her mother for rescue, though Olena could tell how uncomfortable she was, her every muscle tense but not struggling. No, June was looking to Taras, whose drooping eyes couldn't lift from his glass.

"I want to get down," June said in a small voice while Petro hugged her tighter.

"No," Taras mumbled to his whiskey, "youth is wasted on the young."

Petro's hand rose higher on June's thigh.

"Taras!" Olena barked, and Petro peered at her with vaguely startled eyes. June twisted herself neatly away from Petro's slackened hands and the Eaton's catalogue thumped to the floor.

"Why are you yelling like that?" Taras slurred.

Petro shuffled his feet awkwardly, his face red. He glanced briefly at Olena, then down at June, who was picking up the catalogue.

"Here, here." He fumbled at his pockets and pulled out a worn and greasy dollar bill. "Little girls need pretty things. I didn't mean to scare you, sweetheart. I'd like a daughter of my own some day. Here, take it."

June took the dollar bill with her arm stretched out full length, then ran with it into the bedroom.

Olena stomped in after her. June put the bill on the dresser. "It's mine, isn't it, Mama?"

"Yes, it's yours. You could maybe pick out something for your sister too."

"Maybe," June said reluctantly. "If there's anything left from the shoes."

But when Petro was snoring in the daybed by the stove and Taras came to call Olena to bed, the first thing he did was throw a shame-faced glance at her, then stuff the bill into his pants. As Olena knew he must. She could hold his pig friend against him, but not the knowledge that fancy patent shoes must wait for flour, sugar, and maybe salt pork for the winter.

"Well? Did you go to the relief office?"

"I will. Next time I'm in town. I promise."

"Your daughters have no boots for the winter." Olena eased May out of her cot, each whispered word carrying the cold sting of a razor. "I have no flour sacks for dresses that might actually fit them. Leave your pride behind you when you go. You cannot afford it any more." She slid May into the cot beside June, climbed into the warm space her daughter had left, and turned her back to him.

THE MAN NAMED Petro left the next morning before any of them were up. June searched every drawer of the battered dresser in her room for the dollar he'd given her, without success, and when her mother explained that her father needed that dollar when he next went to town, she didn't whine. Even last night it had seemed too good to be true. Besides, her father was staying for several days, and that was worth more than all the dollars in the world. She and May helped him check the traps for fish, the snares for rabbits, and even the days they returned home empty-handed and had only soft-boiled eggs on toast for supper didn't darken June's happiness. Her father bucked the remaining logs, filled the wood box, milked the cow and sprayed warm milk into June's and May's open mouths, praised them both when they tried the milking, even though May's hands were far too small and the most she could achieve was a few drops that were probably what had been left behind on the teat anyway. He dug up more potatoes and May and June competed to see who could first spot the pale glimmer in the earth and pounce on it like miners discovering gold. But when Olena started churning butter, wrapping it in moist cloths and keeping it in a bucket in the cool of the creek, June's heart got heavier. Her father would be leaving, would take the butter with him and sell it for whatever he could get in town.

The morning he left, June and May walked with him to the edge of their property, where he would wait for Petro and some others to pick him up in their wagon. "You be good girls, now." When he pinched their cheeks May smiled up at him, but June hid her face in his pant leg, the tears rising even though she knew he would say, as he did, "Now, now, June, you are too old for this crying. You know I leave because I must. I'll be back as soon as

I can." He disentangled her from his leg, gave her a gentle push, "Off you go now. Your mother needs you." June smiled a watery not quite smile and turned her face toward home. May slipped her hand into June's and gave it a squeeze. "We'll be all right, June," she said in her best grown up voice. June's chest heaved but she squeezed back.

"You'll see." May bounced along beside June, raising clouds of dust and flies. "He always comes back and when he can he brings presents! Remember my dolls? Let's play with them after we eat, that will cheer you up, I know it. You can even have the evening gown."

Their mother had breakfast waiting for them, bowls of bread and milk. May tucked in right away, but June could only stare at hers, until her mother pushed her spoon roughly into her hand. "Eat! Otherwise it goes to the chickens. They'll make quick work of it and you'll have nothing until lunch."

Eyes on her plate, June spooned the pasty mess into her mouth. Did her best to swallow, though it took several tries. Suddenly her mother cried out, "Those damn cows! If your father would mend that fence like I asked!" June looked up tearily to see several of Mr. Maguire's cows meander past the window.

"Leave that!" Olena barked. "June, you come with me. May, you stay right here. Move, and I'll tan your hide." Olena grabbed June's hand and dragged her out the door, snatching up a switch from the porch as she ran.

June stumbled, still snivelling, but knowing better than to outright cry. Her mother was short but she moved fast when she was angry, and she was practically flying through the grasses whipping about her ankles and calves.

"Those damn cows. I'll beat them till they run," her mother

hissed, swinging the switch. *"Stop whining!"* She whirled on June, who sucked in her sob like a hard candy and choked on it so the switch wouldn't swing in her direction. Her mother's eyes startled wide as her whole body twisted beneath her.

"Damn," she said almost as if asking a question, and fell heavily. June saw her foot half hidden in a gopher hole.

"Mama?"

Her mother's fists tore at the dusty grasses by her head.

"Hush now," she whispered, and June was frightened to hear her mother's voice so quiet, almost tender.

"Let me lie still a minute, Junie, yes?"

But she didn't lie still. She rippled. Bent and twisted so that June could only make out a trace line from her temple to shoulder to hip, her mother rippled. Her hands moved down to her belly.

"Sweet Jesus," a groan that was more curse than prayer. Another convulsion.

"Junie," her mother spoke to the earth, her lips smearing with dust and spit. "Run quick as you can, now. Get Mrs. Maguire. Quick now."

June ran, mud forming on her face, a meeting of dust and tears. She ran but couldn't seem to get closer to the Maguire house, which she could see on the horizon. She had a moment of panic that she would never find Mrs. Maguire or her father or anyone. She would just run, forever, until her heart burst. But suddenly the house loomed large before her, white, two-story, tree-lined. The relief of it carved runnels down her muddy cheeks. She could not speak, but she did not need to do anything more than stand at the bottom of the porch steps, dust-streaked and wailing. The door banged open and Mr. Maguire rushed out.

"Your mother?" His voice snapped June out of her wailing enough to let her nod her head up and down. "Christ, and Shena off to Saskatoon for some shopping." He snatched a jacket off the peg inside the door and took the stairs two at a time. And June was running again, but at least now there was an ashen-faced grown-up running with her.

"Mother of God, Olena." He dropped to his knees beside her. "You go off home now, June."

June saw a splotchy red mess on the ground beside her mother. It was like the pig's afterbirth she'd seen last year when her mother helped the sow with her piglets, before they had to sell the sow and her young to pay the taxes. The sow had lain there, eyes glazed over, grunting and not really connected to what was happening at the other end of her, as piglet after piglet slithered out, greyish white beneath streaks of red, June's mother snatching one up, hastily clearing its mouth of slime, then tossing it into the straw to get to the next one, cursing whenever one refused to breathe. Her mother said now what she'd said to June's father then, "Let her stay." With the same bitter tone, but paler now. Tired. "Besides, is over. I know, soon as I fall. Something—snipped. Snapped. Ach, this language." She turned her face to the earth.

Mr. Maguire took off his jacket. "Here, hold that between your legs—it's fresh this morning." The red between Olena's thighs was glistening.

"June, give me your cardigan, girl." To June's mother he said, "We have to wrap the poor wee thing in something." He stooped over the red mass, scooped it into June's sweater. "Do ye think ye can walk?" Mr. Maguire slipped an arm under Olena's shoulders to help her to stand, then they started off slowly in the direction of the house, his arm now around Olena's waist, her feet dragging, June trailing behind and wondering how they would ever get the stain out of her only sweater.

Mr. Maguire settled Olena in bed with some clean towels stuffed between her legs and hot water in a basin at the bedside. May hung back at the doorway, unusually quiet.

"Will ye not let me fetch the doctor? Ye'll be needin' more care than this wee girl can give."

"No. No doctor." Olena winced as she eased back onto her pillow. "No need. Taras, he is gone for vehrk but he is back in few days. I be fine. June, she is old enough to look after me."

"Jesus, Olena, he can't be keepin' ye here like this. It's inhuman..."

"Shh." Olena glanced sharply at June. "I am fine. I have horse ahnt vagon, if need be." She reached for Mr. Maguire's hand. "Tank you, ahnt tanks be to God you vehr here."

"Well, if you're sure." He hesitated. "I'll bury the poor thing before I go. Up by the creek?" Olena closed her eyes. "Make your mother some tea." Mr. Maguire ruffled June's hair as he headed to the door. "And take care of your sister, there's a good girl." June shrugged off his hand, wanting him to stay and take care of her mother, whose white face scared her, but even more wanting him and his friendly hands gone. Hoping he would have enough sense not to bury her sweater too.

The next morning June woke to find Olena still in bed and the fire in the stove almost out. She stoked the embers and threw in some kindling, then helped May to dress. And still Olena did not come out of her bedroom. June stole into the darkened room to find her mother hunched away from her, facing the wall. She turned when June stood by the bed, but stared dazedly at her, as if she couldn't see her, then rolled back to the wall, the rust-coloured stain on the skirt she still wore from yesterday shaking June to her core.

June made tea and toast, set it quietly on the rickety willow table by her mother's bed, then she and May had their usual breakfast of bread and milk. June shovelled hay into the horse's stall, then milked the cow as best she could, ending up with barely half a pailful. Thank heaven there wasn't still the pig to slop. When her father sold it that summer, along with a few of the chickens even though that meant fewer eggs, June and May had cried to see the pig go. It had been almost like a pet, running up to snuffle hello when they carried out the slops and mash, the special treat of a bucket of whey when Olena made butter. But June hadn't cried over the chickens, nasty things, ganging up on the weak ones until their feathers were pecked clear off. Smelly too. June didn't like feeding them, or mucking out the coop that stank so strong her eyes stung and her lungs practically burst with trying to hold her breath. She hated helping Olena with the butchering too, the dying squawk as blood burst from a severed neck, the cloying smell as Olena pulled handfuls of slimy red and purple entrails from the carcass. But the one time she complained, Olena said, "You don't help, you don't eat." After seeing the egg that should have been hers go to May, watching May poke strips of toast into the gooey yolk, eyes closing with pleasure bite after bite, June didn't have to be prodded to collect the eggs, or hold the chicken down if it fought the blade. Now she barely noticed the smell or the noise as she scattered the grain, then gathered the eggs, her mind too filled with worry about her mother whom she had never known to lie in bed even when she was sick.

This routine continued for three days, tea and toast to Olena, who left it untouched for June to pick up at the end of the day; meals of bread and milk or scrambled eggs, the easiest way to cook she could think of, for her and May. While she was doing as many of the chores as she could, May followed at her heels, saying "Let me! Let me! I can do it!" But when May tried to pull carrots her grip was so weak she ended up with only green tops in her hand, leaving June to dig the roots out. And she was nervous around the hens, not liking to put her hand underneath them to search for an egg, afraid they'd peck.

On the third day May was so insistent that June let her try to milk the cow, her tiny hands so inept she couldn't produce even a dribble, and the cow started stamping and turning its head to moo at them, nostrils flaring and eyes rolling. June smacked May's hands away from the teats. "Can't you see the cow's upset? Just go away!"

June got half a pail from the cow, which at least stopped the stamping and lowing. For now. She forked some hay into the stall, then grabbed the egg basket and headed to the chicken coop. The chickens hadn't been laying much, almost as if they knew something was badly wrong. Only four eggs yesterday.

May emerged from the coop, face beaming, holding her skirt in front of her. "I did it! They didn't even peck, and I got three! Look!" Then she tripped at the bottom of the ramp and all three eggs smashed on the ground. Several hens darted forward to pick at the slimy mess.

"Oh, May! That was all we had for supper!"

June bit down hard on the cruel words rising to her lips. "I'm going to the creek. Don't follow me!"

At the creek she found a fish in the trap and, remembering how her father did it, bashed the fish over the head with a rock until it stopped moving and blood leaked from its skull, but then she realized she wasn't sure how to cook it, so she released its corpse to the creek. She dropped her head in her hands and cried, not for the stupid fish but because May had complained this morning that she was tired of eating only bread and milk and eggs and whatever they could eat raw from the garden, and they had eaten almost all the bread and June didn't think she would be able to make more even with instructions from Olena, who still wouldn't get out of bed, and because even though June tried to milk the cow every morning and evening, she knew from the stamping and mooing that she wasn't emptying its udder, and if the udder kept filling it could make the cow sick, maybe even kill it. She crouched by the creek and thought of all her mother did, even when her father was home. Kneading bread in a pan so large May could take a bath in it, then baking enough loaves for the week; doing the laundry in an even larger tub, rubbing the dirty clothes against a board, sweating in the steam coming from the roiling water, refilling the tub with hot water from the stove's reservoir when it cooled. Filling the reservoir again with water from the well. Milking the cow, bucking logs. Weeding and hoeing and harvesting, then putting up the food from the garden: beans and peas, sauerkraut, which she shredded on a board fitted with a lethal blade, into a huge crock, salting each layer, weighing it down with a stone on a plate, skimming the scum that burbled up from beneath. June thought of it all and was appalled. What if her mother never got up again? June had no idea how to send word to her father. Even if she could somehow harness the horse to the wagon and make it go where she wanted, she had no idea where her father was. He should have been home by now, surely. She raised her head from her hands and her gaze caught on a tiny mound, on it a small cross made from two twigs lashed together with string. She could fetch Mr. Maguire. But at that thought she forced herself to stop crying. She would rather die. She would rather her mother died. She bathed her face in the cold creek water, not wanting May to see she'd been crying and get scared. Squared her shoulders and forced herself to her feet, to take the long heavy walk back to the house. But when she got there she found her mother in the kitchen, in clean clothes, putting bread on to rise and acting as though nothing had happened. Olena milked the cow, swatting it to stand still when it tried to kick her, told the girls to fetch water which she heated in the wood stove so she could bathe, then heated more to do laundry, managing somehow to get the dried blood out of June's sweater, thank goodness, though June still got a bit queasy at the thought of wearing it. Or perhaps it was the relief of this miraculous return to order that made her go behind the chicken coop and throw up every scrap of the bread and milk she'd had for breakfast.

 Her father came back the next day, to a house that seemed so normal June thought she had perhaps dreamed it, or made more of it than it was. But over dinner her father kept looking sharply at her mother and sent the girls to bed as soon as they'd finished their last mouthful. June crept up to the crack in the curtain and overheard her mother telling him that the thing that looked like a piglet would have been June's brother, saw her father red faced and smashing a fist on the table, her mother stony faced and rigid. It's all right, June wanted to tell her father, you still have me. I will be more to you than any son. She wanted to go to him, but she knew that expression on Olena's face too well and stayed crouched behind the curtain, mourning her father's loss even while part of her was glad not to have to share him with one more person. At the sound of another blow on the table, May stirred and cried out, and June crept into bed beside her. "Hush, May," she whispered. "It's all right."

May snuggled in close, pulling June's arms around her.

"Shall I tell you a story?"

"The one about the princesses and the shoes?"

"If you like. Once upon a time, in the days when wishing still helped, there were twelve dancing princesses. Every night they went to sleep with brand new shoes beside their beds and every morning the soles were worn right through and no one knew how..."

The next day June's father hugged her to him and pulled her onto his lap. "Your mother told me how well you took care of her while she was sick. You were very brave." June nestled in close until he held her away from him by the shoulders and stood her up so he could look in her eyes. "And Mr. Maguire. He was very helpful too, wasn't he?"

June stared down at her feet. "He carried the thing in my sweater. It was very bloody. He asked if Mama wanted the doctor and when she said no, then he left."

Her mother was still pale and sitting down more frequently between tasks, but she didn't seem to want anyone's help, especially Taras's. "Quit hovering!" she hissed at him more than once when he was trying to take the bucket of water from her to fill the stove's reservoir or carry in firewood from the lean-to. Her father's face would darken and he would go out to buck firewood, even though they had plenty. And when June and May made as though to follow him, he snapped at them to do their chores, even though they had already done them.

It was almost a relief when at dinner Olena said, "You'll need the horse and wagon to go to Norfolk and apply for relief."

Taras gave an irritated sigh. "I know, I know. But how can I leave you here without them? What if you take a turn for the worse? You still aren't yourself..."

"I'm going to send word to Varvara to come stay while you're gone. She is her own mistress now that my father has died. She'll bring her own horse and wagon, not that anything would arise that she wouldn't know how to deal with."

June's father waited only until Aunt Varvara arrived two days later, and then he was gone.

AUNT VARVARA, dressed all in black, was completely crooked, her back bent and her fingers twisted, the joints bumpy and swollen. Even her nose was crooked, and her face so weathered the wrinkles folded in on themselves. When Olena pushed June forward she said politely, if a trifle tremulously, "Hello Aunt Varvara."

"I am *not* your aunt, young lady, I am your great-aunt, and there is no need to remind me of how old I am getting. My bones do that well enough, and plain Varvara will do well enough too."

"That Baba Yaga," June's father often called her, and June could see why. Even though Varvara arrived in an ordinary wagon, June had little trouble picturing her flying through the air in her mortar, steering with her pestle and sweeping her tracks away with a willow-twig broom. When Varvara started poking her scrawny fingers through Olena's herbs and medicines, June was sure that if she wasn't actually the Baba Yaga, she was some kind of relative, for Baba Yaga swooped over fields late at night, scouring them for rare and powerful herbs in order to cast her spells and poison her enemies. June edged away from the herb chest, but Varvara grabbed her with a scrawny and surprisingly strong arm.

"So this is the oldest." She gripped June's chin with her fingers and angled it upward. "She won't be a looker, that's for sure, not with that frown." Varvara rubbed a bony finger across it, then with her thumbs pulled back the lids of June's eyes and peered at her eyeballs until June twisted away. "Ha!" she cackled. "You were such a skimpy thing we didn't waste a middle name on you. Didn't know if you'd survive your mother's meddling. You've proved us wrong." Though the words sounded approving her expression remained more worried than relieved. But maybe the wrinkles just made her look that way.

"Leave it be, Varvara."

Varvara pinched June's cheek, sharply more than affectionately, then swung her around and pushed her toward the door. "Out! Go play with your sister. At least one of you is a pretty little thing. Your mother and I have much to discuss."

June moved slowly out of the kitchen, lingering long enough to hear Varvara say, "Here. I made you this tonic. You're too pale. This will bring your blood back." June slammed the door on images of the bloody sheet between Olena's legs, the bloody mess in June's sweater.

That night they feasted. Aunt Varvara had brought a slab of salt pork and a small sack of rice along with the jug that she banged on the table and poured from while she cooked. "Sit, sit." She pushed Olena into a chair at the kitchen table. "June can help me." So June went to the garden for a cabbage and several onions which she washed under Varvara's careful eye. Then, still under supervision, she rinsed off the pork, which Varvara diced up and put into the old cast iron frying pan. As the pork gave up its fat, hissing and bubbling, Varvara diced the onions. "Here." She handed the cutting board to June. "Toss them in, but watch the fat. It will spit!" June stirred the sizzling onions while Varvara put rice on to boil and cored the cabbage, then put it in a large pot of water. Every so often she would take a pull on the glass of clear liquid she'd poured for herself, lift the cabbage from the boiling water with a slotted spoon, and get June to peel off the loosened outer leaves, her fingers, still smarting from the hot fat that had splashed her, now scalded with every tug. When the lower leaves became cool and resisted being pulled from the core, back the cabbage went to its boiling water.

Once the rice was cooked, and the pork and onion reduced to tiny dark brown bits in a sea of boiling fat, Varvara drained out the bits with a sieve and dumped them into the pot of rice, stirring vigorously with a wooden spoon. Then she and Olena folded up the mixture into the cabbage leaves, layering the finished rolls in a blackened and dented roasting tin, finally pouring all the sizzling fat over them. The smell of the roasting rolls, the cabbage browning in the sweet pork fat, was intoxicating. It had been months since they'd had any meat other than a hen who'd stopped laying or a hare caught in a snare. June could hardly wait until they could sit down to eat, but when they did she was mesmerized by Varvara downing roll after browned and greasy roll and shot after shot of vodka. The stories said Baba Yaga could drink an entire river without quenching her thirst and eat an entire ox without slaking her hunger, and this appeared to be true of Varvara too. June nudged May to see what she thought, but of course,

May was too concentrated on making sure that every spoonful of cabbage roll which Olena had cut up for her had a dark nugget of pork at its core.

"Don't stare, June," her mother said. "Eat your cabbage rolls." But by this time the fat had cooled and congealed and somehow the pork didn't taste as sweet as June thought it would.

To June's horror, Varvara insisted on sleeping with her, saying to Olena, "These old bones can't lie still for ten minutes together. You can't have me tossing and turning all night. June's young and strong. She can put up with me."

June was a sound sleeper and wouldn't have noticed any tossing if Varvara hadn't woken her up early the next morning by tugging on her hair. At first June thought it was by accident, and didn't open her eyes. She was sleepy, and she didn't like Varvara. But the tugs on her hair got stronger and stronger, until finally she opened her stinging eyes to find that gnarled face looming over her.

"You know that you were supposed to have a baby brother, yes?" Varvara whispered.

June nodded, closing her eyes against the image of the bloody piglet. She hadn't felt anything when she'd first seen it, but since then, whenever she thought of it and that it might have been a person, she felt sick.

Varvara's face moved too close to June's, her breath and her skin sour and ancient. "What did your father say?"

"I don't know," June stammered. There was danger here, danger to her father, but she didn't know what it was or how to guard against it.

"Did they argue? Did he ask you how often that man comes here?"

"I was asleep, it was late." June's voice squeaked, loud and sharp with anxiety, and Varvara's face flashed irritation.

"Is that you, June?" Olena's sleepy voice murmured from behind the curtain.

"We're just chatting here," Varvara's kind tones at odds with the frown she aimed at June, and the vicious tug she gave June's hair. "You go back to sleep. It's early yet."

But now May was awake and whimpering at Varvara's strange voice, still too drowsy to remember who she was. To her relief, June heard Olena's feet slap along the floor toward the stove. Without waiting to be asked, June called, "I'll get some eggs!" She slipped out from under Varvara's hands, shuffled into her clothes, and made good her escape, scalp and eyes tingling.

OLENA, wincing as the door banged behind June, plunked down heavily at the table, holding her belly. Two weeks after the miscarriage and she still felt scraped out. Varvara was right. She had to stop these assaults on her body. Somehow. Try to put money aside for the ingredients to make the pessary, though how was she to manage that when they were selling what they could just to buy food? Last winter they wouldn't even have had meat if a hunter, blue with cold and crusted with snow, hadn't chanced upon their cabin in a blizzard and left behind a side of deer as thanks for the shelter Olena provided. She'd salted some and frozen the rest, and it had seen them through the bitter months, small shreds of it giving a wild and glorious flavour to sauerkraut and soup. Not even Taras's jealous rage when she refused to assure him she had not even flirted with the man, staring insolently at his stupid questions until he hit her, not even that had ruined the taste of that meat.

June banged the door open, carrying a basket of fresh eggs from the coop, and Olena felt an unfamiliar struggle between irritation and affection, between the impulse to snap at her for the noise, the untied shoe laces, uncombed hair, and unwashed face, or smile at her for getting the eggs without being asked. Praise her for all that she had done when Olena had simply been unable to leave her bed. This was what bearing children did to you, put you at odds with yourself, as though the body itself forged a connection, a love that went deeper than any conscious or even unconscious desires of your own. Olena had heard that after giving birth, the native women bit the cord themselves and whether it was true or not, Olena could feel the wisdom of it, the need to sever that connection, to remind yourself: this is my body, that is yours, don't think you can cling to me forever, or I to you. But she doubted this was more than wishful thinking. Those nine months changed you, and not just physically. No matter that Olena wanted to be free, unfettered; once that life took root it wound its little fingers around her heart with a stranglehold. Even this one that hadn't had a life had left its mark, in her sadness and the sense of loss that couldn't quite be extinguished by her relief at not having one more mouth feeding off her, by the knowledge that this loss was the very thing she had most desired.

"Go wash your face and comb your hair. And get your sister ready," she said, more harshly than she'd intended, her throat thick. June put the eggs on the table without a word, but from behind the curtain of the girls' bedroom Olena heard her tones duplicated in her daughter's. "May, get out of bed, you lazy thing."

A bony hand pressed her shoulder and, embarrassed, she dashed the tears from her eyes.

Varvara peered closely into Olena's face. "You drank that tonic I gave you? Last night and again this morning?"

"Yes," Olena sighed, "but it doesn't seem to be doing any good." She just hadn't the energy to fight any more, not the farm, not Taras, not herself. The weariness that had pinned her to her bed for three days had frightened her badly, a weariness so deep it had seemed to divorce her from herself, left her observing her inert body from a place of complete numbness. Varvara dragged a chair beside Olena's and she recoiled at the scraping sound.

"Give it time." Varvara put a hand that was somehow both rough and gentle over Olena's. "Taras is away too much, and this place, two children, it's a lot to have on your plate if you have no help."

"There's not much I can do about that, is there? Except try to keep one more mouth from the plate."

Varvara flinched. A look of decision replaced the frown.

"Your father, you know the farm was in his name and mine, that he couldn't have left it to you girls, even if he'd thought to." She grimaced. "Which he didn't, old fool." Olena nodded. Her father's passing the year before had caused barely a ripple in her consciousness, and why would she want yet another crumbling piece of property?

"Well, I'm getting too old now to run the place, even with hired help. The last time I was in Eldergrove getting staples old Boychuk said he was selling the hardware store, moving to Winnipeg to be near his daughter."

Olena felt a flicker of interest.

"If we sold both farms we could buy the store and a small house for me. There are quarters above the store, three bedrooms. Talk it over with Taras. I know my neighbour is keen to buy my land and I'm sure your situation is no different. Even if it is, there are families coming up from the south where the land is so dry all they reap is dust. You'd think this would teach them, but no. The government is offering them money to resettle up here and up they come. Farmers," she snorted. "Always hungry for land."

"But what do we know about running a hardware store?"

"Boychuk will teach you all you need to know before he leaves. Show you the books, give you the list of contacts. I never thought I'd be grateful to Katya for chasing you off to school and putting those crazy dreams in your head, but now look. A life in town, just like you wanted. One thing you can say about Taras, he has turned his hands to many things since coming to this country."

"Some more successfully than others," Olena muttered.

"You cannot blame him for this depression. Although I will say, this land needs a better farmer than he to make it produce grain. You will never get ahead growing only enough to feed the four of you."

"Barely enough."

"Yes. Well. In town you would have people around you. Your girls could go to school. And you would have me to help." Varvara shifted uneasily in her chair. "I'd hoped that you and Taras would have sorted out your troubles by now. Perhaps if you are not so isolated... May, little chatterer, let slip you didn't leave your bed for three days after the miscarriage. I worry..." Varvara's grip tightened.

Olena set her jaw, some of her old resolve stirring deep within, the desire to be somewhere else, even if she could not be with someone else. Mindful of Varvara's arthritis, she patted the old woman's hand. "I will speak to him about the store."

TARAS PUSHED his weathered hat back from a sweaty brow. Wiped grit and salt from his eyes. The shuffling line of mostly men, the occasional woman with tattered children in tow, had inched excruciatingly along the wooden sidewalk of Norfolk for two hours under the hot sun, all of them getting dustier and sweatier by the minute. Like Taras they'd dressed with care, the men in suits, the women in hats they probably wore to church, tarted up with bedraggled flowers, though why any of them should have bothered he couldn't quite figure, given they were lined up for relief. Besides, the threadbare cloth, the patches, and especially the shoes and boots — cracked and faded beyond shining — gave them all away. As he rounded the corner and saw the stairs up to the fire hall, which housed the makeshift relief office, Taras almost turned tail, but steeled himself and stood his ground. He'd held out as long as he could, but there was no money for even the most basic supplies: flour for bread, salt for preserving cabbage and beets and cukes, the smallest sack of sugar to sweeten his daughters' morning bread and milk, enable Olena to put up raspberries and saskatoons. They would probably have to do without meat. Even side pork was too dear for what he imagined relief would provide. At least they still had chickens, too valuable to butcher as long as they kept producing eggs. And the cow, since it could graze while there was no snow on the ground and he was able to put up enough hay to feed it through the winter. No use selling it. With the going rate at only five dollars they were better off with the milk. Besides, the children adored it. At the thought of little May trying to milk it with her tiny hands, he cleared his throat roughly. The man ahead of him turned at the sound, peered at him shrewdly. "Smoke?" He held out a precious cigarette.

"Tanks." Taras shifted his knapsack to one shoulder, feeling rather than seeing the man's slight recoil at his accent. Or perhaps he'd imagined it, because the man still held out the cigarette, lit it when Taras bent his head to the flame.

"Long wait." The man picked a flake of tobacco from his chapped lip. He was younger than Taras had thought, little more than a boy really, with a face creased beyond its years, his ankles and wrists protruding from the frayed cuffs of a suit too small. "They turned us away yesterday, so I came this morning first thing. Should get in today."

Taras nodded, drew smoke deep into his lungs. It had been a long time since he'd been able to buy tobacco. "Hope so. Took all night to get here and I got friends at hotel look for vehrk. Harvest vehrk. They find anyting they leave note ahnt I join them tomorrow."

The door in front of them swung open and shut as people entered clutching hats, and left clutching vouchers, some of the men red faced, some of the women teary. The line shuffled forward a few steps, stopped. The door as far away as ever.

The boy twitched nervously, flicking invisible ash from his cigarette into the street. "You got family?"

"Vife, two geerls. You marrie?"

The boy shook his head no. "I hear they send the young ones like me to camps. Building bridges, roads, that kind of thing, for food and lodging. The camps are far away, my mother won't like it. But my father died a few years back and I haven't been able to find any work. I figure the little ones can help her almost as much as I can, and they don't eat as much."

Taras looked away from the boy's reddening eyes. He hadn't thought of his own mother in years, had left her with barely a backward glance, her only son, so filled with contempt for the peasantry she represented, with revolutionary zeal for a new order that the volunteer teachers had imparted along with lessons in reading and writing. When the war broke out he fled conscription and by the time it ended, when he made an effort to contact her, she'd vanished. He had no idea what had become of her. So many people in the old country had been displaced. Or killed, of course. He wondered if she would have appreciated the irony that after all his efforts to reject her and her way of life, like her he had ended up scrabbling in the dirt for what could barely be called a living, though at least it was on land of his own.

He and the boy smoked in silence until they were next in line. When the door opened, the boy pitched his half-finished cigarette into the street, stiffened his spine and marched up the steps. He really was young, thought Taras as he resisted the urge to pick up the smouldering butt, not to know enough to pinch off the burning end and save the rest for later. No doubt he would learn. Taras smoked his cigarette until his fingers were singed, and by then it was finally his turn.

He entered the dimly lit room and was waved over to the only empty chair in front of four desks. Removing his hat and ducking his head briefly he sat, his chair raking the wooden floor with a screech that turned heads. The place was as hushed as a church, and perhaps the similarity was not accidental: all these whispering people confessing their failure to feed their families. Pleading for understanding. Swallowing mouthful after bitter mouthful of pride.

The man at the desk was about Taras's age, and pasty faced. Probably an office worker from the time he'd come of age. He had long, thin, pale fingers that continually shuffled, then aligned, the papers in front of him. When Taras sat, sliding his knapsack under the chair, the clerk looked up and smiled mechanically. No doubt these were long days for him too.

"Name." His voice barely above a whisper so that Taras had to bend forward, fighting the impulse to whisper as well, as though they were engaged in some nefarious act.

"Taras Zalesky." The man looked as down at heel as the people applying for relief. When he caught Taras staring at his frayed shirt cuffs he hid them under his suit sleeve like a turtle pulling into its shell.

"Zalesky. What is that? Polack?"

"Ukrainian." Taras resisted the urge to say "bohunk." He needed this man on his side.

"And where do you live, *Mister* Zalesky?"

"I have homestedt one, two days from here."

"How long have you been in this country, anyway?"

Surely these were not the questions on the sheet in front of him. He had not marked anything on a paper but Taras's name.

"Ten year."

"They teach you manners where you're from?"

"Excuse me?"

"Ten years. Sir."

Taras turned the brim of his hat, hand over hand, counting the turns. "Sehr," he said as evenly as he could, refusing to look away. The clerk's eyes were as washed out as the rest of him, not a callous on his hand except perhaps for one under that pen he'd been pushing all his life. But under his gaze Taras felt every weathered wrinkle on his face, the sunburned swath on the back of his neck like a brand.

"And I suppose you've got chickens? A garden? Pigs? Cows?"

The man spoke softly, conversationally, even with a faint smile. "Why do you need to come here with your hand out? Don't you have food? People in town are making do with scraps. Yet here you are, asking them to give up even that for you, an immigrant." He leaned forward, his lilting voice becoming a hiss. "Why don't all you bohunks and polacks and commies just go back where you came from and leave this country to the white men who built it."

Taras stood, the chair's scrape once more raking the air. "Sehr. My two geerls, they born here. They not — commies — " he spat the word, as softly as the man in front of him whose face was getting red. "They are Canadian. Who vill feed them if I go back vhere I come from? You? Vhere you come from, eh? How long you been here? You don't look Indian to me." Every fibre of him itched to make a dignified exit, but the thought of Olena's face when he returned, once more empty-handed, forced him back into his chair. "I vehrk here ten years, I vehrk the land and make homestedt, make life. That is vhere I come from and I don't leave until I get vhat I am here for."

The red-faced clerk was about to speak when another man, from the crispness of his shirt and the crease in his pants someone higher in authority, bent down to examine the sheet on the desk. "Problem?" he asked.

"No, sir. No problem at all," the clerk replied. "Just finishing up."

"Very good," the man said easily. "Long lines today, mustn't delay unnecessarily."

"Cow?"

"One."

"No milk ration, then. Chickens?"

"Six."

"No eggs."

"Radio? Car? Telephone?"

Taras shook his head.

"There's no relief if you have luxuries. We can send someone out to see if you have lied to us. And we don't give you any warning so you don't have time to hide anything."

"They vant to come, they can come. They find nattink."

A signature scrawled at the bottom of a page and then Taras was back in the street, clutching his relief vouchers in a hand still shaking with rage. He reached the hotel to find his friends gone. They'd left word with the bartender that they hadn't found anything close by so had gone with a group of men heading farther west in search of fields to harvest. No hope of adding to the meagre amount the vouchers represented, then. Taras stood at the bar fingering the dollar bill he'd stuffed in his pants all those days ago and had resolved to leave untouched, June's dollar bill, hoping against all reason that he'd be able to give it back to her, see her dancing in those shoes, what did she call them, Mary Janes? He had an almost visceral impulse to go back up to that bastard in the fire hall and punch his face in. He could taste the man's bile in his own mouth, it stuck to his skin like tar. What would be so wrong with using some of June's dollar for a hotel room, to sleep in a bed, have a decent wash? Or why not forego the room and spend the entire dollar on booze, leaning up against the polished wood of the bar, the gleaming brass rail, forget the squalor that was his life.

He couldn't do that to June. Olena maybe, but it was June's dollar. He stumbled out into the glaring afternoon sun and walked up and down the street, hoping to clear his head, his lungs, which were choked and throbbing with holding it all in, always holding it all in.

When he finally had pulled himself at least partially under control he went into the general store and a woman behind the counter with crinkly blonde hair and far too much makeup said, "Taras, isn't it? Taras Zalesky? You've been in here before. Don't you remember my name?" She pouted. "I thought I'd made a better impression on you than that."

"Oh, yes." Taras scrambled through his memory. He seldom got into Norfolk and when he did his focus was usually on getting to the bar as quickly as possible.

"Hot, isn't it?" She undid her top button, then pressed her arm against the counter so he could get a good eyeful. There was no one else in the store.

"Hot. Yes."

"Hot, Mrs. Dillon," she teased. "But you can call me Betsy."

"Betsy." He pulled out the vouchers and laid them on the counter. "Vhat can I get with these? Please."

Her eyes narrowed slightly, but then she smiled. "I guess this is your first time?"

He nodded.

"My husband usually does the serving, that's probably why you didn't remember me right off the bat. But he's off for a week, fishing with his brother, so it's just little old me." She riffled through the vouchers. "Hmmm. No eggs or milk, I see. But we can give you salt and flour and tea, even some rice if you like. And if you run across to the butcher after this he'll give you a bit of salt pork."

"Any sugar?" Taras asked, smoldering with the humiliation of being told what he could eat but keeping his temper in check. "My kids, they like sveet tings."

"Yes, there's a voucher for it right here. Brown will be better value." She weighed out the dry goods, poured them into sacks. "How are you going to get all this home?" Though it didn't look like all that much to Taras.

"I got vagon out back of hotel."

"Oh, good." She touched his arm lightly as he gathered up the packages. "Which way are you headed?"

Somehow another of her buttons had come undone, and when she suggested a glass of lemonade at her house — really, he would be passing right by it, only a little ways out of town — Why not, he thought. Why not. She gave him careful directions, and even more careful instructions to pull his wagon round behind the house, out of sight of the road. "You go get that salt pork while I close up," she said brightly. "And here," she slipped a couple of licorice pipes into his hand, her fingers lingering on his, "for the children."

After getting a measly amount of salt pork from the butcher's, he tossed it in the wagon and headed out of town, and before long pulled in behind a large brick house set back from the main road. Betsy opened the door and showed him into the parlour, ushering him to an overstuffed sofa littered with crocheted doilies, and set out a pitcher of lemonade and some cookies. When she offered to spike the lemonade with something a little stronger all he said was, "Tanks."

"I'll just go freshen up a bit." She vanished up the wood panelled hallway. He poured a huge splash of vodka into his cold and sweaty glass, drained it in one gulp, then pressed it to his hot and dusty forehead.

SHE EASED the bedroom door shut, her mouth so dry she had to take a sip from her glass of lemonade. She had never done anything like this before, could hardly believe it when she'd loosened a button on her blouse. Then another. For a labourer, a Uke at that. Her husband would kill her if he found out. But her husband wasn't here to find out, was he? Gone off for his own fun with his brother and warning her before he left not even to go for a drive in the country like she'd done the last time he was away. The price of gasoline being what it was, they couldn't afford fripperies. Over and over he reminded her they were one of the few families in the area who didn't drive Bennett buggies, hitching a horse to a car they could no longer afford to gas up. But God, she was so tired of being careful. So she'd undone those buttons, breathing in the musky smell of sweat and dust, which reminded her, she'd have to be sure to dust off that sofa, remove any traces that might arouse her husband's suspicions. She'd briefly considered bringing the Uke to her bed, but her mind had rebelled — there were limits.

She slipped out of her dress, stripped off her cotton bra and dusted her armpits with scented powder, then slid into her best robe, real silk, bought before this wretched depression. "Don't call it that," she could hear her husband say almost as if he were beside her. "Bennett always says the fundamentals are sound." Well if they were so sound why was there never any money was what she'd like to know. When they'd come out to this godforsaken place he'd promised her they'd be living the life of Riley, much better off than they were at home. To be sure, *he* was living the life of a country squire, off on his hunting and fishing trips while she minded the store like some skivvy. Well, she'd had enough.

Seating herself at her dresser, she rifled around in the bottom drawer until she found an old tube of red lipstick and a vial of red nail polish, bought years ago on a lark but never worn again after her husband told her she looked like a tart. How lucky she'd kept them. They liked bright colours, these Ukes. Garish, savage. She'd heard they were hung like horses. She shivered, blew on the wet nails, used her pinky to mend a slight smudge beyond the lip line. She mustn't keep him waiting too long. Or herself. Standing, she spritzed herself with perfume from an atomizer, folded back her robe to show even more cleavage, staring at her reflection in the mirror. Already she looked different, sultry, experienced, like she should be smoking a cigarette and letting the strands of smoke float past her eyes. Only one thing jarred the image. She pulled the robe back from her hips and surveyed with dissatisfaction her plain cotton underwear. Her husband didn't approve of lacy lingerie, saying why bother when they only ever made love in the dark. Well, a loose woman wouldn't worry about being seen in the light. A woman like that, a hardened adulteress, probably wouldn't even wear underwear. She shivered again. Maybe he'd get so carried away at the scent of her that he wouldn't even undress her, just tear into her and take her with her clothes on. Animals, she thought, and stepped out of the heap of cotton at her feet, rubbing her robe into her moist crevice.

WHEN SHE ENTERED the parlour, if he was surprised to see her change of clothes he didn't show it. He laid her down on the sofa and peeled open her robe, thank goodness for the way the heavy curtains filtered the late afternoon light. After all, she wasn't exactly in her first blush of youth. When he took off his pants she sneaked a peek, but he seemed normal, not that she had more to compare with other than her husband, and it was not even that her husband was not an adequate lover, it was just that she was bored, bored, bored, but then the Uke thrust himself deep inside her and it jolted her right out of herself, just as she'd hoped, and she was crying out things she had never dreamed of saying, "I love your cock," she cried. "Fuck me, fuck me," anything was permissible here, she was a woman who dared all things, she was a woman desired by men who fucked like animals. She was a woman to whom men said, as this one did, flipping her over on top of him so that she was riding him the way you would a horse, "I vant to see you come," and that almost pushed her over the edge. She bounced on him, he must be hot to speak like that, and she had never been on top with her husband, and that alone made this the most exciting sex she had ever had. That and the fact that he seemed to be able to last forever.

JESUS, he thought, why wouldn't she come. One of those damned doilies had worked itself under his knee and was so starched it scratched. Her constant talking and moaning was distracting and her perfume was overpowering. He needed to get done and get out of here. While she'd been "freshening up" he'd had too much time to drink vodka and think about how stupid it was just to be here. What if her husband decided to come home early? What if a neighbour dropped by? Even if she didn't answer the door you'd be able to hear her cries. He'd never been with a woman this loud. Maybe she thought she was encouraging him.

"Oh God," she hissed through her teeth. "Oh, God." Her lips were pulled back in something like a snarl, Christ what was she thinking to wear that lipstick, she looked like a drunken whore, all that red smearing over a powdery white face.

"Moment." He yanked the woman up and flipped her on top. Enough of that doily. "I vant to see you come." He pulled her down hard on his cock. "Ride 'em cowboy," she chuckled and bounced up and down on him, her hands on his shoulders, breasts jiggling.

He reached one hand up, knotted his fingers in the crinkly yellow hair, and pulled that red mouth onto his. Anything to stop her talking.

Now she bucked so violently she almost threw herself off him, and he had to pull her against him with both hands, until she collapsed and smeared red lipstick and spit on his shirt. Christ, his only good shirt.

WHEN SHE CAME there was some credit due to his expert thrusts, his endurance, but what sent her crashing into climax was the image of herself as adulteress, riding herself to orgasm. Life would never be boring again. She would have this image of herself even when she was measuring out dry goods into worn sacks, counting out change, rubbing her husband to erection. In afterglow she slumped against his still hard penis and traced her finger along the raised veins of his arm as though tracing the map of her future. She was brazen, a hussy who rode forbidden male flesh, and that woman said, as a hussy would, "Oh, Uke, honey. You can play hide the kielbasa with me any time."

He yanked out of her — what had she done? Was he angry? He spun her onto her back and hovered over her, his penis now looking huge as it bumped against her lips. Was he angry? He was saying something about her husband and he was shoving his cock into her mouth. She wanted to spit it out, good God it had her juices all over it, she didn't want it, but she collided with this new image of herself as a woman who dared all things, was this what they did? She choked and her eyes rolled back in her head. This was beyond the pale, her husband had never dared — what was he saying, this bloody peasant in his barbaric language, he'd been talking dirty but this didn't sound like sex talk, it sounded like contempt, and the image of herself as powerful adulteress started to teeter, what was he saying, she couldn't get her ears wrapped around the words — Jesus he was bumping against the back of her throat, she was going to gag.

TARAS CROUCHED OVER her head, almost hissing, "You like kielbasa so much, English bitch, go on, taste it." Her eyes rolled white and started to leak from the sides, but Taras couldn't help himself, the venom spilled out of him, "You think my accent makes me stupid? Next time I see your stick of a husband I'll be remembering this —" he yanked his cock out of her mouth and for one moment that white powdered face became the pasty face of the relief officer and he climaxed gloriously, the sluggish liquid dribbling toward her mouth.

WHEN HE PULLED OUT of her all she could think was, thank God I can breathe, thank God he didn't make me swallow it. "You bastard!" she gasped now that her mouth was free. She scrubbed at the liquid on her face then pushed him away with both hands. "How dare you!"

He grabbed her by the chin and forced her to look up at him, then, shifting himself till his mouth was inches above hers, slid his hand luxuriously over her breast, toward the cleft between her legs. With a shock she discovered desire lurking there still. The hardened, glamorous adulteress flared back to life. She was not sure of him, but she could not acknowledge the other possibility of what had been happening here, so she parted her thighs and her lips and started to reconstruct her story. Warily. Just as her hips started to roll toward his hand he pulled away. She closed her eyes and moaned. His tongue slid around her nipple as he eased off her. "I'll be right back."

Drawing her robe loosely around her, she murmured sleepily. "You are a bastard. But don't be long."

TARAS RAN cold water into the bathroom sink, soaked a face towel, pressed it against his face and neck. Christ, he had to be more careful. Lately he felt like the cum he was shooting into the women he bedded was pure rage. But speaking to Betsy like that, treating her with contempt like that, that was stupid beyond belief. At least he'd lapsed into Ukrainian, but even so. He couldn't ever forget what side of the tracks he was on. There had been rumours of the Ku Klux Klan setting up in the south of the province. Not that vigilantes needed an organization, just an excuse. It was so easy for a "Uke" to put a foot wrong. And now he was entangled with this woman, when he wanted nothing more than to make a quick exit. But he couldn't leave her with any reason to regret what she'd done.

"What's taking so long?" a throaty voice called from the other room and he grimaced. Once again that piece of gristle between his legs had landed him in hot water. But it seemed to have a life, a mind, of its own. It fed where it did not hunger, and hungered for what was always out of reach. If he dared, he would wave his cock in his wife's face when he got home, another woman drying on his skin, her garish lipstick still circling the shaft. Prove to her that other women valued what she did not.

He emerged from the bathroom and stood gazing down at Betsy. Even in the dim light he could see beneath the gaping silk robe how her aging breasts sagged away from her breast bone.

"You know, my husband goes regularly to Regina to buy clothing at the year-end sales to sell here. It's not much of a profit, but he says every little bit helps." She pulled Taras toward her lipstick-smeared mouth and whispered against his, "And it means he is often away from home."

TRUE TO HIS WORD, June's father came back three days after he left, the wagon stocked with flour, salt, tea, sugar, and side pork, enough to make June's mother smile. Varvara left the very next day. June was happy to see her go, to be rid of those early morning interrogations, the whispered conversations between her mother and her aunt that hovered just out of June's range of hearing but sounded sinister nonetheless. Mr. Maguire was mentioned more than once. Varvara didn't appear to like him any more than June did, but even that didn't endear her to June. With Varvara gone the house returned to normal. Better than normal, with no arguments for two whole days, her parents working separately, meeting only for meals. Her father doing the milking, mending the fences, bringing the hay in for the cow and the horse. Her mother starting to put up food from the garden, the huge canning pot on the boil all the time it seemed. She sent June and May out to pick saskatoons from the bushes by the creek, and raspberries from the garden, which she canned or made into jam. She got June to spell her off with shredding the cabbage, layering it with salt in the large pottery crock and mashing it with a wooden spoon to release the juices, then burying cabbage heads in the shreds. It took all June's strength just to shred and pound one cabbage but her mother didn't frown at her once for being slow or clumsy. May was too small to do any shredding and ate more berries than she put in the baskets, but she liked to feel she was helping, and besides, Olena said, it kept her from under Olena's feet, not seeming to care that this meant putting her under June's. Or that May invariably got distracted from any task, stopping to count the number of dots on a ladybug if one landed on her hand, "... four ... five ... this one has eleventy, June! It must be very old. Ooh! It tickles!" Leaving June to pick all the potatoes their father turned up from the garden while May kissed the writhing worms that had also been turned up, murmuring as she poked them back into the soil, "There, there. You go back home now. Your children will miss you."

But once the chores were done and the girls went down to the creek to sit in the shade, dabble their feet in the cool water and make mud pies, decorating them with grasses and wild flowers, once June's desire to smack May into paying attention ebbed away, the flow of May's babble — "Do you think bluebells look better than tansy, June? I think bluebells. I like blue better than yellow, don't you?" — blended with the murmur of the creek, and June felt an inexplicable release as she listened, knowing she was not expected to respond, except perhaps to hand over some water-polished pebbles for the final touch.

They were just finishing off one of these pies when June saw her father coming back through the fields from Mr. Maguire's, where he'd gone on his third day home to help with the haying. Puffs of dust and clouds of insects rose with his every step. Something was dangling from one of his hands. A rabbit.

"Mama!" June called as she ran to the house, banging into the kitchen.

"What now?" her mother snapped, but she looked up from the sink as June pointed out the window. Something like pleasure flicked across her mother's face. Something greedy and alive.

"Run quick and get me the vinegar and the salt from the lean-to." Olena pulled the large cast iron pot from the shelf and threw another chunk of wood into the stove, poking at the embers to bring them to blazing. June brought the crock of vinegar, then the sack of salt and set them on the table.

Her father strode through the door, and he and Olena exchanged brief nods. They didn't touch one another, June had almost never seen her parents touch except by accident, but they were moving together in rhythm. To June it was a beautiful thing.

"Still alive?" her mother asked, honing the carving knife, scrik scrik along the stone.

Her father wasted no words, just grasped the rabbit's ears with one hand, tucking its body under his other arm, bending back the rabbit's neck so it extended over the pot. Olena made one swift, decisive incision that slit the rabbit's neck. Her father, holding the hare's legs firmly, bent the neck over the pot just as it started to pulse blood, rapidly at first, then slower and slower, while Olena sprinkled salt and trickled vinegar into the pot, stirring and watching intently. When the rabbit was completely drained, June's father took the body outside to skin it, gut it, and carve it into pieces that Olena tucked into the simmering liquid.

This was a dish of rare good luck, dependent as it was on finding the rabbit almost as soon as it was snared. The first time June had seen this ritual, she had cried for the poor dead animal. Her mother, after a careful stir of the pot, turned on her and slapped her face. "You want to eat? You want to stay alive?"

When June nodded, she returned to her stirring. "Then sometimes you've got to kill things."

She had driven the lesson home again one day when June's father was once more working another man's fields. Olena had gone to check the snares and strode through the door with a rabbit dangling limp from her hands. June's heart pumped in her throat.

"Don't just stand there! Get the salt and the vinegar and pour until I say stop."

Standing on a wobbly stool, June did as she was told.

"There, that's right. Ach!" The rabbit was stirring under her mother's arm. Olena whacked it on the back of the neck, then held her ear to its chest.

"Lucky. Still beating. Get the knife."

Her mother held the rabbit over the pot, throat exposed. "Go on June, you know what to do." June gripped the knife. She could see a tiny flutter in the rabbit's chest, a stronger one at its neck. "There. Right there where the pulse is. Hurry before it comes to. Fast and deep now."

But the rabbit kicked just as she struck with the knife, she only nicked it. A thin spurt of blood arced out of the rabbit's neck, spattering June's hands, the floor, her bare feet. "Again! Deeper!" The bloody knife was slippery in June's hand, and when she stabbed blindly the rabbit let out a terrible shriek as its head rotated toward her, its eyes rolling back in its head and its mouth open, she could see its needly teeth and pink tongue, and a wider flow of blood pumping slower and slower until its terrified eyes were snuffed out, like a doused candle. Even Olena seemed a bit shaken, but all she said was. "You did well, Junie. Go wash now."

That night June managed to eat only as much of the rabbit

stew as would take the edge off her hunger. But the next day she ate the leftovers warmed through and served with fresh mashed potatoes and even sopped up the gravy with a heel of bread. After all, she had often helped her mother butcher chickens, held them down as they squawked, smelled the copper smell of death. The fact that she disliked chickens should not weigh in the balance. As her mother said, if you want to eat, sometimes you have to kill things.

And now as the rabbit stew simmered on the stove, filling the house with the scent of garlic and onion and game, it seemed to weave a magic spell that held them all in its warmth. While it cooked, her father and June hauled water from the well, and her mother didn't even say anything when June spilled some on the kitchen floor, just stoked up the fire to boil the kettle. Olena dragged the bath tub in front of the stove, pouring in cold water from the buckets and heating it with boiling water from the kettle and they all had their baths, first May, then June, Olena, lastly Taras. Then her mother ladled out the meat, so tender it fell from the bone into pools of rich dark sauce, filling their plates. Her father sighed with satisfaction. "My mother used to make this dish in the old country, and she said it held all the flavours the tongue could perceive. The sour of the vinegar, the sweetness of meat, the salt of the blood, the bitterness of death."

The luck of the rabbit held as they soaked up that sauce with bread made fresh that morning, made with flour her father had brought back thanks to something called relief. The luck of the rabbit shone in her mother's small smiles at her father's stories about his time on the road, in May's deep concentration as she wiped up every drop with her bread, her pudgy fingers as careful as an old lady's, her eyes fixed on her plate. It shone when Olena told Taras how brave June had been to help kill the rabbit while he was away, and her father chucked June under the chin, "Good girl." June licked up that dark red gravy and thought how silly she'd been to cry for a rabbit. She felt much more grown up now. Next time she was called on to wield the knife her hand would not falter.

After supper June tugged at her father's sleeve.

"Did you bring a book, Papa?"

"Not this time, I'm afraid. But I'll tell you what I'll do." He pulled June onto one knee and May onto the other while Olena sat in her rocking chair and started sorting laundry from a big basket for the next day's weekly wash. "I'll tell you a story my great-grandmother told me, from the ancient days on the steppes, about a very heroic young girl."

"Was she pretty?" June asked glumly.

"Very! In fact, she looked a lot like you." He winked and June knew one moment of pure happiness.

"Oh! I almost forgot!" Taras stood the girls up again, disappeared into the bedroom and emerged with his duffle bag, then rummaged around inside it, clothes spilling out onto the floor until suddenly he cried, "What have we here?" and held out two licorice pipes, with crusty red candy where the embers should be. Then he settled the girls back on his knee while Olena scooped up the clothes into the basket.

June popped the licorice into her mouth, leaned into her father's familiar smell, moved so she could touch May's feet with her own.

"Once upon a time, in the days when wishing helped, there was a little girl named Vasilisa. She lived with her father on the edge of a great wood."

June's mother inhaled sharply and they all turned to see her staring at a shirt she'd drawn from the basket, her eyes sharp as nails. The luck of the rabbit that had wrapped them in warmth froze up like hoar frost blown from a tree, its invisible shards all about their feet.

"Why was she only with her father?" said May, oblivious as always. "Where was her mother?"

"Good question." Olena's tone matched her eyes. "Usually in these stories, the mother is conveniently dead. She has done her duty, born the children, and her reward is to die before she has lived her life."

Taras's hand on the arm of the chair clenched until the knuckles gleamed white.

"Sadly," Taras glared at Olena, "the mother had up and left Vasilisa and her father when Vasilisa was very small. Sadly, there was not enough love in her heart even for her daughter to keep her at home."

"Papa," May whined, "you're holding me too tight."

"I'm sorry, sweetheart." Taras loosened his grip on the chair enough that the pink returned to his hand.

"Go on," Olena said. "Tell the girls the fairy story. You like your stories, don't you? And they will learn soon enough what real life is like."

To June's great relief her father opened his mouth to continue. "As I was saying, Vasilisa and her father were very sad when the mother abandoned them so selfishly, but it so happened that in the same village there was a woman with flowing black hair, quite a young woman and pretty," Olena snorted but didn't speak, "though not," Taras hugged June close, "as pretty as Vasilisa. She liked Vasilisa's father very much and after a time, saying that if the mother wasn't dead, she was as good as, this young and pretty woman convinced him to marry her. Unfortunately she didn't feel the same love for Vasilisa. You see, she didn't want a child she hadn't carried under her heart for nine months. So she hatched a plan to get rid of the little girl."

"Do you mean she gave her away?" asked May, eyes wide, the licorice pipe almost dropping from her open mouth.

"You shall see exactly what she meant soon enough, little one."

June poked at May to let her father go on, and May poked her back, as if it was a game.

"In those days, fire was very precious. There were no such things as matches that could light a fire — poof — whenever you wanted. Because of this people were very careful always to keep the fire lit in their homes. But this woman waited until a time when the father had to go away on business, and then she let the fire die out completely. 'Now you must go to Baba Yaga,' she told Vasilisa. 'No one else can give us fire.' So little Vasilisa set off into the forest at the edge of the village. She walked a long, long way, with the trees moaning around her, until finally she found a house — a strange house, all the walls crooked, not a straight line anywhere, perched on huge chicken legs in the darkest part of the forest."

"Chicken legs?" squeaked May.

"Yes, all wrinkly and yellow and scabby, the ugliest chicken legs you ever saw. The fence was made all of human bones with a skull at the top of the bony gate that rattled at Vasilisa's approach. Baba Yaga came roaring out of the house. 'Who dares to disturb me?' Little Vasilisa, afraid of Baba Yaga but still more afraid of going home without the precious fire, gasped, 'Please, Baba, but we have no fire in my home and I've been sent to beg some from you.'

"Baba Yaga reached out with her scrawny fingers to pinch Vasilisa's cheek. 'Ach, not enough meat there to keep a bird alive. However, you may enter.'

"So Vasilisa went into the house and when she saw Baba Yaga in the light she could hardly keep from running away. The old hag was dressed all in black and her back was bent. Her fingers had nails like talons and her teeth were sharp as razors. She had just finished eating a huge ox, the bones and fat were filling up the fireplace and the stench was filling the air so that Vasilisa could barely breathe. 'I will make you a bargain,' Baba Yaga said. 'I will give you fire, but first you must complete three tasks. And if I am not satisfied, I will cook you and eat you even though you are so bony you might crack my teeth.' Vasilisa was too afraid to do more than nod.

"'First you must scrub my hearth until it is spotless. Remember, do it well if you don't want to end up as dessert.'

"The hearth was huge and so were the bones, all black and stinking in pools of grease. Vasilisa lugged them to the edge of the forest, then scraped and scraped to get the burnt animal fat off the stone, and carried bucket after bucket of ashes to the back of the hut, all while Baba Yaga picked her terrible sharp teeth with a rusty iron file. Baba Yaga gave Vasilisa only a crust of dry bread and a glass of water, then went off to bed, leaving Vasilisa to finish the hearth. 'And if I find one spot of grease or one feather of ash, you will be my breakfast.'

"By the time Vasilisa took out the last bucket of ashes, the moon had climbed high into the sky and was throwing eerie shadows all around Baba Yaga's hut. Vasilisa was already uneasy but she almost screamed when the skull at the top of the skeleton gate rasped, in dry as dust tones, 'Hello little girl. I thought your bones would be joining mine this night.'

"Now Vasilisa was a very polite little girl, and besides, she was more afraid of waking Baba Yaga than talking to a skull, so she thrust the scream deep in her chest and simply said, 'No, Uncle.'

"'No,' sighed the gate. 'Well, that is a good thing for you, but a sad thing for me. I could use some young bones. All of us are ancient and brittle and we creak something fierce, especially when the wind blows. And of course, the wind always blows.'

"'What if I oiled you, Uncle?' Vasilisa suggested, her skin prickling at the thought.

"'Why, that would be wonderful.' The skull's grin seemed to expand. If he'd had a tongue and lips, he would have been licking them. 'Perhaps you could use the animal grease from the hearth?' And that's what Vasilisa did, and when she had finished, the skull rattled the whole fence with pleasure. 'I haven't felt so loose-limbed since I arrived here.'

"'When was that, Uncle?' Vasilisa ventured to ask.

"'Many long years. Baba Yaga appeared in the shape of a young and beautiful woman with flowing black hair and ruby red lips, and before I could see the hag within the maiden I was as you see me now.'

"'I am very sorry to hear that, Uncle.'

"'Well, we must see if we can make your story turn out somewhat better. You must always remember that Baba Yaga is a great liar, the consort of the Prince of Lies. She will offer you your heart's desire and while you are dreaming of it you suddenly find yourself nothing but bones and Baba Yaga licking her lips and picking her teeth. Now, leave an extra dollop of that grease in my mouth and go to bed before the old witch discovers us talking. If I can do you a good turn I will.'

"But as Vasilisa began wearily to go up the steps she heard another voice. 'Hello little girl.' Vasilisa looked all around but could see no one, so finally she peered under the stairs and the chicken legs said again, 'Hello little girl.'

"'Hello.' Vasilisa was so startled she forgot to say Uncle or Auntie, and wouldn't have known which to use anyway, since the legs had no body or head.

"'Do you think you could cover us with the last of the ashes?' the legs asked, scrabbling in the hard dirt. 'We are so itchy from lice, and ashes are so soothing.'

"Vasilisa scooped up a bucketful of ashes from the heap at the back of the hut and bathed the ugly yellow feet, which sighed their pleasure, even though Vasilisa's gorge rose with every puff of ash. 'Thank you, little girl. You wouldn't think it to look at me, but I used to be as young and pretty as you, so much so that I caught the eye of Baba Yaga's dark companion and when I spurned his advances, he cursed me, and Baba Yaga came to claim me. The punishment for my virtue is that I remain for the rest of my days nothing but ugly legs that can move but never run away.'

"'I am so sorry to hear that, Auntie,' Vasilisa said, now that she knew the legs were female.

"'Well, we must make sure your story turns out better than mine. Listen for my voice very carefully while you are in the hut with Baba Yaga. I hear everything that goes on in there, to my horror. Now go to bed before she finds you out here talking. But on your way, would you tie up the thorny bush with those pretty red ribbons in your hair? When the wind blows its branches scratch something awful.' So Vasilisa did as she was asked and the bush preened herself and rustled her thanks.

"Vasilisa finally slept, on the hard but spotless hearth, grateful for its fading warmth.

"The next morning Baba Yaga shook Vasilisa awake before the sun rose. 'While I'm away you must sort the poppy seeds from that pile of dust or I will eat you, gristly and bony though you may be.' Then off she flew in her mortar, using her pestle to steer and a broom to sweep her tracks behind her. Vasilisa sat down and cried, for the poppy seeds were as small as the grains of dust and there were millions of them. But then a tiny voice spoke from her feet. 'The chicken legs sent us to help you, since you helped her.' And little lines of white lice began to sort the seeds from the dust and didn't eat even one, because of course, lice eat only blood. After several hours they left behind two piles, one of seeds, the other of dust, and Vasilisa hurried outside to bathe the chicken legs in the dust as thanks. 'Careful, little one.' The legs pointed one clawed foot toward the sky. Vasilisa rushed inside just as Baba Yaga swooped down from her travels. 'Here.' She hauled a huge buffalo out of the mortar. 'I have been far afield today, and I am rather hungry. Cook this.' Her eyes flicked in the direction of the poppy seed pile and she frowned a terrible frown but said nothing more.

"Vasilisa cooked the buffalo and this time when Baba Yaga had finished her meal and was picking her terrible sharp teeth with the file, she let Vasilisa sit at the table and eat some of the meat with her bread. When Vasilisa had finished, Baba Yaga yanked Vasilisa's chair right beside hers, so they were almost touching. 'I have one more task for you and then you may have your fire.' She opened her mouth so wide Vasilisa was afraid she might fall in. 'There at the back.' Baba Yaga smiled a cunning smile. 'Take the file and lean into my mouth and get that piece of meat that is wedged in between the teeth.' Trembling, Vasilisa grasped the file, rose from the table and took a tentative step toward the yawning mouth. But just as she did the legs scuttled madly, hissing, 'Run, Vasilisa, run!' She threw the file into the back of Baba Yaga's throat, turned on her heels and ran as hard as she could. Baba Yaga howled and spat out the file, sending it crashing through the window. 'I'll catch you yet!' she roared, but the chicken legs scrabbled so violently the house heaved and bucked and knocked Baba Yaga headfirst into the thorny bush, which pierced her eyes and made her howl even louder. As Vasilisa sped past the fence, the skull called, 'Take me with you, little girl. You will need me to guide you.' She snatched him up from the top of the gate as Baba Yaga, blinded by the branches, screamed, 'Run then, you ungrateful, wicked girl. You aren't worth the eating anyway!' And run Vasilisa did, until she could hear nothing but the trees holding their breath.

"'You have done well, little one,' said the skull. 'Soon you will be home. But first, breathe on that bit of grease you left in my mouth.'

"'Yes, Uncle.' Vasilisa said, because she was a very polite little girl, but truly, she was not looking forward to going home to the woman who had sent her to such a terrible place, especially since she had failed to bring back fire from Baba Yaga. She gave a small sigh before she blew, then started back as the grease leapt to fiery light and the skull glowed so fiercely he scorched her fingers.

"'Now we are ready,' said the skull.

"Toward morning, they arrived at her father's house at the edge of the village.

"The stepmother opened the door even before Vasilisa knocked, astonished to see her, but also relieved, for while Vasilisa had been gone, no one could light a fire in that cold, cold house. 'Finally,' the stepmother snarled, her beautiful face twisted to ugliness. 'Your father has gone to search for you, you ungrateful girl. I will deal with you later.' She reached greedily for the skull in Vasilisa's hand, but before she could grab it, the skull's glare grew tenfold, glowing stronger and stronger, and though the stepmother tried to hide from that brutal glare, in the end she was mesmerized, and stared straight into the fiery eyes and mouth. She began to glow a strange red, and her eyeballs melted and ran down her burning cheeks, and after a horrible screech she collapsed into a heap of ash. Then such a huge fire erupted that it burned the house right to the ground. Vasilisa was so afraid that she dropped the skull and ran into the village where a kindly old woman took her in until her father returned to claim her. Then he searched far and wide for Vasilisa's mother and found her and she was very sorry for all the pain she had caused and he brought her home and they lived happily ever after."

There was silence for a moment. June glanced at May, afraid that her sister would be as frightened as she was, unable to shake the images of melting flesh and shooting flames, but May had fallen asleep, licorice-stained mouth slightly open, hand still clutching the half-eaten pipe. Olena snorted, jolting June from the remnants of the uneasy spell of the story that still clung to her. "Happily ever after. Lucky woman. Dragged back to live with an adulterer and a murderess." She shook May awake.

"Time for bed." June slid off her father's lap, slipping her uneaten licorice pipe into her pocket. "Good night, Papa," she said in a small voice.

"Good night, little one." Her father patted her hand, but did not meet her gaze.

"Perhaps if Vasilisa's father had stayed home more often she wouldn't have been put in such danger in the first place." Olena scooped up May and stomped off to the bedroom.

JUNE'S FATHER stayed on for a few days, he and Olena exchanging no more words than were absolutely necessary. Once more June watched sombrely as he became a tiny dot dissolving on the horizon. If her mother would only be nicer, maybe her father would stay longer. At every opportunity after finishing her chores June would sneak away to the creek to read her book of fairy tales, hiding inside its grimy, weathered cover, wanting to be anywhere else, anyone else, to be Gretel or Vasilisa, vanquishing the witch, or Sleeping Beauty, awakening in her prince's arms.

Almost as if he knew Taras was gone, Mr. Maguire started coming by, to see how Olena was getting on he told them, but he didn't bring Mrs. Maguire. He and Olena would go out to inspect the fence, and Olena always told the girls to stay in the house, they'd only be gone a minute. One day she left them a pot of boiled young corn, tossed with butter and salt. "A treat. You stay here until you've finished it."

June and May ate systematically, starting at the widest end, and chomping in one long run to the narrow end. Chew, swallow. Begin again at the wide end. A ritual of plenty. Then they sucked the naked cob for the sweet marrow, sucked the morsels stuck in their teeth, sucked out every possible taste. They didn't even fight over the cobs, but timed their eating so that they began and finished together.

They were not quite half through when a pounding rattled the door. June jumped up and opened it, expecting to see either her father or mother with arms too full to open it themselves. But the man there was a stranger. June thought perhaps he needed water, as sometimes happened. Every so often a man or boy showed up at their door, hat in hand, asking for work or food. Sometimes they stopped in mid-sentence when they saw Olena's and June's and May's dresses, all faded to the same uniform grey, the cotton so thin you could see light through it if the sun was bright through the windows. Olena always gave the visitors something, even if it was only a morsel. June felt a pang for the pot of corn. She had shared willingly with May, it was too much to ask that she also share with this stranger.

But he didn't have the same humble stance of the men who asked for food. His hat was on his head, and it was not shapeless or tattered. His shirt, a strong red plaid, still had weight and all its colour. His sleeves were rolled up past the elbows, his arms wiry and tanned. In one hand he held a shotgun. Perhaps he was a hunter. With his other arm he held the door open as though to keep June from closing it. A vein in the man's arm was raised and pumping and June was suddenly afraid.

"Where is he!" the man shouted and the breath of his yell broke on June's face. An Angliki.

"Who?" June stammered. Her spoken English was not very good, but thanks to her beloved fairy tales and her father's occasional lessons she could understand as long as people spoke slowly.

"Where is the son of a bitch!"

Her mind a noise of urgency, she shifted her body slightly, hoping to hide May from view. It was the only thing she could think to do, the only thing she knew with any certainty: if Olena and Taras came home to find their children in pieces on the floor it would be June's fault. How could she make this man understand he'd made a mistake? The only thing she could see clearly was the vein throbbing in his arm. It looked incredibly strong and she wondered what she would do if he tried to force his way past her to search for what he wanted inside the house.

The man lowered his face to the level of June's. Another vein was throbbing at his temple. She could count each individual hair in his greying stubble, every pore of his skin. His mouth was huge and the smell of liquor strong in it.

Another man, shorter, stockier, and not so angry appeared in the doorway. "Come away, Jonas." He tugged at the angry man's sleeve. "You know what Eddie's like when he's drunk. All talk."

"No bohunk is going to make a fool of me." The angry man brushed off his friend's hand without taking his eyes off June.

His friend frowned, then with a forced smile lightly punched the angry man's shoulder. "C'mon, man, think! I mean, can you see Miss Hoity-toity having it off with a Uke?"

June scrabbled through her brain for the words to send these men away. Her father. Where was her father? "Verhk," she croaked. "He go verhk."

"Where?" the man barked.

June shook her head mutely.

"See?" the man's friend said. "She doesn't know. But if he's working he can't be with Betsy, right? Come away back to camp. There's only a few days left of hunting and I'm damned if I waste them chasing some drunk's lies." He tugged again and though the angry man again shrugged him off, he did take one step back from June. "You tell that bohunk bastard if he ever dares to go near my wife he's a dead man." Then he spat at June's feet. He flung himself away, not bothering to close the door, and mounted his horse. The other man gave June an oddly helpless, almost sympathetic grimace before mounting his own horse, and then they rode away. June looked at the greenish spit on the floor. She and May must have been too busy eating the corn to hear the horses' hooves. The relief as the man rode out of sight brought the corn up, up and out the huge gaping hole that was her mouth, a bright yellow covering the spit.

Vomiting brought her some sense of balance. After seeing only his distorted mouth, hearing only its rage, she could hear and see the world around her again, and what she heard was May crying. June stepped round the vomit and closed the door, then crouched beside May, whose mouth was still half full of corn, her sobs pushing out little half-eaten mounds that dribbled down her chin.

"Shhhh," June spoke unthinkingly. "It's all right, May. He was looking for his wife. He won't hurt us. He's gone." She hoped this was true. Her mind, frozen with fear, hadn't been able to follow everything the man said, speaking as quickly and violently as he had, and there were words she hadn't heard before. Bohunk? Bastard? But she'd known he was looking for her father. Her father who'd been doing something bad with the man's wife. Surely not. Still, it was better if her mother didn't ever learn about this visit. Because if she did it might lead to another of the ever more frequent fights between June's parents and this time, perhaps, her father would just keep on walking. She grabbed May by the shoulders. "Listen to me, May. Don't say anything about this man." She shook her sister hard and May closed her mouth abruptly in mid-sob. "Don't say anything. It will just worry Mama and Papa. We're fine. Eat your corn. You can have my share." June wrapped May's hand around the cob she'd let fall into her lap.

Pulling the metal bucket from beside the stove, June filled it with a few dippers of water from the reservoir, then knelt to wipe up the vomit and the spit hiding beneath it. The vomit wiped up easily, but it took a lot of scrubbing to get rid of the smell of the spit. Before she got it all tidied away Mr. Maguire and Olena were in the doorway, and May started to cry with terror and excitement and relief at seeing her mother, and within minutes Olena had the whole story out of them. She flushed and asked Mr. Maguire, who was also red faced, "You know who it vas?"

"I think so. Sounds like Jonas Dillon. He owns the general store in Norfolk. He and his brother have a camp north of here where they spend a week hunting every so often, and there's usually a fair bit of the drink involved."

"Which way did the man go?" Olena asked June, shaking her roughly when June just stared at her open-mouthed. "Think, June. Which way?" June thought hard, back to the wheeling horse and the dust trail and pointed.

"North," Olena murmured as though to herself. "And Norfolk to the south. The fool! I should let him rot there." Olena turned back to Mr. Maguire. "Vhere is this Dillon's house?" Moments later she was stomping to the barn, yanking her daughters behind her.

"Sit there and be quiet!" Her voice like the crack of a whip as the girls huddled together in the straw while she hitched the horse to the wagon, hitting it on the head when it resisted the bit, and cinching it almost viciously tight, so that its breath left its body in a sudden whoosh of protest. She bundled the girls into the back of the wagon, even though it was late afternoon and time for milking. She thrust a crust of bread into their hands. "There. That may be all there is to eat from now on."

May chewed placidly while June's heart caved in. In the fairy tale, Hansel left a trail of crumbs in the hope it would lead him home. But the ploy failed, and in any case, what home would there be without her father in it? June's bread picked up sweat from her palm, balling up in her clenched fist. Olena whipped the horse to make it trot faster and the sun sank in the sky. When May finished her crust June handed over her own and May ate it in spite of its grey and mangled state. June wiped the sweaty crumbs onto her coat, and still the horse trotted down the rutted road, the wagon rattling their bones, chattering the teeth in their heads.

"Your father!" Olena spat between slaps of the reins on the horse's back. "Working so hard for that crust of bread!" Slap. "Out in the fields all day, so he *says*, but does he bring home money?" Slap. "No. A sack of flour, a few handfuls of salt or sugar! While we stay trapped on his sorry excuse for a farm." Slap. "How blind does he think I am!"

June was confused. It was a good thing, wasn't it, that her father got the jobs working in the fields? But her mother was no longer talking to anyone but herself, her words like sparks of rage.

"I should let him stay rutting like a pig in shit until he ends up slaughtered like the animal he is. It would serve him right. But then who is left to clean up the mess he will leave behind? Who else but the person who wanted no part in it from the beginning."

June huddled beside May in the thickening darkness, the clopping of the horse's hooves a counterpoint to Olena's intermittent bursts of anger, until the moon and stars shone in the cold autumn sky. Eventually her fear and confusion were overcome by weariness and she slept fitfully, waking to find a weak glow beginning in the east and the wagon pulling up a lane to a tall brick house on the outskirts of a town.

When the horse stopped, June shook May awake, and the girls started to gather themselves to get down from the wagon.

"Stay where you are! Let him see you here, out in the dark and the cold. Let him think for once of something other than himself."

The girls sat shivering in their thin jackets, snuggling close together for warmth. Olena sat like stone, staring at the windows. Every so often the curtains flicked open a crack and a strange woman with frizzy hair peeked from behind them, then let them fall.

"So," Olena's voice after a long silence, startling June. "Maybe this will be your new home. How do you think you'd like that? Maybe this woman will be your new mother, eh?"

June's empty stomach flipped over. May started to cry. And still the heavy wooden door remained closed. May whimpered to go to the bathroom. June's feet had fallen asleep. "Stop fidgeting! The old coward. Does he want me to take you up to the door!"

The sun burst over the horizon like a flame, the door opened, and her father emerged. June could have vomited with relief, but there was nothing in her stomach to come up. Her father climbed into the wagon. He did not look at June or May, nor even at Olena.

"You should be grateful I came. Her husband has been looking for you with a gun and I was tempted to let him have you."

"Did you have to bring the children?" he hissed.

"Just a reminder. Where you go, they go."

Fear clamped June's stomach again. She had thought her father's return meant the end of danger, but the danger was more alive than ever and seated in the front of the wagon, between her parents.

ELDERGROVE

A clear red stone tastes sweet.

You kiss a beautiful mouth, and a key
turns in the lock of your fear.

Rumi, "Where Are We?" The Essential Rumi, trans. Coleman Barks

·1940·

OLENA WALKED May and June to the small wooden schoolhouse, each clutching the lard pail that carried their lunch so they wouldn't bother her at the store. The routine had started because June got lost the first week after their move to Eldergrove, but had continued because Olena liked getting out into the open air, strolling around town before shutting herself in the store all day. It reminded her of her walks as a girl, before she'd ever met Taras, ever had children to escort to school. Of a time even earlier, when she was May's age and walking the long miles to school, dreaming of being a teacher one day, with the same immaculate hands and unpatched clothes, a ruler slapping in her hand to control her students.

Her heart lifted as the door closed on her children, and she headed toward Main. Taras was on a buying trip and she would have the whole day working alone. She still found it hard to believe they'd been able to make the move to town. First, Boychuk had changed his mind about selling the store, hoping to pass it on to his son. Even if they'd found another store to buy, the market for farmland was so slow it seemed they'd never get free. But then, thanks to the blessed war, the price of land had risen, and just as they found a buyer, Boychuk lost his son in a training accident on a base in Québec and was suddenly desperate to sell. It felt like a miracle. They had enough money after buying what was now Zalesky's General Store and Haberdashery not only to settle Varvara in a tiny house and themselves in the apartment above the store, but also to buy Boychuk's third-hand Buick which they just managed to keep in gas. They still had to watch every penny, but at least now they had pennies to watch.

At first, working in the shop was like being in school herself as she wrestled with the pronunciation of the English words for items she'd seen only in the Eaton's catalogue. She understood and spoke English not too badly, so long as conversations didn't stray too far from the conventional, but even at school she'd found the language unwieldy, at war with her lips and brain, and though Taras had tried to insist they speak English on the farm, for him too it had often been easier to switch to Ukrainian. She felt a rare pang of guilt for the girls. May with her quick ear and chatty personality was already speaking with hardly a trace of an accent, but June was struggling with her English and shyness both. In the store Olena had blushed every time customers had to grab whatever it was they wanted to buy and say the word again for her. But she learned fast. Gabardine. Galoshes. Lingerie. Silk stockings. Dollar. Cent. Nickel. Dime.

Taras had worked out that if he shopped the year-end clothing sales at the department stores in Saskatoon and Yorkton, buying dresses, shoes, stockings at a deep discount, he could make a small profit, even once the cost of gas was factored in. "Women like to see before they buy," he said. "And touch too." So Olena started to wear fashionable clothes, twirling in flared skirts, teetering on high heels so alien to feet that had mostly gone barefoot on the farm in summer, heavily booted (galosh-ed!) in winter. Every morning she clacked along the wooden sidewalks, marvelling at the trucks and cars parked in front of the hotel, the hardware, the café, even a movie theatre. So much painted wood siding, and the rust-red brick of the bank. The trains that rolled through daily, up to the huge grain elevators, then away. So many people after so few for so long. Eldergrove had a population of over four hundred.

And whether it was the clothing and makeup, or just the newness of the town, she had recognized another language in the store, one she had begun to learn with Conor Maguire. It started with a shrug of the shoulder, or a flick of the skirt, an answering flick of an appreciative eye. She practised it in the mirror when she fluffed out her home-permed hair and dabbed spots of rouge on her high cheekbones. She was not a pretty woman, but she had an energy that sparked when she smiled, when she moved. On the farm where there'd been only Taras with his rights and needs, his sullen presence, this energy had been banked, barely smouldering, and that only when Conor brushed her hand, or flirted with his eyes. But his wife had kept him on a short leash and their relationship had not gone beyond hurried fumbles. When she finally met Shena Maguire at the farewell dinner Conor had insisted on giving, she realized why. Shena's skin was pale and translucent, her eyes a deep blue, her hair blue-black silk. Beside her Olena felt too solid and low to the ground. She saw her sharp glances at Shena just as sharply returned while Conor looked on sheepishly, and she realized he did indeed love his wife, treating her with a deference he had never shown Olena. Olena couldn't imagine him grabbing Shena as he had sometimes grabbed her behind the barn, clutching breast, hip, thigh. Olena had been quite happy to leave Taras twisted with jealous doubts about Conor and was untroubled with worries about fidelity, but still she could never quite reach the point with Conor she so often reached with Taras, of complete abandonment to her body's urges. Now she realized her body's wisdom. Conor merely wanted to feel more of a man, to impress the little peasant girl in a way he could never impress his wife. Taras made love like he was drowning in her. As in so many things, her body could tell the difference, finding passion with the man she refused to love, and none with the man she'd thought perhaps she could.

    Olena turned the key in the lock, the bell above the door tinkling as she entered. She pulled back the curtains from the side windows to let more light in, then took a moment as she always did to breathe in the place. The polished wood floors and counters, the faint metallic smell of the stamped tin ceiling, the aroma of spices and dried fruit. She threaded her fingers through bins of dried beans and white rice, ran her hands over bolts of cloth and stubby buttons of all shapes and sizes tacked to cards, clanged open the register with its raised brass design and small round buttons, dribbled coins into their receptacles. Relishing this time alone. As soon as she opened the store a slow but steady stream of people, mostly women, would come, less to shop than to gossip. This too was improving her English, for hers was the only Ukrainian family in this town peopled with Irish and English and Scottish: Angliki. She recognized Shena Maguire's cool aloofness in the lack of invitations to join Eldergrove's sewing and knitting circles, which raised funds or sent supplies to the boys at the front, but she didn't resent it, or at least, not much. She had learned as a girl on her father's disintegrating farm to prefer her own company, and life with Taras had driven her more deeply into herself.

The clock above her chimed the hour: nine o'clock. She flipped the sign on the door to Open, straightened her hair and her dress, put on a smile that was only partly obligatory. She had the day to herself, no children or man pulling at her, only herself to please. Except customers, of course. And so long as they spent money, that pleased her too.

JUNE PAUSED at the entrance to the school and watched her mother stride away. Living in Eldergrove was strange in so many ways. Some she liked. Both she and May enjoyed helping in the store. May liked talking to customers, but June was happiest in the storeroom where it was dimly lit and cool, and she could sneak a few tastes from the huge sacks of raisins and brown sugar, or bury herself in her fairy tales until her mother called her away. Customers like Mrs. Logan frightened her. On June's first day helping in the store, while Mrs. Logan was picking up and putting down cans June had carefully organized, creating havoc of June's neat arrangement, an Indian came into the store and ordered some tea from June's mother. As he was leaving, Mrs. Logan sniffed and said, loud enough for her voice to follow him out of the store, "Well, at least you won't get too many of *them* around here. The reserve is closer to Norfolk so they mostly shop and get up to no good there, thank goodness." Yet as far as

June could see the Indian had done nothing except order his tea politely, wait while it was weighed out, pay, and then leave. The town seemed full of snares and pitfalls June could not recognize, invisible rules she seemed always to be violating.

When her mother released her from the store, June would climb the stairs at the back of the building to the second floor where their apartment was, to sit on the landing and read, occasionally looking down on the back yard with its small garden, outhouse, and rain barrel. No room for a cow or chickens, so now they bought milk and butter and eggs from a farmer who came into town every week. No milking or egg gathering, and so much less weeding to do. Best of all no more hoisting water in heavy pails up from the well, lugging it to the house and inevitably splashing some on her feet, her clothes, the floor. They had a pump right in the kitchen and a laundry machine now too, with a stick that you swung back and forth with all your might to get the clothes swishing around, and a wringer that took the puffy wet clothes and pressed them flat as boards, grey water gushing from them back into the tub. No more washboard and no more of May and June taking either end of a sopping wet sheet and twisting and twisting to wring out the water, half the time May's weaker hands dropping the sheet in the dust and condemning them both to their mother's wrath. No more standing on a stool to hang the clothes on a line strung between two poles. Here they had a clothesline that worked on a pulley so on a fine day you could clip the clothes on the wire and then send them out to wave above the garden, or hang the parlour's multi-coloured paisley carpet and beat the dust out of it. There was a bakery in town but Olena scorned its fluffy white loaves so she still put up a huge pan of bread every Sunday, enough for the week, and though they bought their milk, Olena still made cottage cheese, the bulging bags that leaked sour-smelling whey into the sink a reminder of home.

But June missed the creek, with its skinny aspen trees and fragrant wolf willow, its cool shade even on the hottest of days, the fish in the trap, the faint rattle of birch leaves in the fall. The small patch of earth she had known with every fibre of her being, never putting a foot wrong. She had not known she loved this patch of earth until she lost it. It had been the backdrop to her life, almost invisible, but now she could bring it to mind, to all her senses, by closing eyes that soon began to sting with sorrow. She even missed May, who on the farm had for the most part been a small nuisance and care, but here in town was June's only ally, until she began running off with friends she was already making at school, leaving June to hide out on the landing like a treed animal.

Beyond the yard she could see the whole alley behind their house, the cats scrounging in dustbins, the shadows of life behind the curtains of the rooms above the other stores. Mr. Barker's hardware. The McTeers' bakery. Sometimes when she was sitting on the tiny landing at the top of the stairs with her legs dangling over the edge, she would set aside her book just to listen to all the bustle, the voices floating from open windows, music from a radio, the occasional squeal of an unlucky mouse. All in contrast to the inside of the house where the wooden floors made her footsteps echo in what seemed always to be an ominous hush. Now that all the rooms had wooden doors, not just curtains, sounds became muffled and somehow more threatening. Occasionally one of those doors slammed. But then the ensuing silence settled grimly. When the strained whispers and smothered thuds seeped from under her parents' door at night, and with no one to comfort since May now had her own bedroom, June would creep to the living room. There she would pull the crocheted afghan from the sofa, wrap herself in it and, in spite of her father's orders not to waste battery power, press her ear to the round black mesh on the front of the radio, twisting the knobs from voices to static, voices to static, until she had drowned out the sounds she did not want to hear. Nothing had ever been said of the night in the wagon outside the strange woman's house, or the scary man who had been looking for her father. June had practised shooting cans on the fence so that if he came back, she would be ready. But he never did. Still she couldn't shake the sense of danger. Even though with the move to town they'd left the frizzy-haired woman far behind them, every time her father went on one of his buying trips, she fretted that this time he wouldn't return. That the man with those dreadfully pulsing veins would find him and kill him and she would never know, just wait forever. Every time her father walked through the door she felt she'd been given a reprieve, however precarious.

The school bell rang, and June squared her shoulders before entering the building, forcing herself to keep her eyes straight ahead while the sniggers and whispers of "bohunk" swirled around her like demons. The first week in town, she'd gone for a walk down Main Street as far as the trees at the very end, hungry for a sky uncluttered by buildings. She had wandered among the poplar and birch, sucking up the smell of leaf and green, the sound of bird and frog song, missing the creek at home so badly, and when she finally walked back to town, she couldn't remember which of the store fronts was theirs. A roaring filled her ears as she walked up and down the street, trying to remember and too ashamed to ask anyone, her small store of English eaten up by panic. The third time she passed a group of kids lolling outside the Full Moon Café, they started taunting her with the word she didn't know then, but would become all too familiar with later, on the playground and in the schoolyard.

"Hey hunky, what's your problem?"

"Maybe the little bohunk is lost."

"Look, it's crying."

"Crybaby bohunk. Cry hunky baby bohunk." They all took up the chant while June just stood there, silent and wary. She'd seen what happened when an animal was threatened by a pack of coyotes. While the fawn or raccoon faced them, they held off, snarling and yipping and dancing, but once you turned your back, they were on you in a second. On the farm she'd known how to shoot since she was seven, though the most she'd ever managed was to wing a coyote, but here in town she had no weapon at all. Yelling in Ukrainian would get her nowhere, and her English had flown to the back of her brain. She thought longingly of the coyote she'd shot, the bright spurt of blood and how it ran off, limping and whining and dragging one leg, but still not letting go of the chicken in its mouth. May had cried for the coyote, but June had simply quoted her mother. "You want to eat, you have to kill things. Now there will be fewer eggs."

Finally a Chinese man came out of the café and shooed the kids away, yelling something at them in English as fractured as June's. June stared at him mutely until he took her hand in his and led her to her parents' store. The kids, delighted to have new prey, followed behind, alternating "chinky chinky Chinaman" with "hunky baby bohunk" until he deposited her at the door of the store. When he turned to face them they finally scattered, though strains of their chant drifted above the ring of the door's bell as she entered. The next day at school the story had leapt like lightning from mouth to mouth as the joke went round about the farm girl so ignorant she got lost on the two-block main street.

June paused at the door to the classroom. May was already in the desk they shared, beckoning over her shoulder in agony in case June should be late again, and made to stand in the corner like last time. Eleven years old but because of her lack of schooling June was forced to sit with the six-year-olds. May, at eight, should have been equally out of place, but she was small for her age and had a way about her that somehow disarmed the teacher, the other pupils. She was already staying after school to perform the coveted task of banging chalk out of the erasers, then playing in the schoolyard until suppertime, while June walked home alone with eyes red from the taunting she was learning to understand better with every English lesson. Even the teacher made fun of her accent. "Tanks, June? Tanks are what our brave boys are driving overseas. Say after me: tthh-hanks. Tthhh." The whole schoolroom sniggering. Whenever the teacher called on her, her mind twitched and froze before the question like a mouse facing one of those alley cats and the answer stuck in her throat. Sometimes May would try to help her and then the older students would snicker again.

Two weeks into her first term at school her father sat beside her at the table where she was doing her homework and twisting her hair until her eyes leaked tears. When he lifted her onto his lap she gave a deep sigh and buried her face in his chest, her thin ribcage inflating and collapsing. He held her face in both hands, raising it gently to meet his gaze. "Do you think those children are better than you?"

Her lower lip trembled, but she gripped it between her teeth until she could speak.

"No..." She did not sound fully convinced even to herself.

"Well, I know they are not," he said. "And shall I tell you why?" She nodded, hopeful that a story would keep her from the dreaded homework for at least a short while.

"I'll tell you why. Those people at school, even the teacher, don't know it, but you come from a nation many hundreds of years older than this one. Its story is full of great warriors, and glorious battles for control of the steppes, heroic resistance to preserve our heritage. Brave students would travel from town to town, like the salesmen who come to Eldergrove, but they were giving, not selling. They were teaching the peasants to read, something that was illegal back then, telling them their history, and reading the poems of Ukraine's greatest poet, Taras Shevchenko." Closing his eyes he intoned:

> Oh bury me, then rise ye up
> And break your heavy chains
> And water with the tyrants' blood
> The freedom you have gained.
> And in the great new family,
> The family of the free,
> With softly spoken, kindly word
> Remember also me.

He opened his eyes. "These people are ignorant. They look at you, they don't see you, they see what they need to see to feel better about their ignorance. This gives you great power, because only you know who you really are inside. Do you understand?"

June nodded, baffled.

Taras smiled and sighed. "You will, little one. You will." He picked up one of her hands and touched it to his chest. "For now, understand that at least one person knows who you truly are, and who you are is kept safe in here." He tapped his chest with her hand. "And the other one who knows is here," he moved her hand to cradle it against her chest. "You cannot get lost if you always look in those two places." He closed his eyes again and rested his chin on her head, as though praying that what he'd said was true.

"So." He placed her back on her stool at the table where she shivered in the sudden chill. "You show them what a person who knows herself can do."

Now June sucked her breath deep into her chest, feeling like Vasilisa stepping into Baba Yaga's hut, keeping her eyes and ears open, biding her time until escape was in her grasp. Her father had told her she could do anything these other ignorant Angliki could, and even more because she could speak the language of the Cossacks, who had been not Russian as these ignorants thought, but Ukrainian. She would not let him down. She took another step, another breath. Her stomach settled, her ears cleared. The teacher was shushing the class for the singing of God Save the King, whose photograph, along with the Union Jack, hung above the row of letters taped above the blackboard. Aa Bb Cc. June slid into her chair beside May, who squeezed her hand as though she were the older sister. June squeezed back but stared straight at the blackboard. If she stared hard enough into that black square, sometimes she could see through to the end of the day.

TARAS EASED THE CAR out of the alley into the parking spot behind the store. He always came the back way, not wanting Olena to know he had arrived, and since he never told her how long his buying trips would take, she couldn't anticipate that arrival. He sat for a moment inhaling the faint aroma of saddle soap, running a hand over the brown leather seat that he conditioned regularly, trying to bring its cracked surface back from the ravages of age and prairie air that sucked the moisture out of everything. On impulse he angled the rear-view mirror toward his own leathered features. Only forty-four, but the prairie sun and wind had worn their way into his skin too. He was pretty much the same age now as Metro and Varvara had been when he first met them, when he was determined never to be as ground down as they. And that thought brought Varvara's wrinkled face to mind, as she'd told him what June would never have revealed: how Olena didn't get out of bed for days after the miscarriage, how June had carried the burden of the farm on her own. "Olena is too much alone. The girls too, they need school. They need friends." Varvara held up one gnarled hand to stop his protest. "Olena, she told me there have been times when she has thought of arranging an 'accident.' I have a plan, and unless you want to come home some day to find her blood on your conscience, you will consider it very carefully." And he had. Terrified as he was that Olena would find someone else if she were free of the farm, would find a way to leave him, he was more terrified of a world without her in it.

Shaking off the memory, he opened the trunk and hauled out a couple of cardboard boxes full of the dresses, and even some lingerie, that he'd bought at the year-end sale in Yorkton, getting an even deeper discount for taking the entire lot off the manager's hands. A wry smile twisted his face. The devoted communist had turned out to be a better capitalist. In the end he had soured on communism when news started filtering in to Canada of the Holodomor, the Great Hunger Stalin engineered in Ukraine in the '30s, starving almost four million to death in one year. Since then Taras had divested himself of loyalty to ideology, did what it took to survive, perhaps eventually even to thrive. He had developed a knack for bargaining, honed in those years when that knack had meant an extra relief ration, or the scale tilted in his favour by a kindly proprietor. Now he was the proprietor. No longer clad in tattered coveralls held together with patches, or work boots whose cracks — no matter how often he mended them or treated them with beeswax when he could afford it — let in mud, dust, or snow, depending on the season. Now he wore a suit and tie, and leather-soled shoes that he polished faithfully every Sunday, never tiring of the gasoline smell of the polish, the whisk of the brush, the coal black gleam that rewarded his efforts. Just as he never lost the thrill of miles whipping by beneath his wheels, remembering all those years on foot or in a wagon dragged by a horse one step away from the glue factory. Luckily no gas or food rationing so far, though if you believed the rumours it probably wasn't far off. Even if these trips hadn't yielded the profit they did, he doubted he could give them up.

Balancing the boxes carefully on one knee, he pried open the back door and lugged them into the storeroom. The usual odd assortment of sizes, styles. But it seemed to appeal to people. They never knew what bargains they might find, what items of clothing or makeup he would be able to scrounge up. As long as the price was good, most of them didn't care — couldn't afford to care—that it was last year's fashion. He slipped one box to the floor, stole up to the door, straining to hear male voices, female laughter or low murmurs, the familiar roar in his chest. He told himself he didn't regret the move to town. Olena was more animated here than he'd seen her in years. But he did regret the days when he'd been the only one able to get away, when he'd always known where she was, what she was doing. Often he'd had to take the horse and wagon when looking for work or buying supplies, and after the crash he was almost relieved when they couldn't afford a second horse, though even if they could have, where was she to go? The Masiuk homestead had been the only one within visiting distance and they'd sold up to the Maguires before the families had a chance to get to know one another. Shena Maguire had made it plain she wasn't interested in visiting, the flimsy excuses Conor initially offered out of politeness floating away eventually like so much poplar fluff. Still, Olena had never complained about being lonely, either because she refused to show any weakness or because she just didn't have any desire to leave the farm once Taras wasn't on it.

Boychuk had taught only Taras to drive the Buick before he left so Taras was still the only one who could get away. But now when he drove off, Olena was in a town where so many men wandered up and down the streets, into and out of the store. Men younger than he, with more money than he. The thought tormented him, drove him to sneaking up on her in ways he'd never been able to on the farm, where his approach could be seen on that flat landscape for miles. But what he'd realized shortly after moving here was that the town was keeping a careful eye, and ear too. From the gossip he overheard in the store, he was acutely aware of the proximity of all those apartments along the alley, how secrets seeped out of the windows, even when they were tightly latched. The whispered arguments this proximity forced upon him and Olena seemed somehow more vicious than the all-out fights they'd had on the homestead, though the end result was the same: the excuse of work, the destination a bar in a distant town. Seeking not the company of men — he could find that, and did, at the Eldergrove hotel bar — but of women more tractable than the one he'd married.

The front doorbell rang out and so did the laughter he'd been dreading. He burst through the storeroom door, still clutching the box of lingerie, which cracked open, spilling brightly coloured panties all over the floor. Olena looked up sharply. The store was empty save for her and June behind the till, then the bell rang again and May ran laughing through the door. Taras gathered up the lingerie, stuffed it back into the box, and offered it to Olena almost as a kind of peace offering. He was a fool. A fool at war with himself. He wanted, needed, people to come to the store, women *and* men. He'd forgotten that May never tired of the sound of the bell, or of darting in and out of the store just to make it ring. And Olena would never be foolish enough to carry on in the store, under the eyes of the town, her children, her husband.

"PAPA, YOU'RE BACK!" June ran from behind the till and tried to throw her arms around him, impeded by the box he was holding out toward her mother, who had not moved from the counter.

"Careful, June, you'll make me drop them again!"

June stopped short, arms stiff at her side.

"Don't just stand there, June. You can start folding those panties your father brought back."

June's father handed her the large cardboard box, then disappeared into the storeroom. One by one she pulled out silky slips or panties, willing herself to focus her blurry gaze on how their lustrous textures slid through her fingers, how their jewel colours brightened the dim store. Her father appeared not to have missed her at all.

"May!" Her mother barked as the doorbell rang once again. "Stop that right now or I'll give you a reason to stop!" She turned to follow through on her threat only to pull up short at the sight of Mrs. Logan, head of the Women's War Effort Committee, coming through the door, May trailing behind her. June wasn't sure what the Women's War Effort Committee did, but it must be important because Mrs. Logan never failed to remind anyone she came across in the store about it, practically bullying them to join. Except for June's mother.

"So sorry, Mrs. Logan." Olena snapped her fingers at May and pointed to June with an unmistakeable order. "Can I help you?"

"Tea." Mrs. Logan pressed her hand to her huge bosom, which was heaving with every breath. "I'm right out of tea. Don't know how I let that happen and himself will be fit to be tied if it's not on the table at five o'clock sharp." She glanced at the delicate gold watch biting into the dimpled flesh of her wrist.

Before June's mother could even reach for the tea caddy, the bell chimed again and Mrs. McTeer, secretary of the committee, scurried in. She was as skinny as Mrs. Logan was fat. Mrs. Logan, whose husband ran the bank and who lived in a large house at the edge of town, had made a point of telling June's parents that she bought all her clothes in Saskatoon, but Mrs. McTeer was always first in line for the discounted items Taras brought in, usually trying to find the kind of print dresses with big shoulder pads that Mrs. Logan favoured, and which didn't really suit either of them. The first time May saw the two women together she made a drawing of them, one shaped like a barrel, the other a triangle. June had stifled a smile, then made May rip the drawing into small pieces and stuff them beneath the kindling at the back of the stove. There was nothing invisible about the rule not to offend Mrs. Logan, who had a habit of telling jokes about Ukrainians that June didn't understand, but that made her father stiffen even while at his most polite, and that seemed to embarrass even Mrs. McTeer, though she always laughed.

"I hoped I'd find you here, Imogen. You'll never guess who's come home. Tom!"

"Tom? Tom Barker?"

"Yes! Terrible limp he has, and scrawny! But they finally let him out of the hospital."

"Oh, thank heavens. It's a shame the boy won't make it overseas but he still behaved very bravely." To Olena, Mrs. Logan said, "Tom went east for military training with Mr. Boychuk's son and they were both in a terrible accident. Tom wrote from hospital. I guess Ed Boychuk was fooling around with a grenade and Tom tried to save him before it went off but he couldn't get there in time and the blast killed Ed and landed Tom in hospital all these months. Old Mr. Barker *will* be pleased to have him home, so proud of him he was."

"Well, you might think so but you'd be wrong! LeAnn, down at the depot, said he was smiling about as much as he ever allows himself to when Tom stepped off the bus, but then Tom helped down a young lady, sporting a ring that looked like the one Mrs. Barker used to wear, you know the one, all crusted over with little stones, and the smile wiped clean off Old Man Barker's face. Tom's brought home a wife! *And* she's French! LeAnn heard her accent."

"No!"

"I know! And apparently not a peep about it to his father until today. Old Man Barker took one look at her, not a word or a hug, just grabbed the luggage and marched them over to the apartment, then minutes later was in the store flipping the CLOSED sign to OPEN. LeAnn says the girl is quite lovely, olive skin and dark hair, beautifully waved, very chic. Still," she pursed her lips, "French, you know."

"Well!" Mrs. Logan exclaimed. "Old Mr. Barker won't like that. He won't like that at all. A young Mrs. Barker. Imagine."

June wondered why Mrs. Logan said "a young" Mrs. Barker, since there wasn't an old Mrs. Barker. She had died just before the war broke out. Perhaps that was why Old Man Barker could not make his face smile, though the deep grooves in his face looked like they'd been there far longer than a couple of years. Whenever he entered the store June retreated to the stock room.

"Girls!" Olena called, in Ukrainian. "Mind what you're doing. June, keep an eye on your sister!"

June looked down to see that May had taken all the lingerie out of the neat lines June had arranged according to size and was fanning them out in multi-coloured jumbles.

The door chime interrupted June's cry of dismay and a wiry young man with a limp stepped into the store, followed by the most beautiful girl June had ever seen. Young Mrs. Barker, for it had to be her, looked like she had stepped out of one of June's fairy tales, or would have if she hadn't been so stylish. Her sleek black hair, bright lipstick and matching nail polish, her trim suit and hourglass figure threw Mrs. Logan and Mrs. McTeer into pasty relief. Beside her, still in his khakis, Tom Barker looked dull and a bit anxious. Perhaps it pained him to walk.

Mrs. McTeer moved toward the couple with her hand outstretched, but before she could speak Mrs. Logan stepped in front of her, saying, "Welcome home, Tom dear. So sorry you were wounded, but so happy that you are back safe."

"Thank you, Mrs. Logan. I only regret I couldn't bring Ed back with me."

"And I hear congratulations are in order." Mrs. Logan took Young Mrs. Barker's hand. "What a lovely ring! Isn't that your mother's, Tom? Such a distinctive design and of course, she always wore it."

"Yes, she gave it to me for luck just before she died, and it certainly did the trick."

"I believe you are from France, my dear?"

"Yes," Tom cut in before his wife could reply, "she lost her whole family early in the war and managed to get onto a boat to Canada, to my great good fortune."

"How did you meet?" Mrs. McTeer asked.

"She nursed me in hospital, didn't you, love." Tom squeezed his wife's arm. "Only thing that kept me alive."

Young Mrs. Barker blushed, twisting the ornate ring round and round on her finger.

"You seem terribly young to be a nurse," Mrs. Logan said.

"Yes, but I was in training. Tom, 'e exaggerate my abilities, I think." As if to change the subject, she pointed out the lipstick that June's father had brought back on his last buying trip. "Mais voilà, chéri," she leaned into Tom with a sparkling laugh. "It is called Patriot Red. Surely it would be treason not to buy it, non?"

Tom's anxious expression melted into a teasing smile. "Well, if it helps the war effort. Silly me for thinking we could get out of here with only the bottle of aspirin we came for." He fished in his wallet and handed her a couple of bills. "Do your worst, but don't forget the aspirin. I'll be at the hardware."

Astounded at her boldness June crept forward from the back of the store and cut off Mrs. Logan, who was saying, "You must join the Women's War Effort . . ." "Vill you like to try sample, Mrs. Barker?"

"Really!" Mrs. Logan sniffed. "Don't interrupt, little girl."

June stepped back, face burning, eyes fixed on the ground, but Young Mrs. Barker tilted June's face upward with two gentle fingers, the same laugh in her eyes as her voice, "Oh, ma p'tite, you make me sound so old! I am only nineteen, which I think is not so much older than you. What do you call yourself?"

"June," June stammered, trying to imagine a time when she too might be able to speak so animatedly, to smile so freely.

"Well, I think, June, we must be friends. And between friends there are few formalities. You will call me Marie, yes?"

June could not have said, or cared, if Mrs. Logan or Mrs. McTeer were still in the store. In a daze, she agreed with Marie that the lipstick was just the thing for her colouring, then helped her pick out a pair of open-toed shoes, red and white patent leather. In a daze she eased a shoe onto Marie's delicate foot, the red-tipped toes matching the painted fingernails. In a daze she wrapped up Marie's purchases and watched her leave the store, completely incapable of returning Marie's little wave goodbye. That night, curled up with her book of fairy tales, whenever she encountered a dark-haired heroine, she pictured Marie, and felt a faint stirring of hope.

THE VERY NEXT DAY, Marie was back, and June rushed forward to greet her only to be cut off by Old Man Barker, who steered Marie to the counter, plunked the shoe box and the Patriot lipstick down. "Mrs." — a slight hesitation as his jaw set and lip curled — "Barker will be returning these." Tom hovered behind the pair with an even more anxious expression than the day before.

"Is that right?" said Taras, not best pleased. "And vhy should this be so? The shoes they don't fit?" Olena came out of the stock room and gazed thoughtfully at Marie.

All of Marie's sparkle from the day before had vanished. "Non, they fit mais..."

"But they are too extravagant for a veteran's pay, for one thing," Old Mr. Barker cut in. "And I don't hold with open-toed shoes. Nor with red lipstick."

"The lipstick ve don't take back." Olena pushed the tube back across the counter. "Rules of healt."

"Anht the shoes." Taras examined the soles, which were lightly scuffed. "These been vorn. Ve cannot sell if they already been vorn." Old Mr. Barker's scowl deepened and his jaw worked as though he wanted to spit, or swear, and as he jutted that jaw across the counter toward her father, June's stomach flipped over. But June's mother laid a hand on her father's arm. "Perhaps ve vehrk someting out." She smiled at Old Man Barker, though June noticed the smile did not reach her eyes. "These geerls," nodding at June, and May who was peeking out of the storeroom, "they are young to be vehrking the store. Maybe Mrs. Barker she vehrk some hours here to pay for shoes."

Please, June prayed, please say yes.

"She has work to do at the hardware, with Tom." Old Mr. Barker jerked his head at his son without bothering to look at him.

"Yes, yes. But maybe vhen hardvehr is closed. Ve open late Fridays. Maybe Marie she vehrk then."

Old Man Barker grunted his displeasure but stomped out of the store, shooing Tom ahead of him. Marie followed, throwing a nervous smile over her shoulder at Olena, who nodded. "Ve see you Friday."

Taras glanced at Olena, looking puzzled and a bit irritated, but before he could say anything Olena said, "Only until the shoes are paid." But June heard her mother mutter under her breath as she headed back to the stock room, "And after that we'll see."

WHEN OLENA SHOWED Marie around the store the following Friday it was soon apparent that the girl was a quick learner, handy with numbers and the till, but at her best when charming the customers, laughing and cajoling the men into buying a special little something for their wives, pointing out to those wives that the expensive cinnamon was worth it when making a pie for *such* a husband. Offering to carry the kerosene lantern closer to the bolts of cloth so the true beauty of the colours and textures could be seen. Of course, everyone had heard of the new arrival and wanted to check her out, so the store was busier than usual and the air swirled with whispers about Marie's lovely skin, kissed by the sun of the South of France, her stylishness, so French. Women clustered at the till, asking for Marie's makeup tips.

Olena watched with amusement as June mimicked the toss of Marie's hair, the small pucker of Marie's lips as she debated which hat, which shade of lipstick was most becoming to a customer. When Mrs. Logan called Marie away from June to press her to join the Women's War Effort committee — "Only the first families, you know, my dear. Mr. Barker, such a long-standing resident." — June's face fell into gloom, but after Marie offered prim thanks, Olena saw her wink at June behind Mrs. Logan's departing backside. June, her frown almost erased, winked back, at least she tried, and was rewarded for her lopsided facial expression with Marie's teasing laugh. She was a bright presence in the store, dusting shelves without being asked, chatting with Olena about how odd it was to be married while they stacked cans of tomato soup. "You sign a paper et voilà! The next time you sign something you are not you any more, you are a new person with a new name." Even mimicking Old Man Barker at one point — "I don't 'old with lipstick" — her jutting lip and scrunched-up scowl so exactly like his that Olena felt a prickle of fear even as she laughed, and glanced round the store to be sure no one else had seen. As soon as Olena flipped the store sign to CLOSED, Old Man Barker appeared, without Tom, and all Marie's mischief disappeared behind a bland expression. Olena measured Marie's pay into Mr. Barker's outstretched hand, Marie thanked her politely, then followed her father-in-law into the street. Olena stared at the door for some time after they left.

JUNE NO LONGER had to be coaxed to help in the front of the store. She lived for Fridays, especially for the times when business was slow and Marie would try to teach her a French song, or show her how to put on lipstick, though June had such thin lips she found it hard to "pucker up," as Marie commanded. "'ere, like this," Marie muttered through her own pursed and glossy lips, then dabbed at June's with the Patriot Red. "You look very nice, chérie." She sat back to admire her work, handing June a Kleenex and showing her how to blot her lips, then angling her small compact mirror so June could see. "It is a good colour for you, I think." June thought her lips looked like a thin slash across her face, nothing like Marie's bow-shaped mouth, and sighed. "No, no, little one," Marie stroked the space between June's eyebrows. "No frowning. The world prefers a 'appy face. Beauty is not so much what you 'ave as what you do with what you 'ave, tu sais? And we all can 'ave a smile, yes? Next Friday I show you 'ow to put on rouge, and some concealer for this little crease between your brows."

Marie snapped the compact and lipstick tube shut and dropped them into her pocket as a frown wrinkled her own brow. "I 'ave to go to one of those 'orrible meetings tomorrow." She shivered dramatically. "They are the worst you can imagine. Even the 'ardware store is better, I tell you. And I know they want for me to 'ost one of these teas, but 'ow can I? Mr. Barker 'e keeps the good china locked in a box. I may not know much, but I know not to serve tea on chipped china." June nodded, trying to look as though she understood, wishing she could say something to help and fighting the impulse to bite the sticky lipstick off her lips.

The next day she raced home after the store closed and sat on the landing, staring across the alley to the window of the apartment above Barker's hardware store, hoping for a glimpse of Marie. Finally, she entered the apartment, removed a small blue hat from her dark curls and kicked off her shoes, then opened the window and took a deep breath. She seemed very tired, but when June waved she smiled impishly and put one melodramatic hand to her forehead. After disappearing from view for a few moments, she opened the door and stepped onto the landing. She had changed into a black bathing suit with a heart shaped bodice and a skirt that flared out just over the top of her thighs. As she leaned against the metal railing, soaking in the sun, it was as if one of the models had stepped out of the Eaton's catalogue. When she lit a cigarette and blew tiny rings of smoke towards June, June was fired with a wish to some day smoke as elegantly.

Suddenly a voice hollered from inside the apartment. Marie jumped, threw the cigarette to the alley below, ducked into the apartment through the open window and banged it shut, but not before June heard Tom yell, "Why do you have to make such a spectacle of yourself, to antagonize him? You know he doesn't hold with women smoking! And in a bathing suit!" Even through the closed window June could hear Marie yelling back, "Do you ever once think to tell 'im to stop antagonizing *me?*" "Tell *Him*," Tom hollered, "*Him*, not 'im. How hard can it be to tell the difference?" and then a slamming door. Moments later, Marie returned to the window, drawing aside the curtain and blowing smoke defiantly through freshly lipsticked lips into the air above the alley. But she was wrapped in a dressing gown and did not look in June's direction, just drew deeply on her cigarette as though she wanted to inhale its glowing tip.

AS THE WEEKS PASSED, Marie stayed on at the store, even though June was sure she must have paid off the shoes and lipstick by now. She overheard Marie telling Olena while they were shelving stock, "The old devil says I may as well bring in some money, and I think also he does not want to see me any more than he has to."

Old Man Barker still dourly escorted Marie to work and picked her up at the end of her shift, collecting her pay from a stony-faced Olena at the end of each week. Tom nowhere in sight. June's resentment rose each time he failed to appear. How could he just abandon his wife to his ogre of a father? Marie stood by meekly, her face washed clear of all expression, just as she had the first time Old Man Barker dragged her into the store to return the shoes. She was careful to pronounce her *h* words correctly, with a little hesitation before each one that made her accent even more charming. She didn't wear the open-toed shoes she had worked so hard for, but kept the lipstick in the till and put it on when she first arrived, always taking care to remove it with cold cream before closing. Old Man Barker didn't hold with hairstylists, she said, making a face, but he couldn't stop her pincurling her hair at night after he had gone to bed. For all he knew she had naturally wavy hair. She showed June how to do pincurls and June spent a restless night with pins poking into every inch of her scalp. It would be worth it if her straggly brown hair could be transformed into Marie's silky curls, but when she went down to breakfast, May asked, "Why is your hair all kinky?" June could not comb her hair straight before school, so the sniggers, which had dropped off for a while, started up again. After school she retreated to the landing, gazing blearily at Marie's window. It was ages before Marie's shift. Maybe June should just put her head under the water pump. But then, as though like had called to like, loneliness to loneliness, Marie appeared in the window. She took one look at June, pointed to the storeroom door and June clattered down the stairs.

Marie's face was alight with warm laughter as she ran a hand over June's hair. "Oh, ma p'tite, I think perhaps pincurls are not for you. Come, we'll do you up with braids, it will be beautiful, truly. I brought my brush and comb, and some ribbons, see?"

She held out a jumble of bright red satin, the kind Vasilisa must have used to tie up the thorn bush's branches. Which, June thought bleakly, was how her hair looked.

Marie settled June on a stool in the storeroom and stood behind her. "This is called une tresse française, a French braid." With her comb she snaked a part down the centre of June's skull. "And not because I'm French but because it is très chic, like all things French. Those girls at school will be jealous when they see you."

Marie's fingers teased apart strands of hair, leaving tiny shivers of pleasure in their wake, gently tugging the strands to snug up against June's scalp. June closed her eyes and sighed.

"You know, June. I too had a difficult time in school. But it does not last forever."

And under those hands June could almost believe it was true.

When Marie finished the braids she secured them with elastics, tied a ribbon round each one, then stood in front of June to inspect her work. "Voilà! Come see."

"What do you say, Olena?" Marie steered June to the mirror on the counter. "She is transformed, non? She looks just like that girl in the movies, the one who clicks her heels and goes anywhere she wants, you remember, the girl with red slippers."

June shook her head shyly. "I haven't been to the movies."

"Oh, well no matter. You look like yourself and that is even better. Isn't that so, Olena?"

Olena nodded. "You look very vell, June. Better than this morning, for sure."

June gazed at herself in the mirror and while she could not see a pretty girl, she did see a girl with glowing cheeks and eyes, and thought perhaps she looked a little bit, a very little bit, like

Vasilisa. She turned those glowing eyes to Marie, "Tthhhank you so much."

"It's nothing, ma p'tite. I used to do this for all the girls ..." She stopped abruptly.

"Your sisters?"

"No. Just some girls I used to know. I have no sisters." Her face lightened. "But if I did have, I'd want them to be just like you." And June's happiness was complete.

BUT ALL THROUGH the following week Marie's window remained empty, its curtain drawn. Raised voices often leaked from behind the pane, not just Tom's but Old Man Barker's, almost never Marie's. Every night since Marie had traced her frown, June had followed the path of her friend's finger with her own thumb, trying to rub her brow smooth. Now she felt it settling into deeper grooves.

JUNE WOKE to hear Marie singing, at the top of her lungs, a garbled version of the song she'd tried to teach May and June: Père Barker Père Barker, dormez-vous, dormez-vous! After every "dormez-vous" there was a loud crash, and when June crept to the window where her parents were silently watching, she saw Marie tossing pieces of china off the landing from a large crate beside her. Lights shone from all the windows along the alley, shadowy figures watched from behind twitches of curtain. Tom was trying to drag Marie back inside, but she shook him off as though he were a mosquito and the crashing and singing got louder. Old Man Barker yelled from inside the apartment, "If you can't keep control of your woman, I'll be forced to. Useless! You were always useless." Then an arm reached out that even seen from across the alley reminded June of the angry man who'd come searching for her father, its veins standing out in stiff ridges, its muscles taut and menacing. That arm plucked Marie up as though she were made of cotton and pulled her inside. The window slammed shut and all was quiet except for June's muffled sob. "Go to bed, June." Her father took her hand and led her away from the window. "There's nothing we can do." In the morning, June, half believing it had been a dream, went down to the alley to find a heap of shards from a beautiful set of china, creamy white sprinkled with tiny blue flowers. June picked up a fragment of what had once been a saucer and tucked it into her pocket.

"OLD MAN BARKER is fit to be tied," Mrs. Logan said to Olena that morning as soon as the store opened. "In the bar. Drinking with the men. My son Mitch and his friends saw her there, the monkeys. Underage the lot of them." She laughed. "But the nerve of the girl! Sneaking out while Tom and Mr. Barker were asleep and coming home rip-roaring drunk. And that china! It was Mrs. Barker's pride and joy, only came out at Christmas, Easter, and Thanksgiving, and with her gone Old Man Barker doesn't bring it out even then. God knows how the girl got her hands on it. You mark my words, there will be trouble over this."

And there was, but probably not the kind Mrs. Logan had imagined. The next Friday Marie came to work with her sleekly styled hair pulled over one eye, but even so Olena could see a purple shadow. So did June. "Marie, I think you've mussed your makeup," she said, but shut her mouth abruptly at the sharp look Olena gave her. "June, I need to talk to Marie. You go . . ."

The door burst open so violently the little bell practically flipped upside down. Mitch Logan and a couple of friends spilled into the store, all of them stinking of booze and lurching into one another, laughing raucously. Marie backed away from them behind the till.

"Hey, Frenchie," Mitch hooted. "Why so shy? Why don't you come over to the bar with us? We miss you!" And when Marie shook her head, her face so pale the bruise stood out like a scar, "I thought all you French girls were always up for anything. You know if Tom can't give you what you need, you don't have far to look!"

Olena banged the till savagely shut just as Taras entered the store from the back. He took in Olena's red face and Marie's white one and strode to the front. "Vhat's going on here?"

"Hey, never mind," one of the other young men grabbed Mitch's elbow. "We were just jokin' around."

Taras yanked open the door and the young men left, but Mitch, once well out of Taras's reach, turned back and called, "See ya round, Frenchie! You know where to find us!"

A strangled sound burst from Marie's throat, and she fled to the storeroom. June started to follow but Olena said, "No. I'll go."

When Olena entered the stock room Marie was huddling between the large burlap sacks of raisins and sugar, her knees hugged to her chest. Olena shifted the raisins far enough to sit beside her, careful to stare straight ahead.

"I can't bear it," Marie whispered. "C'est insupportable. The three of us living on top of one another, no room to move, to breathe. I just want to *breathe*."

Olena offered her a handful of raisins, then took one herself. Recognition thrummed through her. All those walks taken when she'd been a girl not much younger than Marie, that restless need to get out. Away. But she also felt a surprising gratitude.

For all the times she'd inwardly railed against being trapped on the homestead at least she'd had periods of reprieve when Taras went to work the fields. And now, his forays to buy discount items offered that same release from his constant presence. She would encourage him to make those trips even if there were no profit in them.

"Do you know Mr. Barker, he has a house at the edge of town? A house! Four bedrooms, a parlour *and* a dining room."

Olena nodded, chewed thoughtfully.

"Tom, he said we'd live there, he told me all about it, the family dinners, la Fête de Noël, Pâques — how you say — Easter. He didn't tell me that after Mrs. Barker died, Mr. Barker, he shut up the house and moved him and Tom into the apartment above the store. Tom says it is from grief but me, I think it is because the old man is a miser. He has no soft spot in his soul. When Tom asked if he and I could move into the house, the apartment is so small for three, the two of us newly married, Mr. Barker, he laughed. No. He spat! He said ... he said ..."

Marie started to shake, no tears, just a dry shaking. "And Tom, he said nothing."

"I know you cannot go back to France but you have nobody back in Quebec, the hospital vhere you met Tom? No friend you could go to?" Olena had an insane thought of stealing money from the store and sending Marie to safety, if safety could be found.

"Non. Personne. No one. There's never been anyone. Only Tom." Marie contemplated her handful of raisins. "He was so kind when I met him at the hospital. I would clean his room and feel sorry for him, injured so badly and never any visitors. No flowers or cards. When he could walk again he would take me to a little café at the edge of the hospital grounds. We would have un peu de vin, a meal, he would make me laugh. But he's changed, his father is changing him. The longer we are here, the worse it gets. Tu sais, I asked Tom to go with me that night, the way we used to, but he said 'I don't hold with women drinking.' That voice." She shuddered. "So I got mad and went anyway. And then when his father gave me this," she lifted her hair to reveal the bruise, "he did nothing. Rien. What your husband did for me today, it is more than Tom has done in all the time we've been here. So you see, there is no one. And the worst is that Tom is not the only one changing. His father, he is chipping away at me too." She dropped the raisins back in the sack, stood with an air of resolution, brushed the wrinkles out of her skirt. "You and your husband are very good but it is for me to deal with. After all," a bleak smile shadowed her face, "the old man cannot live forever."

JUNE AND TARAS stood by the till, avoiding each another's gaze. The clock ticked slow minutes so loudly June thought her brain would explode. Her father too appeared to be watching the clock, though he tried to hide it by polishing the brass railing on the counter beneath it. After ten minutes he said, "Enough!" He rang open the till and plucked out two dimes, dropped them into June's hand. "No work today. You take Marie to the movies. Go in the back way. No need for that Barker son of a bitch to know. Be sure to be here by closing."

When June slipped into the storeroom Olena was straightening Marie's lovely hair over the terrible bruise. "Good," she said, when June told her about the movie. "You go try to forget all this, at least for a vhile."

WHEN JUNE AND MARIE entered, the theatre was in darkness and the newsreel was already playing. June tiptoed to the front to pay, then joined Marie at the back in one of several empty rows just as the movie began. June could never have imagined anything like it, a whole life played out in black and white. Cowboys rode back and forth on splotchy horses. A covered wagon driven by a screaming woman lurched toward them, followed by streams of Indians that crowded round the wagon and looked like they would burst out into the cinema. The screen swarmed with thundering horses, grey dust filled the air, bangs and pops exploded from guns, arrows whizzed past cowboy hats and ripped through the covered wagon. Every time a cowboy fired, Indians shrieked and tumbled to the dust, twitching, then lying still. It was all very exciting, though by the time the movie ended, June couldn't help but notice that the pretty blonde woman ended up with the hero, while the dark-haired woman ended up back in the saloon. She sighed and turned to Marie. It was getting late and her father had told them not to linger but even though the credits were rolling, still Marie stayed in her chair, staring at the screen.

"You know that movies are only make believe, yes? That those weren't real Indians?" June nodded, though she hadn't really noticed until Marie mentioned it, having spent all her attention on the fate of the dark-haired woman. But it was true. The Indians on the screen looked like no one she'd ever seen, with their strange, harsh faces and inhuman yells, the braids that were so obviously wigs. The Indians who occasionally came into the store looked more like the movie cowboys, with their short hair and cotton shirts and jeans, but without the guns.

"And you also knew they were just playing dead?"

June nodded, confused. Wasn't it all pretend?

"Ah yes, but you are eleven. When I was little, maybe six or seven, a man who gave money to the orphanage took some of us young ones to the cinéma. It was the first time I ever saw a film. A western. It was magic, but something troubled me. I could see, tu sais, that the Indians weren't real. But the dying, that was different. I heard the gunshots, I watched men fall. I could not understand why any man would volunteer to get shot. So I decided the movie company must be sending someone to the prisons, to death row."

June nodded wisely. She had heard about death row. On the radio, on one of those nights when she couldn't sleep. An announcer had said a man who'd killed his cousin had been taken from death row and hanged by the neck until dead, and all she could think of was the time her mother strangled a chicken that had been pecked almost to death by the others, the dreadful squawk, the crack of the bone under her mother's pragmatic hands. Her father had told her that men who were going to be hanged got to eat a last meal of all their favourite foods, but it didn't seem like much compensation. June wished Marie would hurry up with her story. People were filing out of the theatre, and the fewer there were inside, the more there would be outside to see them leave and tell Old Man Barker what Marie had been up to. Again.

"This man — I always picture him fat and chewing on a cigar, like W.C. Fields — anyway, he would walk into this room full of condemned men, and he would say, 'Okay. We all know you have to die.'" Marie spread her hands and shrugged, miming the fat man's attitude, that it was too bad but there was nothing anyone could do.

"And then he would say, 'But I have, how you say? une proposition. You can either go quietly and get hanged off by yourself.'" Marie's shoulders slumped, conveying what a lacklustre option that would be. "Or..." and here Marie, still playing the fat man, waved her arms so enthusiastically June thought his cigar would surely have gone out, and worried that they were drawing attention to themselves, completely against her father's instructions. She held her finger to her lips.

Marie dropped her voice. "'Or,' he would say, 'you can go out with a bang. A bit of fun.' And then he would let those men talk it over and sure enough they'd decide it was worth it. Vraiment, who wants to go like a sheep to a death chamber, to die all alone. This way, you get to put on war paint, ride a horse, have some fun yelling and shooting arrows, and then you will be dead. I did worry about giving these criminals, men with nothing to lose, giving them guns. What if they decided to kill the cowboys and ride away on their horses? But today I understood. The Indians, they have only bows and arrows, and the cowboys, they get the guns. The game, it is already rigged. Funny, the things you think when you're a kid, non?"

June didn't really think it was all that funny, but as she laughed obediently she was startled to see in the flickering light from the screen a tear trickling down Marie's cheek. Feeling utterly inadequate, she tugged on Marie's arm. "We'd better go. Papa told me not to be late."

EVEN THOUGH it had only gone nine, the day was unusually sultry, sweat already slick between Olena's breasts and thighs, both rubbing together as she walked. The apartment had been stifling, the store would be stuffy and she wanted to take some time in the sun and open air. A chance to clear her head of its worries about Marie. It was not in Olena's nature to interfere, but that young woman was on a road to ruin and there seemed no way to help her. Olena thought wryly back to when Varvara had told her it was the lot of women to do, not what they wanted, but what they must. How had she put it? Eat from the plate put in front of you. It still rankled. How could she say the same to Marie, essentially tell her to surrender? But those bruises, bruises she appeared to court. The other night howling up at Old Man Barker from the alley at midnight, daring him to come down and face her. After what he did to her for smashing that china too. Craziness. For all these acts of rebellion, Marie did not strike Olena as strong. It might be true that Old Man Barker couldn't live forever, but he showed no sign of dying any time soon, and in this battle Marie was losing ground.

Olena unbuttoned the collar of her dress in a vain attempt to allow some cooler air to reach her skin, then stopped mid-stride.

Music was pouring out of the upper window of the hotel. Music such as she had never heard, the voices unearthly, alien, either soaring high or swooping low, and the words not English, that ugly language with all its short sounds. This language was as liquid as the music itself, pouring round her like a stream tumbling over and around a rock. It became the slickness between her breasts and thighs, part of her rhythmic movement against herself. Olena's lips parted and the opening of her mouth was only the smallest part of the opening blooming inside her. She thought back to the day when the notes of Conor's violin had floated across the fields and pierced her clear through with longing, and this was the same, but closer. Here on her street. From the window above her a black and curly head jutted out, black eyes blinked at her, the man's mouth was open and music spilled out of it before he could stop himself. Olena was too startled to do more than stare, her mouth open like his but silent. Then the head vanished, the music shut off, and Olena hurried to the store where she knew Mrs. Logan would be waiting, abuzz with the latest gossip.

The curly-headed man was the new owner of the hotel and bar. He was an Eyetie, Mrs. Logan said, chatting to Mrs. McTeer while Olena weighed out their weekly orders of tea, imported Irish breakfast for Mrs. Logan, ordinary bulk pekoe for Mrs. McTeer. "Not fresh from Italy of course, because of the war. From Toronto."

Mrs. McTeer nodded. "I hear that in Toronto they've been locking up fascists, like they did commies in the last one. Maybe he's one of those. Fascist, not commie."

"Really, Fiona." Mrs. Logan waved aside this theory. "What would a fascist find to do in a town like Eldergrove? It's not like we have any state secrets to steal or vital rail lines to blow up."

"Yes, I see what you mean," Mrs. McTeer said regretfully.

"Of course, there could be other problems," Mrs. Logan mused. "A lot of Eyeties are in organized crime and everyone knows about their loose ways with the women."

"He's hosting a dinner on Saturday, a kind of opening night, at his expense. He dropped off invitations all over town. Do you think perhaps we shouldn't go?" Mrs. McTeer looked anxiously up at Mrs. Logan. Given that the McTeers, like the Zaleskys, lived above their store, Olena guessed treats like a dinner out weren't often offered.

"Oh, no, we should definitely go. Of course we can't socialize with them, but it's a nice gesture and it can't hurt to see what he's done with the place."

"Yes, that's what I think too." Mrs. McTeer's relief was palpable.

"I wouldn't worry if you don't get invited, my dear," Mrs. Logan said to Olena as she scooped up her change from the counter. "He's probably hosting people he knows can afford to pay later."

Mrs. McTeer's face flushed mottled red.

Olena suddenly heard Conor all those years ago — "You know the Irish are the bohunks of Europe, don't you?" — and had to pretend to drop a coin so Mrs. Logan couldn't see her biting her lip to keep from laughing out loud. Just as Olena had wiped the smile from her face and closed the till on the stray coin, who should walk in but the Eyetie, who introduced himself as Antonio Bruni, come to invite Olena and Taras to the dinner too, handing her a small poster with all the details. Olena had no doubt this gesture sprang from his desire to guarantee the best prices on supplies, but still, she couldn't resist throwing a glance of triumph at Mrs. Logan's backside as it swayed out the door.

That Saturday almost everyone in town except for the Barkers — Old Man Barker didn't hold with foreign food — made their way to the hotel to find part of the bar transformed into a restaurant. Small tables draped with checkered cloths, each with a candle set in a china saucer as its centrepiece. From a record player in the corner came the music that had moved Olena so strangely. Mr. Bruni — "Call me Tonio" — lit the candles at the tables and explained the unfamiliar words on the menus he handed round. He was clever, Olena thought, choosing to serve mostly familiar food — ham steak and French fries, fried chicken and mashed potatoes. For the more adventurous there was something called spaghetti, with a rich tomato sauce, or tiny pillows like dainty perogies stuffed with cheese and spinach, and a roasted chicken basted with lemon and rosemary and — with a finger over his lips and a wink of his eye — a secret ingredient. When Olena tasted it she chuckled and he caught her eye and winked again. Garlic. Clever indeed. To the Angliki garlic was the sign of the peasant and they refused to touch it. Yet, since they had no idea what they were eating, murmurs of pleasure from the tables around her rose and fell in waves. Taras refused the wine Mr. Bruni offered, ordered instead a glass of neat rye. Olena didn't like to say she too would prefer rye, and took a long time to sip her way through the wine, but she enjoyed twisting the stem to catch the light from the candle in the dark red liquid.

After dinner Mr. Bruni turned off the record player and brought out an accordion. He played and sang, his voice filling the room. On her way to the ladies' Olena could hear the puffs of air the accordion shot out from between his arms, an instrument that breathed like a human. To top off the evening he brought to all the tables small glasses filled with clear liquid alight with blue flame and when he counted three they all tossed the liquid into their mouths, drinking fire. But the taste was only of licorice which Olena did not like very much. Still, she accepted a second glass because of the thrill of the fire. It was only on the walk home that she realized his wife had not once emerged from the kitchen.

Soon the click of high heels and squeak of stiff shoe leather along Main was a common thing on Friday and Saturday nights. Of course, he bought supplies for the restaurant from the store, usually appearing when Taras was on a buying trip. Her hands and eyes met Mr. Bruni's over the flour, salt, and sugar she started putting aside for him as it was in such short supply. He bought canned tomatoes by the crate.

Music streamed from the kitchen, rode the rich smells

of garlic, tomato. He leaned out the kitchen window one day, beckoning to her, and she stood on tiptoe, her breasts pressing against sun-warmed wood siding, as he offered her a taste of tomato sauce mounded on a wooden spoon. She blew on it, licked. Olena felt the heavy presence of his wife somewhere in the shadow of the kitchen, slaving over the sauce that was seducing her tongue, but she didn't care, she didn't care.

He brought her a small Italian cookie once just as she was flipping the CLOSED sign on the empty store — biscotti he called it. As she crunched her way through it, a flavour reminiscent of the fiery liqueur teased her tongue. "You like?" he asked. She did. Fading afternoon light filtered through the plate glass store window, touched the hairs on his arms with faint gold as he leaned against the counter and, in English as broken as hers, told her how his wife was unhappy, how her unhappiness often made her take to her bed. "Her father and brother, they get hauled off as fascists, sent to a camp outside Toronto. She never get over it." She had insisted on getting away from the big city, terrified Tonio would be next, no matter how often he told her that he'd never been a member of any fascist group. "But now she hate this prairie too, and she still afraid to go out in case she get snatched. She want me to stay inside also but I tell her we have to eat, make a go of the restaurant. It's a lonely life." Olena wasn't sure whose life he meant.

"I am so sorry to hear that, Mr. Bruni."

"Tonio," he insisted. "Antonio, say like this."

The name slid on her tongue like music, a melody she whispered to herself long after he'd left the store. Twenty-nine years old and she had never known this pulsing, this urgent call of body to body when a man walked into a room, willing him to look up, to come to her, through whatever barriers, as though they were air. Antonio was not even particularly good-looking. But as she spoke his name, she chose him, had chosen him from the moment that strange music had poured out of his mouth and worked its way deep inside her.

When Taras was out of town Tonio began to follow her on her Sunday forays for berries or wild herbs, suddenly appearing and walking beside her with his slightly rolling gait, that and his short stature the result of childhood scoliosis. He did not touch her, never forced himself on her, but there was such a pull between them she could feel the hairs of her arms rising to seek him. He wore white shirts, the sleeves rolled up, his skin dark against them, his hands always moving, stripping off the heads of wild grasses and scattering them on the breeze, running nervously through his hair, or expanding on his halting English. His hair was wiry and springy, threaded through with grey. As they walked he told her about Italy. The heat like this, but moister, heavier.

One day he stopped her on a slight rise of ground and pointed to the sky, streaked with feathery wisps of grey that strayed from clouds above but didn't reach the ground below. "See there? The air so thirsty it suck up the water before it can even reach the ground. Everything here so thirsty." Olena could almost hear the hiss of the vanishing rain. He reached to her face, at the edges of her eyes, and she felt faint grit beneath his touch. "Look," his voice as soft as his fingers, "salt. The air steal even the moisture from your face." He raised his fingers to his lips and tasted the salt taste of her. Almost without her willing it, her hands moved over the bones of his face, cheek, jaw, over hair finer than she could have imagined.

"You are so beautiful, so beautiful," and the English for once was easy. He laughed, for both of them knew he was not beautiful at all, but short and stocky and sweating through his crisp white shirt, but his laugh was a sharp intake of breath that pulled her against his body and mouth.

JUNE AND MAY clumped down the wooden sidewalk to Varvara's. "You go keep that old lady company," their mother had said, as she did so often lately when their father was away, glancing at the curly-haired Eyetie hovering by the tools at the front of the store. It didn't seem fair. It was Friday, June's one chance to spend time with Marie. "Don't whine, June. Varvara doesn't get out much. She'll be happy to see you." Except Varvara never did seem happy to see them, often muttering about extra mouths to feed while sourly poking a stick into the firebox of her huge iron stove to bring the embers alight. If she was in a good mood, she told stories of the old country, which were not exciting like the Baba Yaga stories, but mostly grey and black and hungry and cold and always ended with her telling the girls how grateful they should be for what they had. It was almost better if she was in a bad mood, for then she just grumbled to herself and made them sit in the cramped front room and listen to the radio, to *Carry On Canada!*, the show that gave the news about the war, which was boring but which at least distracted Varvara from their ingratitude. Varvara wouldn't let the girls speak while the radio was on, or even squirm much, which usually got May into trouble as she *would* forget and start humming tunelessly, playing the itsy-bitsy spider game with her fingers. Today she started almost immediately after Varvara had told her to be quiet, twice. Every muscle in June's body tensed as she waited for

Varvara's wrath to burst over their heads, like torrents from the thundercloud that was her face. Varvara marched over to May, who was so deep inside her game she didn't even see the black-clad figure towering above her.

Two weeks before, as Varvara was leaving the store to walk home, the pack of young boys who taunted June so mercilessly converged behind the old woman, pointing at her flapping black dress and hooting at her hobbling, arthritic gait. June, watching from the safety of the store's window, felt a twinge of pity for Varvara, so small and hunched. But Varvara stopped and turned to glare at the boys, raised her bony finger and pointed, motionless, menacing, silent. The boys stopped laughing, stared at the ground and scuffed their feet, finally turned tail and ran.

Now Varvara stood stock still until May suddenly raised her eyes and stopped mid-note, her mouth a round O. June watched for the inevitable disaster, but Varvara's face cleared and to June's wonder, Varvara laughed. Laughed and switched off the radio, then hobbled into the kitchen without a word. June was relieved but also a little jealous. May was like that, she did things at home, in the classroom, and now here with Varvara that if June had done would have earned her a hiding, or at least a sharp reprimand. But May just smiled her sunny smile and got away with it.

Varvara settled the girls at the kitchen table with milk and bread in a bowl, and even a bit of sugar to sprinkle on it.

"Your mother, she works hard at the store, yes?" June tried not to stare at Varvara's hooked nose and the wart sprouting above one eyebrow, tried not to hear her father saying "that Baba Yaga!"

"Yes, Varvara," she answered politely.

"Your father, he's gone again?"

"He left yesterday," May offered, scraping the bottom of her bowl with her spoon and gazing hopefully in the direction of the pantry.

"Hmmm. She sends you here a lot lately, your mother. She doesn't need help at the store?" Varvara's eyes narrowed, and June's stomach clenched the way it used to whenever her father had casually asked her about Mr. Maguire. The way it had on that long, black night in the wagon. She clamped her gaze to her plate and her tongue between her teeth.

"She says you're lonely and need company," May chattered, trying to spin her bowl with her spoon.

"Does she." Varvara stopped the bowl's spin with a heavy hand. "Put that in the sink and bring a cloth to wipe these drops. Does your father know she sends you here?"

But neither girl knew the answer to that. Varvara sat for a minute staring into space, then muttered something beneath her breath and turned on the radio. May stole the last bite of June's bread and milk while June was staring at Varvara's back and trying to still her churning mind.

OLENA AND TONIO scrambled up the hillside to the top of the butte. She was nervous, wanting for the first time since she was a girl to be beautiful so that he would feel how right it was to betray his wife, her husband, her children, the world if necessary. She could see the whole of her small world from the butte, and she would trade it all for him. Her fear gave her courage and she slid out of her cotton dress, an old one she wore for berry picking and herb gathering, the one part of her brain that still functioned having told her that she couldn't afford to get grass stains on any newer clothing. And that she should insert a pessary just before leaving the store.

He gasped. She was not beautiful, but she was what took his breath and she knew a moment of pure gratitude. She pulled him down onto her stained dress, buried her tongue in his mouth. She had not known until this moment how hungry she was, how tired of being always hard, always cold. She had been a rock beneath Taras's rock-hard, demanding body. But this one folded round her hot and yielding, pressing into every contour of her. Slid into her like a hot knife into butter, her melting vulva slick and smooth around him, and still his entry split her open as none of Taras's pounding ever could, a slippage shift along a hidden fault line and release, release, and all within her was slippery, molten, hot surprise of magma underneath. She opened so wide she felt she could suck him whole inside her, and keep him there forever, she opened so wide even her mouth fell open, there wasn't a part of her she could close off. For one long moment she held him still in that opening, wanting to stay this way forever, completely full yet famished, then they started to move slowly, both with and against the other at one and the same time. So this is what it means to have a body, she thought, before all thought stopped.

Later they lay naked, letting the wind and sun lick the sweat from their bodies, delaying the inevitable dressing and descent. A pebble that had been beneath her throughout all their lovemaking nudged her, and she pulled it out without rancour. One side of it was rounded and rough to the hand, but when she turned it over to the flat side she saw an explosion of circles within circles. She cradled it for a moment, showed it to Tonio. "This is how you make me feel."

He took the stone from her hand with his mouth, rolled it round his tongue, then kissed her, passed the stone between their searching tongues, from his mouth to hers. She clenched the stone in her hand as he once more covered her body with his, calling forth cries that rose from her deepest self.

The next day she ached in every muscle across her chest, through her arms. He suffused her every motion, every thought, she couldn't sit still but couldn't stick at any task, leaving the float in the till half-counted, the new supply of women's lingerie half-unpacked. She was all body, a mesh of sensation without boundaries of sight and sound, touch and taste, hearing or speaking, everything was fired with an energy that spun her, bounced her off every mundane task, that infused even brushing her teeth with magic. A dozen times a day she picked up the stone, its circles within circles like exploding stars, the universe contained in the palm of her hand.

He told her they could start over somewhere else, open another restaurant. His wife could go back to Toronto, where she still had family, and once the war was over, most likely to Italy, she'd be happier there anyway. He drew a map of Alberta on Olena's breasts and belly. They could go there, or maybe even to British Columbia where you could really grow things. Think of what he could cook then. By this time she knew what she had earlier suspected: his wife did all the cooking; the rich sauce he'd used to seduce Olena had been simmered by his wife, the crunchy biscotti shaped by her hands. He would have to steal her recipes before he packed her off. Olena didn't know if he even knew how to cook — perhaps he expected her to learn this Eyetie food from recipes in a language twice removed from her. She didn't care. When he talked she really believed they could do it. She didn't give a damn about his wife. Let her go back to the old country. Let Olena claim the new.

Olena saw one chance at survival here, one chance to go back to who she had been. Could be. She could cut her ties to her children without more than a twinge, it was frightening the ruthlessness she felt when she was with Tonio. They were not her children then, they belonged to that other woman, the stone woman, not the molten woman who belonged to Tonio, who emerged when he so much as lifted his eyebrow. Even at home with June and May, she couldn't quite make them real, had to work to bring their faces into focus. Somewhere deep inside her was a flicker of guilt, but she doused it. She hadn't chosen this life, it had been thrust upon her, thrust into her, forced out of her with every birth and stillbirth of these last fourteen years. Taras would take another wife, the children would have a mother. And Olena — Olena could not imagine herself into the future like Tonio could, she only knew she didn't want this present. It had been bearable, just, when she'd been dead on the surface, but now she was alive in every pore, and the tension was stretching her beyond all bearing. It had to give. Soon.

She was not crazy enough to think Tonio loved her the way she loved him — ruthlessly, single-mindedly. Why should he? He had known many women. Olena even knew she might be just a fling, she had heard about Eyeties from the whispers of the English ladies in the store, their hot blood, their roving eyes. She had seen him flirting with Marie, even with prim little Mrs. McTeer, who blushed and giggled like a girl whenever he smiled at her. Olena didn't care. Her love for Tonio was, in some way she didn't quite grasp, incidental to Tonio. It was a love for the woman he created when he moved against, inside her — for this love Olena would sacrifice anything. Maybe he would love her for only a year, maybe he would leave her in this Alberta or

British Columbia. But he would have to hold her to leave her, and by the time he did she would be somewhere else. *Someone else.*

JUNE OPENED her mouth as wide as she could, leaning in to the mirror and peering down her throat. She had been having trouble swallowing since supper last night, as though some morsel of food was stuck, but hadn't told her mother because today was fair day and fair day marked the end of the school year. Six whole weeks of freedom. Her mother would make her stay home if she thought June was sick, but June refused to be kept from her very first fair. Through the window came the banging of hammers and the scraping of saws as men erected booths in the playground behind the school. She tilted with more determination toward her reflection. The livid red of her throat was coated with white streaks, and at one spot a large white lump of what looked like cottage cheese. Picking up her toothbrush by the bristle end, she poked at the lump with the handle, trying to pry it loose. But all she accomplished was a sharp stab of pain that brought tears to her eyes.

"June!" her mother called. "The parade is starting!"

June put the toothbrush back in its mug and wiped her eyes. Marie hadn't appeared on the landing all week and had missed her shift last night. There had been rumours in the store about a salesman causing some kind of ruckus at the hardware and since then neither Marie nor Tom had emerged from the apartment, not even to go to work. But surely even Mr. Barker could not be so cruel as to stop them going to the fair. Marie had told June there would be cotton candy, such a pretty pale pink and so fluffy, like eating a cloud. Today June would wait all day at the cotton candy booth for Marie if need be, and even though her throat clenched at the thought of eating something as dry as cotton, she would swallow that cloud if it killed her.

"NOW," her mother said, when May and June joined her and Varvara at the front of the store. "After the parade you girls go to the fair. I'm going to be doing inventory all day and I don't want you under my feet. June, you keep an eye on May and remember you're staying the night at Varvara's. She'll be giving you supper so don't be late."

June nodded, then turned away to hide her wince as the tiny movement wrenched her throat.

"You girls go outside to watch." Varvara pushed them toward the door. "I need to talk to your mother. We can see well enough from here." May rattled out the door and sat down on the curb, just as the first of the parade vehicles, mostly trucks and tractors decked out with streamers and paper flowers, began their slow, diesel-belching procession. But something in Varvara's tone made June take her seat on the bench just outside the door, which was slightly ajar to let the air circulate.

"People will start talking," Varvara said grimly.

Olena was counting coins into the till, clang clang, her voice almost as metallic as they. "Let them talk."

"You can't be so foolish, Olena. Flirting is one thing, but to be doing what you're doing, this is dangerous. For now people are distracted by that foolish French girl but that can't last forever. Those long walks you take. Don't you think someone will notice who always goes at the same time? It is wrong, Olena, and the wrongs we do, they find us out."

"And what of the wrongs others do to you? What of them?"

Olena sounded almost as though she was laughing, her breath coming in gusts, and the coins plinking faster into the till. She couldn't be counting them, could barely be noticing them.

"So. You throw away your husband, your children, your whole life?"

Olena banged the till shut. "What life?"

"The life God gave you."

"The life *you* gave me, more like," Olena spat. "Not of my choosing."

"So this is what you choose? To behave like a slut and set the whole town to laughing?"

"*I* am the one laughing," Olena hissed. "*Me*. He looks at me and my whole body smiles. He touches me and I laugh in my soul."

"Romantic foolishness!"

"So you say. It is so nonetheless."

"Olena." June was startled to hear Varvara's voice almost pleading. "This cannot last. You will lose everything."

Olena's voice was cold. "I do not lose it. I give it away."

What did her mother mean, give her life away? And who was this man who made her smile in her soul? Certainly not June's father whose slightest touch made her mother either stand still as stone or give the tiniest of shudders.

"It is not so bad, what you have. A man not so old, your children. The store is managing, you have a home, a car. You live in a town, work in a store, not breaking your back on some godforsaken farm. It is not so bad what I did, and what I did, I did for you. Sometimes to survive you must do hard things. I acted for the best."

"Perhaps. But I cannot live a life that is 'not so bad.' Maybe for you it was enough, but I *need*." This last word tore the air like a knife.

"Ach," Varvara exclaimed. "There's no reasoning with you." She slammed the door of the store behind her and marched down the street without a glance at the girls.

Even though the sun was blaring June shivered, and her hand crept to her throat. Need what? She could hardly ask her mother. June's entire life was teetering and one wrong word could plunge the family into ruin. Her father was gone for who knew how long. There was only one person she could turn to. She closed her eyes on the parade, and prayed with all her might that Marie would be at the fair.

JUNE HOVERED by the cotton candy kettle, where a man was winding pink cobwebs onto a cardboard cone. Marie had been right: it was very pretty. But it was too frivolous for June's desperate mood, and the chugging sounds and belches of exhaust from the generator running the machine made her head ache and her stomach queasy. May was off racing in a potato sack alongside some of her friends, all of them collapsing in a heap of giggles far before the finish line, then running off to the next game: balancing eggs on spoons. The shrieks of laughter from the contestants and shouts of encouragement from the spectators cut through June's brain like a knife. And still there was no sign of Marie. June wondered if she could be brave enough to stand beneath Marie's window and throw pebbles at it until she emerged but knew she couldn't risk attracting Old Man Barker instead. Now even her eyelids ached, from being pressed tight over burning eyes.

A bang echoed from across the grounds, followed by a splooshing sound and a huge cheer. A figure in a black bathing suit, black hair streaming down her face, clambered out of a huge tank of water and climbed some rickety makeshift stairs up to a wooden stool suspended from a beam by thick ropes. The figure climbed awkwardly onto the stool and clung to the ropes with one hand, pulling strands of hair from her eyes with the other. Marie. Mascara running halfway down her cheeks, lipstick so smudged her mouth looked swollen to twice its size. June crossed the grounds, barely noticing the races she was cutting through, ignoring the yells to get out of the way. A long line of young men snaked through the crowd at the tank, and at the head of the line was Mitch Logan. He reached down for a baseball from the bucket. "All in good fun," he called as he wound up with the baseball. Bang against the wooden lever. Sploosh into the tank. "Don't forget to breathe, Frenchie," he yelled as she sputtered to the surface.

Marie crawled back up the steps and onto the stool, got hauled up again, hung there limp, dripping. She did not look like she was having fun. A fiery ache started in June's chest and spread up to her throbbing brain.

Mr. Logan was next. He hardly waited for Marie to settle on the stool before hurling a ball. His aim was good, and down Marie went again. The crowd of spectators was growing, among them Mrs. Logan, who gazed fondly at her husband and son.

"That should teach her to try to pass." Mrs. Logan and Mrs. McTeer chuckled companionably.

Bang. Sploosh.

Pass? June thought. But Marie had been out of school for ages.

"What a time to be away at my sister's!" Mrs. McTeer exclaimed. "I missed it all. Were you there?"

"Not me, my husband." Mrs. Logan was delighted to tell what was obviously a well-rehearsed tale. June crept closer, hovered behind them, willing herself invisible. "He was in the hardware buying nails when a salesman came by trying to sell some new kind of drill and Tom went white as a sheet. Turns out they knew each other from the training base and the salesman was injured in the same accident. Old Mr. Barker rushes up proud as a peacock to meet one of Tom's army buddies but the army buddy wasn't at all happy to see Tom. Not at all! Turns out Tom was the one who caused the accident! Fooling around with a grenade, showing off. Got his friend killed and several others injured, including himself. The great war hero! Old Man Barker was fit to be tied. And that Marie! A nurse? Hah! A skivvy more like. Emptying bed pans. Very romantic. As for being French. She's from Montreal!" Mrs. Logan pursed her lips as though tasting something very sour. "I always thought there was something fishy about her. No matter how much she gussied herself up, you could just tell. A half-breed of some sort, the salesman said. She'd probably been with everyone in the camp by the time Tom got to her. You know what they're like. Imagine! Old Mrs. Barker must be turning in her grave."

"Goodness. Poor Mr. Barker. His son putting one over on him like that!"

"Yes, but it's Marie he's most angry at. It was bad enough when he thought she was French. Now he's beside himself. The dunk tank was his idea. My husband trained the whole ball team to pitch for the past week and made sure they all came. And for all Mr. Barker doesn't hold with makeup, he made sure she was wearing it today. If the shoe fits!"

Bang.

Sploosh.

Mrs. Logan and Mrs. McTeer clapped their gloved hands.

June hated these women as she had never hated anyone, not Mr. Maguire, not the frizzy-haired woman, not the bullies at school. Hated their shoulder pads and print dresses, the nylon stockings and white gloves they wore even on a hot July day. The noses they were always looking down. She stared helplessly at Marie, at the black streaks of mascara and red splotch of lipstick that made her look like a sad clown.

Next up was Old Man Barker, who had bought a whole bucket of balls. As he took throw after throw, Mitch Logan called, "Parlay-voo Frenchie?" and his friends quickly got into the act. "May no, monsoor," one of them howled, "Parlay-voo kerplunk?" The dunk tank was the busiest booth at the fair.

Bang.

Sploosh.

Old Man Barker badgered Tom into taking a throw with the last ball in the bucket, and he did, shamefacedly, missing by a mile. When he walked away, he shot a glance of pure loathing at his father, but he did nothing to help his wife. June wished her father was here, to stand up for Marie like he had that time in the store. To stare down that crowd of faces all alight with greed like coyotes staring at a cornered rabbit. For one terrible moment, Marie gazed full into June's eyes, and June knew she should do something, anything, to protest, to show her loyalty to her friend.

Bang.

Sploosh.

But suddenly and appallingly, June's anger flared at Marie. How could she let herself get into this situation, just when June needed her so badly? June, who had thought no one could be lower in the pecking order than she was herself. Who had wanted to slip somehow beneath Marie's skin, no longer plain and gawky, but beautiful and graceful. And now look at her. She was as bedraggled as the hen that got pecked on the farm until its back was a raw and quivering red. The one Olena had to throttle because there was no saving it. Filled with revulsion, June turned and ran, back to the races to find May flushed with triumph, a whole egg slipping from her spoon to smash safely past the finish line. June grabbed her roughly by the arm and croaked, "We have to go."

JUNE DRAGGED HER FEET along the wooden sidewalk, dragged May along behind her, each step taking them further from the shouts at the fairground, the relentless bang of the dunk tank that echoed through her skull. The sun was slanting thick over the town, the dust and heat pressed on her chest. Her whole body was throbbing. Part of her wanted to go back to the dunk tank and yell at all those people to stop, another part wanted to fire a ball at the tank herself. But all of her didn't want to stay the night at Varvara's, in her stale-smelling spare bedroom with its bed so narrow May always ended up sleeping on top of June and half suffocating her. She rubbed at her throat as though massaging the outside would ease the pain on the inside, in her heart. The buildings seemed to crowd in on her, watch her every movement with shuttered, accusatory eyes.

May would not stop dawdling, now to pick up a bit of dandelion fluff to hold to the light, now to poke a stick in a small puddle of mud and draw a picture that ended up lopsided when June hauled her away. All that dawdling meant June saw Olena slap down the CLOSED sign and tap off down the sidewalk away from them. Something about her mother's feet, almost dancing, made June afraid. Even more afraid than the night in the wagon waiting for her father. Or the nights when the muffled but venomous voices and thuds thrummed from her parents' bedroom, and June would wrap herself around May's rigid body, cover May's ears with her hands, leaving her own ears exposed.

She had thought nothing could be worse than those sounds, but she was wrong. Lately, the silence, especially from her mother, had been eerie. It was as if her mother was there but not there, as if she barely saw or heard them, and when she finally did, had to take a moment to remember who they were. She didn't react to Taras's digs at Varvara. She didn't snap at the girls when they made too much noise. Just yesterday June had dropped the red cut glass bowl, the one beautiful dish they had, that her mother took great care of, not letting the children wash or dry it, but always handling herself, polishing until its facets danced red light around the kitchen. She'd had it since before June was even born and had kept it through their poorest times. It had not a chip, and then June dropped it and it shattered. She had trembled before Olena, waiting for punishment, but Olena had only shaken that faraway look out of her eyes for a moment, and said without heat, "Don't just stand there June, get the broom and pan."

And now here was her mother, after telling them she would be working late, here she was heading up the road away from town, hips swaying and feet occasionally skipping, as though they wanted to break into a run. "I give them away," she had said. And June could do nothing about it, not daring to call out to her mother, to let her know she'd been seen. A fury of helplessness swept over her. At all of them, her friend, her mother, even her father. All of them abandoning her.

"Come *on*," June snapped, and yanked May out of the muck,

where she was happily pushing mud into mutant shapes only she could recognize and getting herself filthy so Varvara could blame June for that too. At least when Vasilisa was sent to Baba Yaga she didn't have the added burden of a younger sister. May cried out in protest but allowed June to hustle her up the street to Varvara's before their mother could turn back and see them. "Slow down!" May pleaded, as she stumbled on the uneven boards, and would have fallen if it hadn't been for June's unrelenting hand, which held her up even as it wanted to slap her. May gave her a sideways glance. "Once upon a time there was a little girl called May. She had a big sister called June who had *very long legs* and was *very bossy*." And then, of course, even though she still wanted to slap her, June had to smile, and slow down.

They paused at Varvara's gate. The house was gloomy, even in the late afternoon sunlight.

"Maybe she'll have some candy," said May, ever hopeful. June just snorted, her face twisting at the pain that caused.

"Well, I bet she tells us stories again."

"Terrific." June opened the creaking gate and pushed May through. The last time Varvara had told them bedtime stories May was awake for hours after lights out, desperately pinching June every few minutes so she wouldn't fall asleep and abandon her little sister to the monsters Varvara had planted in her head. June knocked, and Varvara opened the door slowly, peering round it suspiciously.

"So. You're here. Better late than not at all, one *could* say."

There didn't seem to be any answer to this, so June said nothing, but rubbed at her throat.

"You're not well." It was not a question. "Just like your mother to send you to me sickly." For a moment, June was so desperate she considered telling Varvara what she had just seen, but Varvara cut her off, saying irritably, "Enter, enter. My house is losing its warmth." And this appeared to be true, for June was shivering in spite of the heat of the sun.

Varvara seated them in her small kitchen by the big black stove, opened the oven door and poked some baked potatoes out of the glowing red with a long fork. She split the potatoes with a knife and doused their steaming insides with cottage cheese and a pinch of salt, then plunked two plates in front of the girls.

"Here. Eat." She sat down to the biggest potato herself. June was very hungry, but even though the potato was baked to a crisp just the way she liked it, her throat ached when she thought about trying to swallow. She cut tiny pieces and flinched from every bite, torn between the pain in her throat and the pangs of her hunger.

Varvara peered at her. "The food too good for you?"

June shook her head, then, afraid she had been rude, nodded, then, confused, ducked her head, her hand creeping to her throat again.

"Sore?"

June nodded. On this point she was not at all confused. Every time she swallowed or spoke the pain brought sharp points of light to her eyes. She looked up at Varvara and nodded again.

"Just a minute." Varvara moved to the stove, lifted one of the round lids and set it aside. With a long black ladle she dipped into the fire, the dancing flames tossing her shadow huge against the wall and throwing her hooked nose and chin into high relief. She took a tin mug from the shelf above the stove and dropped a live coal into it, then poured some water from a stone jug over the hissing coal and thrust the mug into June's hand.

"Here, quick. Sip all round the edge, like this." Varvara mimed with her twisted hands.

The coal sent scummy bits of ash to the surface, but June was too afraid of Varvara to do anything but what she was told. She began to sip the warm potion in the smallest possible sips, round and round the rim of the cup, pulling back from every swallow because even though the water was only warm, not boiling, what if there was a piece of live coal lurking there and she swallowed it, and it burned her from the inside out like Vasilisa's evil stepmother, the one who was really Baba Yaga in disguise. Maybe that was what Varvara intended. But when June had drunk only half the murky water, Varvara took it from her, saying, "Good."

Varvara scraped the potato and cottage cheese mixture out of the crisp skin and mashed it with a little fresh water to make a paste. "This will be easier." And it was, but June found that, where she had been shivering, now she was sweating and not much interested in food. She felt Varvara's dry hands cool on her face, and then she was being led to the bed not in the spare room, but in the corner of the kitchen where Varvara could keep an eye on her.

"You sleep down here where it's warmer."

"Me too," yelped May, and June could tell she didn't want to be left sitting alone at the table with Varvara.

"Only until bedtime, then you go into the spare room. We don't need you kicking your sister and keeping her awake."

May opened her mouth to protest but closed it again when Varvara snapped her fingers.

After tucking the girls beneath a fraying quilt, Varvara finished all the potatoes — her own and what June and May had left behind. She ran her finger over the surface of every plate to get the last of the juice from the cottage cheese, licked her finger methodically. Then she pulled up her rocking chair beside the bed. "You want me to put on the radio?" she asked, her hand on June's forehead.

June shook her head at the thought of the noisy laughter and music that would shoot like arrows out of the radio. Like the dreadful sounds at the dunk tank.

Varvara sat in silence for a moment, rocking. "So. What shall we talk about?"

June knew it was her job to avert disaster, but a red haze of pain was enveloping her and disabling her will, even though she knew what May would say, which was the last thing their father had said before heading out of town this morning. "Ask that old witch to tell you a Baba Yaga story." He had glanced sideways at Olena as he spoke, but she was combing her hair in a distracted way and didn't even notice, though she did jump when he slammed the door behind him.

Sure enough. "A Baba Yaga story? Papa thinks you might know her."

Varvara gave a crack of laughter. "Really. He might be nearer the mark than he knows and should be careful where he treads, eh?" She leaned in close to the girls, and though she was laughing, her eyes flickered dangerously. "In my story Baba Yaga tells Vasilisa she must give up a year of her life for every question she asks."

As if that would stop May. June pulled the blankets up around her neck.

"I know about Vasilisa," May rattled on. "She burned up her family. My father told me. Do you know that story?"

"Maybe, maybe not. I know one story about Baba Yaga giving

to a man everything he desired, but in the special way she gives, which is not always so good."

"Tell that one," May ordered.

"Once upon a time," Varvara began, "there was a man who loved a woman beyond reason, a woman with hair as black as ink and lips as red as blood. But she scorned the man because he was not rich. And Baba Yaga, who sees all things, knew he would do anything to gain his heart's desire. So she came to him in the guise of his beloved, and told him she would marry him, bringing with her a stupendous dowry, if he would do this one small thing. Slit the throat of her little sister, who had hair like spun gold and eyes like the bluest sea, and bring her the heart. A heart for a heart, she said, my sister's for mine." June closed her eyes, drifted in and out of the tale. Behind her eyelids the little girl's blood was spilling, an angry red haze, and Varvara's voice pulsing in it like a heartbeat, "Such a little neck, such a sharp knife, one swift cut, then all is yours." Someone else saying, "I give them away, take them, Baba Yaga, they are yours." And Varvara coming toward June with a huge ladle that became a knife. The rabbit turned its vacant eyes to June: "You want to eat?" And suddenly June was staring into Baba Yaga's maw, its iron teeth studded with clots of blood and when June tried to run Baba Yaga was both before and behind her. "Run!" and it wasn't a rabbit being offered up to Baba Yaga but May, her throat stretched back, her eyes wide and vacant, and June was plunged into terrible darkness, a darkness in which faces floated in and out of a red-black haze. May, her eyes now full of fear and her tongue utterly stilled, then Varvara, holding not a ladle but a cup that mercifully contained no fire, just some foul-tasting grassy bits, saying, "Drink, it will make you better." And the drink did make her sleep but she didn't feel any better, except occasionally when she clawed her way out of nightmare to find her mother at her bedside, bathing her forehead with a cold cloth and an unusually soft touch and voice, saying, "Hush now, it was only a dream. You've been very sick, June." And then, holding the cup to June's lips, "Drink." Too weak to protest, even to turn her lips from the cup, June drank. "Don't leave me," she whispered before dark waters closed over her again.

WHEN SHE FINALLY surfaced her parents told her she'd been sick for days, and it was only thanks to Varvara's careful tending and knowledge of herbs that she'd survived at all. Her terrible dreams they called delirium, caused by her high fever, and told her over and over that May was safe. When June sobbed that she needed to see Marie, to apologize, to make sure they were still friends, her parents said at first that June was too sick for visitors. But on the day she was well enough to leave Varvara's and go home, her parents told her that the night of the fair Marie had run off, most likely with the owner of the hotel who had vanished the same night. When June wept for the loss of her friend, of the chance to make amends, her mother smoothed the hair from her forehead saying with a catch in her voice and an oddly twisted expression, "You know she wasn't happy in this town. We must hope she'll be happier where she is." Then, straightening both her face and her voice, "You must put it out of your mind, Junie, and do all you can to get better, to get stronger. No more crying."

June tried, but even though she drank Varvara's potions faithfully, ate every bit of food her mother pressed on her, she got another fever, then another. She missed the beginning of school, and when she did return, her brain was heavy with a kind of pall, a whisper of horror she couldn't quite dispel. It followed her into the schoolyard, where she was even more isolated than before, sitting alone watching the others play, so thoroughly shunned the other students didn't even taunt her. June began to look forward to the mornings when she woke up with a scratchy throat and didn't have to go to school, or to the store, even though she knew that within a day she would be crying and clawing at her throat in pain, and fear that Varvara would make her drink fire again, or the potions that gave her such terrible dreams. Dreams that sent her down the stairs and out into the alley where she would wake to find herself shivering in her nightdress, looking up at Marie's empty landing. Her mother beside her, calling her back to herself.

FINALLY, her father came home one night and announced that he'd talked it over with Dr. Gibson and they'd decided June needed to have her tonsils out. "Bargain rate." He was weaving slightly on his feet, the familiar yeasty smell floating around him. "He owes me at cards. I told him he could work it off."

So June ended up on a table in the doctor's room. Olena and Taras accompanied her, and asked to be with her during the operation, but Dr. Gibson wouldn't allow it.

"She has bad dreams, nightmares," her father said.

"Don't worry." Dr. Gibson placed a cup over June's mouth and nose. "I'll make sure she sleeps deeply enough."

He dribbled something onto the cup, saying, "Just breathe normally, my dear, and you'll have a good long sleep." It smelled all wrong, like death, like a black pit opening beneath her, or maybe within her, but before she could raise her hand to signal her alarm, sleep overtook her.

FORT SAN

The fathers have eaten sour grapes and the children's teeth are set on edge.

Ezekiel 18:2

·1941·

THE TRAIN RUMBLED beneath June, rolling through endless, mesmerizing prairie. Her father sat in the seat across from her, staring out the window, glancing at her every now and then, but on those occasions she did not meet his gaze. She was so tired she had to prop her head against the window, and when she pulled the rough woollen travel rug more tightly around her, it did little to ease her chills. The effort caused the air to rasp in her lungs, and her father moved toward her infinitesimally, only to stop short at her minute gesture of refusal.

They had been on the train for hours, and the landscape had hardly changed. Except for the rocking motion, she could almost have believed that a scroll of scenic paper had been winding past while the train sat still. In the Eldergrove theatre, in what seemed another lifetime now, after the news reel of the war in Europe, she and Marie had watched cowboys and Indians on stiff-moving horses ride past the same pile of rocks over and over, as though they were chasing one another in circles, not across the broad expanse of the plains. Riding and riding, getting nowhere. Now the same scraggy poplars, the same brown and chunky cows, the same dry stubble fields scrolled across the train window, round and round. The land flat in all directions as far as the eye could see. From the hill at the outskirts of Eldergrove, you could see for miles, but miles of undulation, where scruffs of bush and stands of trees poked out of shallow valleys. June turned her blurry gaze from the window and it accidentally snagged her father's. He smiled faintly.

"Need anything?" he asked. "A drink? A sandwich." He pulled out the flour sack that was stocked with a jar of tea and the wax-paper packages her mother had wrapped this morning in a futile effort to tempt June's appetite: egg salad sandwiches, dill pickles, a tomato from the garden.

"No," June said. "Nothing." The effort of talking set the gurgles in her chest into their own private conversation with her fears, her resentment. Her father settled back into silence, his eyes bleak, his face drawn, the beginnings of grey showing in the stubble on his chin. June shut her eyes. He was sending her away. He could look however he liked.

She slept, if you could call a troubled murkiness sleep. She was so thin even the rocking of the train bruised her tail bone, nudging her dreams toward nightmare. She had been so tired for so long, but never with a tiredness that allowed her to sleep deeply. The operation to remove her tonsils had cured her sore throats, but she never got completely well. Over the past months her steps had slowed, her breath shortened, the gentle slopes of Eldergrove had become mountains. She missed more school than she attended, and whether there or at the store, seemed always to be seeing things through a haze, not able to grasp or remember numbers or words, or even events people assured her had happened. But it was her loss of weight that finally made her father take her to a doctor. Not the one in Eldergrove who had removed her tonsils. The doctor at the hospital in Norfolk. That was the moment at which June had first felt fear. The Norfolk doctor took only cash. Something must be seriously wrong.

At the doctor's office the nurse in stiff white told her to undress to the waist, then pressed June's naked chest against a cold, hard surface, getting June to lift her arms, one behind her, one to the side, then take a deep breath and hold it. And she did, but it wasn't enough and the nurse asked her to take a deeper breath, until June started coughing, and the nurse, shamefaced, wiped June's lips and told her just to do her best. Then the doctor, also in white, told her he was going to listen to her lungs with a stethoscope, and when he did, his face settled into deeper wrinkles. "You get dressed, my dear, while I talk to your father." June peeked around the corner, but the men were talking in very low voices, the doctor showing her father a shiny black sheet with white marks on it. When her father saw her, he stopped the doctor and called her to him.

"Do you really think . . . ?" the doctor said.

"Tell her vhat you telling me," her father cut him short. "They are her lungs."

The doctor explained that the black sheet was an x-ray, the spidery white lines were her ribs and spine, encasing her lungs. Healthy lungs barely showed on an x-ray, but June's had white shadows over most of one lung, and part of another, and in some spots there were bright white dots, as bright as dimes, but larger, more like quarters, or a fifty cent piece.

"These white shadows mean you have TB." The doctor pointed at them with a pencil. "Tuberculosis. The round spots are where it has gotten very bad, the disease is eating holes in your lungs and so they try to fill the holes with scar tissue which is why it's been getting so difficult for you to breathe. Your lungs have been working very hard to fill all these holes so they need a good, long rest. That means you have to go to a place called Fort San, near Regina. For a long time, maybe even a year."

One look at her father's frown told June this was no time for crying, or compromise.

"How much does it cost?" Desperate not to be sent away, she grasped at the one excuse that had always worked before now to contain desire, whether for shoes, or dolls, or books: too much money.

The doctor blinked away her feeble hope. "We are very lucky here to have a group of men, the Associated Canadian Travellers, who raise money for the San. It won't cost your family a thing. You go see the nurse, now." As June left he said to her father, "Brave little thing." At that, the pressure in June's chest built and built until she thought surely it must burst through all those holes, a mess of phlegm shot through with blood, like what came out of her in her worst coughing fits. She slumped against the door frame to gather herself, and despite the pounding in her ears heard the doctor say, "That fool Gibson. Gave her far too much ether and weakened her lungs so badly they became the perfect breeding ground. The least exposure..." He sputtered to a stop, took a breath, and muttered, "They should have pulled his license years ago, drunken fool."

Her father raised his head, the stricken expression on his face swiftly replaced with anger when he saw June still in the doorway. "What are you doing there? Do as you're told and go see that nurse!"

Now as the train rattled her out of reverie, rattled her ribs until she thought they must be tearing those holes even wider, she could feel the old stinging, but then noticed her father looking at her, and willed her eyes dry.

"Won't be long now," he said.

But when she gazed out the window, the land was empty for as far as she could see. No signs of any town at all: not a grain elevator, nor a church steeple, no houses. On land this flat you'd be able to see a coyote a mile away. June thought for one wild moment that everyone had been lying to her. She wasn't as sick as they said, she was being punished for some nameless crime that hovered in the haze just beyond her memory, her punishment this endless train ride, always travelling but never stopping, never giving her bones rest, in spite of their talk of a "rest cure." Her breath snagged at her lungs, she could feel the gurgle building there, the rasp at her throat, the blood rising in her cheeks, as she fought not to cough. Just at that moment, the land opened up beneath them. The train crossed a trestle and a town appeared by magic down below, houses and grain elevators snugged between hills and the edge of a deep blue lake. Moments later the train pulled into the station, and her father went to find a driver to take them to Fort San.

THE NURSE at the admitting desk took one look at June and barked for a wheelchair. When June stood to get into it, the nurse clapped her hands at the orderly, who promptly whisked

June into his arms and scooped her into the chair. June started to tremble. Her father looked shocked but did nothing.

"No movement for you, my girl. You need to keep very still." The nurse turned to Taras. "It's best if you say your goodbyes here, sir. We need to get her to bed as quickly as possible."

"I vant to say," her father's voice faltering, uncharacteristically humble, "she don't sleep vell, she has bad dreams..."

Still kindly, but more firmly, the nurse said, "We'll take it from here, sir."

Taras folded June into his arms, the stubble on his chin scraping her cheek, the hug choking off her breath for one ecstatic moment, before he released her and ruffled her hair with a hand rough from emotion, looking long and hard into her eyes. "Goodbye, my yastrup, my little falcon. Always remember. There is a reason they call this place Fort San. You are here to fight, little one, and you must be strong. This is a fort. *Fight.* I..." He turned on his heel, and was gone.

The orderly wheeled June out a side door, then slowly up a wooden walkway that ran along several buildings.

"You may call me Nurse Gillam." She had a good-natured, well-scrubbed face, and a voice that eddied over and around June in a wash of sound. "Normally you'd be in the children's pavilion, but I think they'll be too rowdy for what you need, so we'll put you in the women's pavilion. It has a lovely view for patients during rest hours. You can see the grounds, and clear down to the lake." She bent down and touched June's arm. "You mustn't cry, my dear," she said, even though June was not crying, just biting down rather hard on her lower lip. "It's very important not to cry. You can't get better that way. You must keep as cheerful as possible." Whether the comment or the touch was to blame, the tears broke past June's defences and spilled over her cheeks, the salt stinging her lip where she'd been biting it. The holes in her chest seemed cavernous when she thought of her father and his long train ride home. Of herself so far from all the people she'd tried to keep close.

The orderly wheeled June into a room with wide windows open to the chill air, curtains drifting in the stiff breeze. Everything was white. Not just the walls and bedding, but the lockers and metal bedsteads, even the concrete floor. Seven narrow lockers but only one bed. The orderly pulled June's wheelchair to a stop beside it. "The women have all been rolled out onto the veranda," Nurse Gillam said. "Chasing the cure, we call it. You'll see what that's like tomorrow." She started to unbutton June's coat, saying, "No, no," when June tried to help, gently but firmly placing June's hands in her lap. "Don't move, dear. I'll undress you and put you in a nightdress — you did bring one, didn't you?" She was already rummaging through June's one small piece of luggage, a hand-me-down from Mrs. Logan, so decrepit it would barely latch. "Ah, here it is. Very pretty, too." But it was just June's old blue flannel nightie, which had been getting too tight for her and should have been passed down to May, only there was no money after the doctor's visit and the train trip. Beneath the nightdress Nurse Gillam found June's book of fairy tales and pursed her lips as she laid it at the bottom of the bed, out of June's reach. "This will have to keep, I'm afraid. You won't be sitting up to read until we get those lungs stronger. No, don't raise your arms. Just sit while I do everything. That will be all you have to do for the next long while. Learn to be still and let us do for you. It's what we're here for." She slipped June's coat down over her shoulders, then carefully removed her sweater without letting her arms go over her head, talking all the while. "Lifting your arms is exertion. Reading is exertion, even thinking is. From now on you must lie as still and as flat as possible. Not even a pillow, I'm afraid. If you do really, really well, we'll let you roll over on your side and turn the pages of a book. But only if you show us how hard you're trying. Do you understand?" June tried to look as though she was paying attention, but could not keep from shooting nervous glances, face flaming, at the orderly, who was watching from the doorway. Nurse Gillam followed her gaze.

"What are you doing there, Dale?" she snapped. "You know you're supposed to stand outside until I'm done here. Wait till I call." The orderly left the room and June smiled a wobbly smile at Nurse Gillam.

"I'm sorry about that. I get talking and I forget my name." She dimpled at June as she manoeuvred June's arms into the nightie's armholes and smoothed it down over June's legs. "But you won't be shy after a few months here, I can tell you." She called coldly to Dale, "You can come back now." Dale once again scooped up June in his arms and laid her on the bed.

"Light as a feather, this one." Dale winked at June, who blushed and looked away. He was not much older than she, maybe fourteen or fifteen, with friendly black eyes, and a hint of black fuzz at his lip.

"That will be all, thank you, Dale." After he'd gone, she smiled. "He's a cheeky lad, but harmless." She opened the locker at the side of the bed, slipped June's book inside and pulled out a metal pan. "No bathroom privileges for you for a good while. Everything goes into this bed pan, and when you need to use it, you call for one of us. No stretching over and reaching for it. And no lying around with your arms over your head. Keep them at your side. When you raise your arms, you raise your heart rate and that, my dear, is not part of the rest cure. You must keep still."

Over the next few days June learned a lot about stillness. The doctors poked and prodded, not even letting her turn herself. The nurses stuck needles into her, occasionally wiping the tears that continuously leaked from her eyes. They lifted her over the bed pan to catch what leaked from down below too, sharply reprimanding her if she tried to sit up to help keep the urine in the pan. "Don't move. You can't get better if you move. You are a very sick little girl."

"I'm twelve," June insisted, but when they weighed her, they told her she weighed less than a child of ten. "Nothing but skin and bones," said Dale with another of his winks. He had picked her up, carried her to the scale, then stood holding her while the nurse fiddled with the metal weights along the metal beam, taking them lower, then lower, then lower still. Once Dale had settled her back in bed, he stood on the scale alone, and the nurse frowned.

After a week, June started asking about a bath, but baths were not allowed either.

"No tub baths," Nurse Gillam said. "Can't have you catching cold from damp hair. Far too dangerous." June was allowed only bed baths, a thorough sponging of specific parts of the body uncovered, washed and rinsed and carefully dried, then on to the next area. Her body did not seem to be hers any more. It belonged to whoever was bathing it, pressing stethoscopes against it, poking needles into it, shifting and lifting and laying it down. June retreated deeper and deeper into her mind. Only to find that was not allowed either.

"Try not to think," said Nurse Gillam. "Or if you must, think happy thoughts."

But how can you not think, June wondered. Even trying not to think meant thinking of not thinking. It was the same with the nightmares that had plagued her whenever her tonsillitis flared, when the pain and fever turned into Baba Yaga's iron-toothed mouth yawning at one end of a long tunnel and some shapeless, far-worse horror at the other. She had tried and tried not to slide into them, forcing herself to stay awake long past the first sounds of May's soft snores coming through the thin wall between their rooms, but it never worked. Though here, where everything was so frighteningly strange, her bad dreams appeared to have subsided, as though vanquished by a greater threat than they.

Nurse Gillam was not helpful on the subject of not thinking. "I don't know, I'm sure." She slipped the sheet from under June's head. "But you must *try* to stop crying. This is the third time I've had to take this sheet out from under your head, and your hair's wet quite through. We *cannot* have you lying here with wet hair."

But how could she keep from weeping every time she pictured her father's face, so grey and haunted by what she now realized was fear. Fear for her. And she, she had not given him one word of affection, had let him go almost before she realized he was gone, while she sulked like an infant. It took every scrap of her will to keep from flying out of bed and running all the way home to throw her arms around him, beg his forgiveness, burrow into his chest and stay there forever. There was nothing left over to keep her from crying. The other women in the room tried to talk to her, to keep her mind off her grief, which was kind, but they were all so much older than June, talking about children and husbands and other things June had no interest in, and besides, she couldn't lift her head to see which voice was attached to which body, so after she returned nothing but polite monosyllables, they ended up talking over and around her, and she was left to her own disallowed thoughts.

At the end of the second week, Nurse Gillam shaved June's head. Dr. Jameson ordered it. It didn't much matter. Her hair was dry and brittle and coming out in clumps whenever the nurses brushed it. June wasn't allowed to do that either. "I'm very sorry, my dear." Dr. Jameson laid a kindly arthritic hand briefly on her head. "But we mustn't attempt to wash your hair. Health before fashion, eh?"

June lay as still as she could, which was not very. For one thing, she itched. Everywhere. First her finger, then her toe, but most of all her head. Her bald head, sheared once a week, as if she were a boy. An ugly boy. Even though she tried her best to eat the huge meals that were set before her three times a day she always felt hollowed out inside and her body seemed not to accept the food she ate: she lost so much weight that her breasts, which had been just starting, sank away to nothing, barely bumps under her faded nightdress. She longed to stretch herself completely, just once, but even stretching was forbidden. She had wicked thoughts of lifting her arms right up over her head, scratching her baldness madly and long, then reaching further to grasp the iron railings of her bedstead and pulling, pulling, until she was sitting completely upright. When the itching got really bad, she imagined rolling from side to side like a great old sow in mud, rolling and scratching herself in a frenzy of relief. The more she tried not to think about it, the worse it got. And then she had the even more wicked thought of reaching to her locker and taking out her book, not to read, just to hold, to smell the pages that smelled like home, to absorb the stories she knew so well through the worn cover and hide herself deep within them as she'd always been able to do. But the one time she tried, tried only to reach for the locker's latch and the precious book behind it, she just couldn't stand one more minute, she had barely raised herself onto her elbow when a wave of weakness and coughing took her, and blood sprayed from her mouth in a wide arc, drenching the covers, even spattering the white floor, bright red drops that pulsed with danger. One of the women called for help and when Nurse Gillam came running June thought she would be scolded but the nurse just quietly washed June's face and put her in a hospital gown, then stripped the bed deftly, barely moving June at all. When she was finished, Nurse Gillam spoke in a whisper with one of the doctors outside June's door. He stood by June's bed looking grave, and read to her from the Fort San pamphlet: *Part of the cure is the development of a spirit of faithful endeavour, helpfulness, earnestness, good humour, kindliness and forbearance.* June could hardly hear him; it was taking all her concentration just to breathe, to push down the cough and her terror to a place so deep inside herself they could never come back. For the first time she thought she might actually die.

That night a beautiful young woman with long dark hair appeared at her bedside, holding out her hand. "I know where they are," she said. "Come." Flooded with relief, her exile over, June rose from her bed. The woman was holding a rabbit that was kicking against her grip. "You want to live?" June looked down to see a knife in her hand and knew she had to feed the family, but the fish in the creek was dead so she sliced down with the knife, blood spurting in a wide arc and now the woman holding the rabbit wasn't young and beautiful but was an old hag, crooked and bent, pointing a gnarled finger at June, and the rabbit's shriek was her cackling laugh, her mouth red and pulsing and filled with iron teeth and now June was running, but the rabbit's blood clouded her eyes, clogged her lungs, and she had lost the skull that was meant to light her way.

"Keep still," a voice from somewhere above her. "You must keep still." Hands pushing her down, struggling to grasp her frantic wrists.

"June, dear," a soft, vaguely familiar voice, "open your eyes."

She opened her eyes. Nurse Gillam's kind face staring into hers, Nurse Gillam's kind hand stroking her cheek. But when she tried to lift her hands to hold onto Nurse Gillam, an orderly was tying her wrists to the bed railings. "I'm so sorry, June," Nurse Gillam said, "but it's for your own good. You've been walking in your sleep and we can't have that, you know. I'm doing all I can to convince the doctors not to put you in a body cast, so you will try to be good, won't you? For me?"

To stop her disturbing the other patients, and to give her complete quiet she was moved to a rare private room and from then on, June lay as still as death in her bed, flat on a thin mattress like a board on a board, her body a slight bump ruffling white linens. The ceiling above her, the room around her white, like death. Her wrists tethered to the bed, her only movement the pale tears that coursed down her cheeks onto the sheet, the only colour in the room the one she could not see — the flaring red of her cheeks. Consumption. TB. The white plague.

EIGHT MONTHS June lay flat on her back without even the thinnest of pillows, staring at the ceiling and weeping. She had to be spoon fed like a baby, but had no appetite, and since nutrition was part of the cure, she had to force herself to eat. Three meals a day and two snacks, all accompanied with a glass of milk. But the food was bland — porridge or pallid toast strips, turkey with gelatinous grey gravy over pasty potatoes, even the eggs lacked colour and flavour. Every meal only added to her homesickness, her longing for one more taste of her mother's hearty bread dunked into a bowl of homemade cottage cheese with green onion picked fresh from the garden.

Like all the patients, she was supposed to sleep several hours a day, and twelve hours a night, but she found herself fighting to stay awake, terrified she would sleepwalk and have to be put in a body cast.

At the end of the eight months June got her first letter from home, in May's childish script. "Dear June. I am fine. Mom and Dad are fine. They say to be a good girl and do what the doctors tell you. The store is busy. P.S. We miss you." The letter did nothing to feed her deep longing for home. But when Nurse Gillam sat beside the bed to write down June's reply, June could find no words that were not as empty. What could she say other than that she wanted to go home, wanted her father to fetch her. Wanted the impossible. She took refuge in the same kind of non-letter May wrote: "The nurses and doctors are very kind. I am trying to get well. I miss you."

As for her hope of a visit, which set a flutter along the wards no matter whose the visitor, June knew there wouldn't be enough money after the expense of the train trip and the Norfolk doctor's fees. But knowing this brought no relief from the prospect of loneliness unbroken for months, perhaps years, and her eyes would start leaking once more. They had taken her book away, not to punish her, but for her safety, or so they told her. "We'll keep it for when you are better," Nurse Gillam had said. "But for now it's just too much temptation for you, I'm afraid." Healthier patients and volunteers put on plays and concerts, there were even movies once a week, but June wasn't allowed to raise her head to see them. When they wheeled her bed onto the open-air pavilion she could only gauge the changing seasons by the sky, and the tree branches high against it: the yellow leaves and bright blue of October, the bare white branches and stony grey of November, the softness of December, its pale blue dotted with falling snow, the luminescent green leaves of spring that mocked her with their bursting life.

The months slipped by almost without her noticing. Dale snuck in all the treats he could think of: chocolate bars, jelly babies, candied hearts that read "I'm sweet on you" or "Be mine." They stayed on her nightstand until he took them away. Not all his small kindnesses, nor all the nurses' and doctors' entreaties could stop her tears or night terrors, until one day, just after she turned fourteen, outside her door she heard one of the new doctors, Dr. Wilkes, talking to Dr. Jameson, the only doctor June liked. She craned her head and through the crack in the door saw Dr. Wilkes holding sheets of paper with numbers on them, showing them to Dr. Jameson, who was frowning through his glasses. Dr. Wilkes said dismissively, not even bothering to lower his voice, "She won't see the fall." Dr. Jameson whispered something sharp, then a hand reached out to shut the door.

The next day Dr. Jameson visited her on his own, a file folder tucked under his arm. He sat at her bedside and took her hand in his. "You are in deep trouble, June. All this weeping. Is it because you are alone in a room? It is for your own good, you know."

June fought hard and succeeded in keeping the ready tears confined to her eyes. She shook her head, but didn't trust her voice to tell Dr. Jameson that she had always felt alone. She had lost May to the school, Marie to the Eyetie. Her parents had sent her away, abandoned her to this illness that was eating her from the inside. What did a room matter in the face of all that?

Dr. Jameson patted her hand, then gave her an x-ray he dug out of the folder. "These are your lungs. You can see why we are so concerned. One is completely diseased, the other has only about three quarters of healthy tissue left."

June stared at the white shadows clouding the x-rays, feeling as though she were back in Norfolk, receiving her first diagnosis. Over a year and a half on bed rest and she was no further ahead. Perhaps Dr. Wilkes was right about her after all.

"I have a proposition for you."

June felt a glimmer of interest.

"There's a new treatment called pneumothorax that's been having quite a lot of success. We use a needle to insert air between the lung and the pleural lining. This collapses the diseased lung so it can get complete rest, leaving the healthy lung to do all the work. The difficulty in your case is that both lungs are diseased, so we'd have to collapse them alternately." He leaned forward in his chair, the wrinkles in his face deepening. "I wouldn't suggest this if I didn't think it absolutely necessary. But I won't lie to you, June. Normally it is not advised to collapse even one lung when the disease is bilateral as yours is. I don't know if it's been tried more than a few times, and the outcome is by no means certain. The board was very reticent but your condition has deteriorated so badly that I can see no other alternative and in the end they agreed."

"All right."

"Good girl." Dr. Jameson squeezed her hand. "We will be in it together, yes?" June found herself squeezing back. He had convinced the board, perhaps he could persuade her body to make the long climb out of the holes her lungs kept digging.

"Would you like to have a listen?" He hooked his stethoscope into her ears then pressed the metal end to the upper part of her right side. "What do you hear?" She listened very hard, not wanting to disappoint him, but in the end had to say, "Nothing."

"That's good!" The long hairs of his greying eyebrows wiggled their approval. "It means this part of the lung is healthy." He moved the metal circle farther down her side. "Now?"

A fine crackling sound, like tiny balloons bursting, filled her ears. It was as though something was moving around within her and she was tracking its passage. "I can hear it . . . like munching, or no, something else . . ."

"These are what we call rales. Fluids build up in your lungs because of the disease and they make a sound that can tell us where the disease is." He pressed the stethoscope against several places on her right side and the crackles followed his movements. "This is not so good." He took the earphones from her ears. "What we want is for these areas," touching the noisy parts of her chest, "to sound like this one." Touching the upper part of her right side. "I'll come back every week with this," he indicated the stethoscope he was sliding into his coat pocket, "and we shall see how you do with this new treatment, yes? And perhaps if you are doing well, we will allow you a small pillow, maybe even your book, yes?"

June nodded as vigorously as she dared.

"But you must help me, June." He took her cold hand once again in his warm one. "All the treatment in the world won't help you while you are still so very sad. You must try to be more cheerful, for the sake not just of your tired heart," gently he tapped her hand against her chest, "but your tired lungs. Can you do that for me?"

"I don't know how," June whispered, her ragged voice a betrayal of her growing desire to please him.

"I know it is a lot to ask you to be happy here, but surely there is a time, a place you can remember, from before, when you *were* happy, yes? What I want you to do is focus on that memory any time you feel like crying, and tell yourself that you can get back to that place. That you *will*."

His tone, the way he cradled her hand, made her think of her father. Yastrup, he had called her before he left, little falcon. Fight, he had said, and the unfamiliar expression on his face as he'd said it had been fear. Fight, he had said, and had she? Had she taken Vasilisa's courage as her example? No. She had been pining away like some useless chicken waiting for the block. Well, no more. She was staring into an abyss far deeper and blacker than Baba Yaga's voracious mouth. But she would not let her father, or Dr. Jameson, down. If her family could not come to her she would will herself back to them.

BUT WHEN SHE tried to follow Dr. Jameson's instructions, call up happier times, her mind winced away as if from an open wound. Every pleasant memory led to pain: Marie gently braiding June's hair, tying it up with red ribbons, making her feel briefly like Vasilisa, only for her to cravenly abandon Marie at the dunk tank; her father chucking her chin and praising her for helping to kill the rabbit that now stalked her in nightmares. But then a memory surfaced that she'd almost forgotten. The winter before they moved to Eldergrove, two years before the spring when she started getting so tired, dragging her feet behind her. That winter had been cold and dry, almost no snow, and the family had gone to Quesnel Lake in the wagon, wrapped in blankets, the rocks Olena had heated in the stove under their feet. June sat happily with May tucked against her in the back, her parents jostling one another in the front. All of them together. A perfect day.

Olena and Taras had taken with them an ice auger and several fishing lines — even a family holiday had a practical purpose. But the girls took their ice skates, culled from the latest Red Cross box when her father went again for the relief vouchers. June's were too big. She had stuffed the toes with a pair of Taras's socks, and wore three pairs of her own just to keep the skates on her feet. The lake had frozen so clear she could see to the bottom. May and June squealed as they slipped and stumbled over the cracked ice at the shoreline, sliding on their bottoms until they reached level ice, then staggering to their feet in wobbly circles. They clung to each other like drunks and shrieked. They stood on nothing. The ice could have been a foot thick or a mere shaving. Even Olena hesitated, testing the surface with a rap of her outstretched toe before striding off toward the middle of the lake where the fish would be.

"See here." Taras pointed and they followed his finger to see where the ice had cracked, feathery white boas dragged through the glassy surface, pure white bubbles suspended in dark green, delicate shell shapes like mollusks gone astray. "It's plenty thick."

Taras thumped the ice. "Six inches for sure." But June could still see the contours of lake bottom, the dull green of algae near the shore. The fish swimming right under her feet. A whole other world and life that played itself out beneath her with no thought for her presence. She fell to her knees and knocked at the ice to see if she could get the fish to turn, to look up, to see her there watching them. It struck her almost like a pain that this was always here, that the same world existed under the creek at home too, the patterns of the ice, the movements of the water plants and fish — it was always here but covered with snow, so no one could see. Like magic. She lay flat on the ice and pressed her face as close to this world as she could, insulating her cheek with one mittened hand.

"Here, here." Taras stood first June and then May up straight. "Keep your ankles stiff, like this — see?" He thumped their ankles through leather softened with many years of use, its white polish flaking away. And he was right. The straighter she kept her ankles, the straighter she flew across the lake, cutting her path in white scars on the glassy surface, sending out white chips like sparks behind her, or, when the wind changed, snowy shavings drifting ahead of her like lost souls. Every once in a while the ice cracked and sent a shuddering *thwang* through the air, thrilling against her insides, feathering through the ice, but holding firm, not opening up to swallow her as she feared it would.

Olena and Taras caught six trout in time for lunch and they all went ashore to fry them over a small fire, blowing on their fingers first for cold, then for stinging heat when they picked singed flesh off the bones. "Your cheeks are red, little one," Taras rubbed one of June's cheeks with his scratchy finger, and wound a blanket more tightly around her. "Ready to rest?"

But June was exhilarated beyond speech and merely shook her head till the lake whirled before her.

"Come on then!" Taras unwound her from the blanket, lifted her to the lake's surface where her skates bit surely into the ice, and kept her steady even though the wind was picking up and whipping against her body like a heavy pillow. Taras gave May one end of the blanket and June the other end. The wind blew the blanket out like a great sail. June had time to toss one glance at her father before her feet began to move beneath her and the girls were sailing across the lake. No sound except for her gusts of breath and the cut of her blades, no sound because they were moving at the speed of the wind. She and May, blown by the wind to the far end of the lake, faster and faster, ankles barely keeping straight, bodies stiff and hurtling.

"Let go! Let go!" May was screaming at her, but June wanted to do this forever and May had to let go first, falling behind her suddenly, leaving her trailing the blanket like the tail of a great kite, and she dropped the blanket because it was slowing her down, and spread her arms out like wings and still the wind blew her, fish flying beneath her feet, her skates spitting ice chips in front of her, the bare trees coming up to meet her, branches outstretched, white against deep blue. She felt as though she could toss herself into those branches, lifted up on a gust of pure, soundless joy.

THE FIRST TIME she was wheeled in for treatment and saw the huge needle she almost changed her mind, but she wouldn't show weakness in front of Dr. Wilkes, who was there to observe, so as Dr. Jameson instructed she lay on her side for the first time in over a year and waited. When he approached her, needle in hand, she shut her eyes tight so she wouldn't see the moment of entry, then there was a dreadful sound like a knitting needle going through heavy cardboard as he punched the needle between two of her ribs. She started, but it was more from shock than pain. Given that horrible sound, she'd expected far more than just one piercing moment. She lay still while Dr. Jameson forced air through the needle into the pleural cavity, wondering why she couldn't feel her lung falling in on itself like a punctured balloon.

When Dale wheeled her back to her room he gave her a pink candy heart and she tried to return his wink as she crunched it to sweet powder. Every week after that she was wheeled up to the pneumothorax machine, one week for the right lung, the next for the left. As weeks stretched into months she devoted herself to becoming an ideal patient. Hungry or not she ate every scrap of food the nurses offered, no matter how bland, letting them fatten her up like a turkey for the slaughter. Porridge, eggs and toast for breakfast, then meat and potatoes for lunch and again for supper, an eggnog every night. She drank her warm milk without protest, coughed with a will for the morning sputum test then quietly chewed her ice chips to halt any further coughing, willing her fluttering lungs into stillness, then going one step further and willing them into health. On the veranda she didn't waste her energy in idle conversation, instead gazed out over the grounds to the lake, and as the snow melted to grassy and leafy green, and pelicans swooped over the glistening blue, she willed her eyes dry, her heart drained of bitterness. She almost laughed out loud in triumph at Dr. Wilkes's face when just before her fifteenth birthday he and Dr. Jameson stood over her bed to tell her the good news. Her numbers had improved dramatically. Dr. Jameson beamed as he placed a narrow, two-inch pillow under her head. And the even greater reward: she was to be allowed to read. "Only lying on your side, mind," he intoned with mock severity. "No sitting up just yet, young lady." If she continued at this rate, he said to Dr. Wilkes as they left the room, she could be returned to the general ward.

But when she tried reading the fairy tales that had been imprisoned in the white locker for as long as she had been imprisoned in her white bed, they did not hold the same magic, and she set them aside for the delights of the library cart, which Dale wheeled through the wards once a week. Dale had always joked with her, winked at her, but now June noticed his hand lingered on hers whenever he gave her a candy or handed her a book. Occasionally he dropped a piece of chocolate, or a rare and marvellous grape, into her open mouth, then stroked her cheek as though to remove a bit of food both of them knew was not there.

Usually she asked for books by Mazo de la Roche, a saga in an endless stream of volumes about a family living a life of luxury in far distant Ontario. But one day Dale brought her a book by an author she'd never heard of and told her to keep it hidden. "The nurses might think you're young for it, but I don't." She sneaked it out whenever she was alone, her body reading it as much as her mind, for in it a young woman met a young man and there were long descriptions of their kisses, their embraces. When the man put his hand on the woman's thigh, June slammed the book shut and slid it under the sheets, sure her flaming cheeks would give her away if a nurse came in. Her breath was racing in a way that should have been uncomfortable and frightening but was exhilarating. The blush seemed to be spreading from her face throughout her entire body. She didn't know how she'd look Dale in the eye when she saw him again, but she couldn't wait to see him again. When she did, neither of them winked, or even smiled. Like the man and woman in the book, they stared deeply into one another's eyes, and, careful to make sure no nurse was hovering, he bent down and kissed her, not on the mouth, he would never do that, but little whispery, barely there kisses on her forehead, cheeks, even her nose and chin. He began sneaking into her room at night. His kisses on her throat, his fingers playing on her breasts through layers of nightgown and blankets, caused her to soar beyond the confines of her narrow bed, her feeble body. She had to lie very still and not make a sound, for discovery would be dreadful, and she was still bound by the rest cure. But it was almost impossible not to writhe with pleasure, not to urge his fingers lower, ever lower to the ache that pulsed and expanded until it took her over completely.

On the night he finally entered her she almost fainted with the joy of it. His fingers sliding inside her were cold, like the ice chips slipping down her hot and aching throat after her morning cough, but instead of quelling her breath they made it huge in her chest, as though she could never suck in enough air to encapsulate this feeling. She impaled herself on his fingers, silently urging him deeper and deeper, riding the ecstasy of danger and soaring joy until suddenly she tipped over an edge she hadn't known was there and her body shuddered and shuddered until she was sure it would bring the nurses and doctors running. The fingers withdrew, Dale was gone and she was left in the dark, trembling and afraid she would never get enough air in her lungs to recover what had torn out of her.

ONE YEAR LATER June celebrated her sixteenth birthday with numbers that at last were positive. During that year her love for Dr. Jameson had animated her days, and her love for Dale had brightened her nights, the first love open, the second secret, and her will to live blazing through both. A year in which she ate and read voraciously, her body and mind equally hungry. A year in which they allowed her finally to sit up to read, to grow her hair again. To take short, supervised walks, her legs giving out beneath her like toothpicks the first time she stood, Dale laughing and stealing a grope of her breast under cover of setting her back on her feet. A year in which her breasts slowly filled out and, to her embarrassment, she got her period. The war, which she'd barely noticed, so absorbed in her own struggle, finally ended and it seemed that on v-day the whole world was celebrating June's victory, and the way that world was opening up before her.

The only sour note in all this good news was that she was moved back to the women's ward. But luckily Dale was often the one who supervised her walks, and though their meetings were harder to manage, the anticipation made them all the more exciting. The danger, the scent of tree bark when he pressed her against it, the scent of her rising from his fingers as they played havoc with her body while his eyes kept a sharp lookout over her shoulder. When Dr. Jameson began to talk cautiously about sending her home, her first reaction was reluctance. She didn't know what the word meant any more. Home. The infrequent letters hadn't kept her tethered to Eldergrove, which had never felt like home after they left the farm anyway. She was a different person, she hadn't spoken Ukrainian in all the time she'd been here, she had no friends in Eldergrove and though she didn't have any here either, she had Dale. What would she do without him? Perhaps they could marry. Why not? Her mother had married at fifteen. June felt brave enough for anything.

Dr. Jameson's visits became more erratic, and when he did come by he looked drawn and pale, his breathing laboured, his wrinkles deepening, his manner with her distracted. One day when Nurse Gillam was taking June's morning temperature, her eyes were red, and when June asked why, she said Dr. Jameson had taken ill and had been ordered to leave work immediately. His heart was dangerously weak. He was long past the age of retirement and his wife was terrified to lose him. She hadn't even let him return to collect his things or hand on his records to Dr. Wilkes, who would supervise June's treatments from now on.

On the heels of this blow came another. Several weeks later Nurse Gillam, anxious and stern, drew up a chair beside the bed and, staring searchingly into June's eyes, asked, "Has Dale been up to anything with you?" A tiny grimace of disgust crossed her face, almost imperceptible, but enough to send danger signals to June.

"What do you mean?"

"Well, has he been ... touching or ..." again that grimace, "fondling you in any way?"

"No!" June forced an expression of shock onto her face. "Why would you ask?"

"He's been told to leave. One of the women complained, and then it turns out he's been trying it with others, but they were too afraid to say anything."

One moment of numb disbelief, then shock, anger, and shame flamed through June. She had thought she was living a romance but all along she had been a dupe. She felt almost physically sick to think she had been such a fool as to think he meant marriage when all the time those fingers that gave her such pleasure were exploring who knew how many others. Her mind spun away from the pain of that thought and as the murky weight of tears moiled in her chest she instinctively began her breathing exercises. No one must ever know.

"He only brought me candies and books and things," she murmured, fighting to keep her face decorously appalled.

"Well, that's fine then." Relieved, Nurse Gillam patted her hand. "I'm sorry to have to trouble you with this. I didn't think he would take advantage of a mere girl, but I had to ask."

How could she have been so gullible? He must have been laughing at her all this time. What if he talked with the other women about her while he did the same things to them that had once made her so ecstatic? What if they were all secretly laughing at her while they were lined up on the veranda taking the air? She had troubling dreams of Dale with other women, women with lips as red as wounds, moaning, sighing. Of Dale turning to look at her, his face blurring and dissolving into her father's, and she woke swamped with shame and horror at herself. Her father. She had betrayed him, all but forgotten him in the depths of her ridiculous infatuation. He would never forgive her. He must never find out. But this resolve did nothing to help when her body raged and her fingers crept down to ease the terrible ache between her thighs.

Now with her days and nights so empty, with the coldly intellectual Dr. Wilkes taking over her primary care and only the memory of Dale ravaging her nights, the emptiness invaded her insides. She lost her appetite, grew listless and apathetic, the tears she had driven out of herself for years returned all the stronger for their absence. Her numbers plummeted and she was put back on total bed rest.

She retreated far into herself, buried herself so deep that even her nightmares could not find her. Under white sheets she lay like the princess whose name she could not be bothered to remember sleeping in a glass case, like the fishes trapped beneath the ice in the memory that no longer had the power to make her feel happy, to make her feel anything at all. Now and then someone came to thump on the ice, speak a few muffled words, read a brief letter from a dimly remembered place called home, but nothing reached her. She lay buried under white, the disease feathering scars through her lungs, digging holes the doctors once again feared would swallow her whole.

·1949·

MAY PLUCKED A PIECE of Dubble Bubble out of the glass jar on the counter, unwrapped it as quietly as possible and popped it into her mouth just as her mother emerged from the storeroom. "Ach," Olena said. "You're chewing up all our profits. I wish your father had never brought those things into the store. Everywhere you go these days you find gum, stuck under tables and chairs, on the sidewalk, sticking to your shoes. Disgusting." May's only response was to blow as big a bubble as she dared, then suck it in before it exploded and stuck to her carefully made-up face. Carrie Logan had shown her a new method for putting on rouge and powder that looked so natural Taras wouldn't notice. Examining her reflection this afternoon, however, May had had her doubts. Her father had forbidden her to wear makeup. Months ago when he found her trying on a new shade of lipstick, he swore, grabbed a hankie, and rubbed her bright red lips so hard they burned. He threw the tube out but she retrieved it and tucked it into her purse. Her first stop at any social event her father was not attending was the powder room.

Footsteps sounded on the stairs from the apartment and Olena shrugged. "Don't let your father see." May slid the gum from her mouth and tucked it behind her ear, careful to avoid any hairs straying from her meticulous updo ponytail. Another tip from Carrie. "No point throwing gum away until you've sucked out every last bit of flavour." May had completely agreed, but the first time she tried the technique the gum got so embedded in her hair that Carrie had to cut it out with her father's razor, both of them giggling so hard May worried she'd be scarred for life. As it was, she had to wear her hair down for weeks.

The minute hand crawled around the clock and May sighed, willing it to move faster. When would her parents learn no one came into the store late on Friday nights? Every Friday Carrie invited a few select schoolmates for what she called a "social" and May got antsier with every minute that elapsed before she could flip the sign on the door to CLOSED.

Everyone would have been dancing for ages by the time May got there. She was wild to hear Carrie's latest records, which could only be bought in Saskatoon, and which May would have killed to own but could only listen to on the radio's *Saturday Night Hit Parade*. Frankie Lane, Perry Como, Peggy Lee. Her mother would never allow her to turn the volume up loud enough for the music to pulse through her body the way it did at Carrie's as she danced with a string of boys, but mostly with Mitch, who would put his mouth up close to her ear and croon along to the songs: "Some Enchanted Evening," "I've Got You Under My Skin," "I Can't Give You Anything but Love."

"What's that on your face?" Her father's voice so close to her ear she jumped, quelling the impulse to put up a hand to cover the gum and give herself away.

"What do you mean?"

Taras ran a finger down her cheek, held it up to show her the telltale red powder, then grabbed the mirror that customers used when trying on hats or testing makeup and held it to her face. A long white streak etched by his finger on her painted cheek.

"It's only a bit of rouge. All the girls wear it. I am seventeen after all."

"I am not interested in all the girls. Go wash that muck off."

"But I'll be late for the dance!"

"What kind of dance starts at eight o'clock? No wonder you drag in at all hours."

"How would you even know? You live here and you never come to Varvara's. Mom doesn't mind, why should you?"

"Maybe so. But I hear things. Makeup, late-night dances, running around like a tramp."

"At least I'm doing my running around before marriage. You're not the only one who hears things."

Taras's face turned white. He slammed the mirror on the counter and started round the corner for May, hand raised.

"Taras!" Olena barked. She was looking not at him or May, but at a Mountie who had entered the store. May hadn't even heard the bell. "How can ve help you?"

The man looked too young for his uniform, with ears that stuck out almost at right angles from his head, and an Adam's apple that wobbled when he spoke.

"I am Constable Miller. I've been making inquiries in the area." He blushed under May's stare and reached into his pocket.

"To see if anyone recognizes this." As he held out his open palm all three leaned in to examine a diamond-encrusted ring. May had a sudden image of it being twisted round and round a finger on a hand far too delicate for such a weight.

"But that's Frenchie's!" she gasped. "Marie's, I mean. Why wouldn't she have taken it with her?"

"Marie? Taken it where? Marie who?"

"Marie Barker, yes," Olena said, almost reluctantly. "She vehrk here some time ago, but she has been gone years now."

"And Mr. Barker? Does he still live here?"

Taras stepped forward. "The Barkers, they leave shortly after Marie. Vhat is this about?"

"I'm sorry to say this ring was found on some remains a farmer discovered near a dried-out slough on his property. A number of miles from here. I've been to Norfolk, and High Plains, and no one recognized it."

"You found her body?" May breathed. "But we all thought..."

"More a skeleton than a body, I'm afraid. Not much to identify her except the ring. Oh," he pulled out a small bag from another pocket, removing a scrap of material with a faded paisley pattern. "And this. Have you seen it before?"

May's mouth opened but a sharp glance from Olena shut it again. "No, I don't tink so," Olena said.

"And you, sir?"

Taras shook his head.

Constable Miller glanced at May, but Taras cut in, "This girl, she vas too young to know anyting back then. Ve can tell you all you need to know. May, go on to Carrie's now."

May grabbed her purse, coat, and hat and skedaddled before he could change his mind.

MRS. LOGAN answered the door on the second ring. "Hello, May." Her tone polite but cool. "They're just about to start dancing. Such a shame you have to work. Late, I mean. Do come in."

"Thank you," matching Mrs. Logan's tone exactly. As she surrendered her coat and hat May felt her usual ripple of satisfaction. Not once had her mother set foot inside, yet here was her daughter being ushered into the parlour where the table was laden with refreshments. Being urged to sip punch from a cut crystal cup, to nibble on fancy crustless sandwiches — egg or ham salad, canned asparagus on cream cheese — not homemade but ordered from the McTeers' bakery. Jiggly tomato aspic studded with bits of olive, celery, tinned fruit, which no one ever touched, but which was always set out as a reminder that the Logans were one of the few families who could afford their own refrigerator. "Thank you, Mrs. Logan. It all looks delicious. Maybe later."

"How are your mother and father? And your aunt? I take it you and your mother are still looking after her?"

"Yes, we are." Mrs. Logan never failed to take some kind of dig at the Zalesky's unusual living arrangements. "She has good days and bad. Mostly she knows us, but she really can't be on her own." *As well you know, you old bat.*

"May!" Carrie called from one end of the room where she and Mitch and a few others were rolling up the carpet. "You're just in time!"

"I'll be right there," May called back as she headed to the powder room.

When she emerged, makeup repaired, Mr. Logan was walking through the front door. He often worked late too, at the bank. "Hello, May. You're looking radiant tonight." He chucked her under the chin and followed her into the parlour where Carrie was putting on the first record.

"There she is!" Mr. Logan pulled his wife against him and twirled her once round the floor, then planted a showy kiss on her lips. Blushing, she pushed him playfully back and straightened her hair. "Get away with you! Your dinner's waiting on you, dear. Let's leave these young ones to their fun and games."

"Righty-ho." Mr. Logan put one arm around her waist as they ambled up the corridor to the kitchen. May watched them with curiosity and a tinge of envy. She couldn't remember ever seeing her parents touch one another with such casual affection. Even before May and Olena had moved in with Varvara, her father staying in the apartment over the shop, her parents had at best maintained a polite distance. Which was certainly better than the fights May dimly remembered from when she was a little girl. But still.

Mitch lifted the needle off the record mid-song and put on "Four Brothers," her favourite dance tune. Following him onto the floor, she felt as though sparks were flying from her heels, her eyes, her lacquered red lips. With the music thrumming through her, it didn't matter that she wasn't able to drive like the other girls into Saskatoon or Yorkton for the latest fashions, that she made her own dresses, staying up late into the night, pins between pursed lips, tacking Butterick tissue patterns by the light of a kerosene lamp onto remnants of material that hadn't sold even at heavily discounted prices. It didn't matter how many times her shoes had been mended. At least, while she could imagine the snide remarks the girls made when she was out of earshot, it didn't matter to the boys. They all wanted to dance with her. All except Albert McGrath, who just leaned against the wall watching her, an appreciative smile playing on his lips and sometimes meeting her eyes. Even before the war he had been an unusual friend for rambunctious Mitch, and now that he had come back wounded and walking with a cane, he was even more quiet, never joining in when Mitch regaled them with improbable war stories in which he somehow always managed to be the hero. Albert's mother had died while he was overseas, his father long before then, so after the war Albert had spent a few years in Europe helping with the reconstruction efforts, only coming back to sell the family home. Rumour had it he was going to Toronto on a scholarship to study engineering.

When Mitch finally allowed her to catch her breath, May plopped down into a seat beside Carrie, fanning her face ineffectually with her hand. All the windows were open to the cool spring evening, but it didn't offer much relief.

"Here you go." Albert limped up to her, holding out a glass of ruby red punch. "You look like you need this."

"Thank you, Albert, that's very kind."

"I'd have brought some sandwiches, but as you see, I'm a bit hampered." He grimaced at his cane.

"No, no, this is lovely, truly," May said in some confusion as he turned away.

"Don't get too stuck on yourself," Carrie said, eyeing May over the rim of her punch glass. She'd sat out a few too many dances while May never left the floor. "I heard my mom say to Mrs. McTeer last week that you were really coming along, not a trace of an accent. But it doesn't mean she'd ever let Mitch get serious with a Uke." Something about May's expression made her add hastily, "Besides, Mitch is bad news. You're too good for him."

May smoothed her features into her disarming smile. What did Carrie know?

"That's enough sitting!" Mitch pulled May out of her chair so suddenly that the last drops of her punch sprayed his shirt and she just had time to hand the cup to Carrie before he spun her onto the floor.

"How soon can we get out of here? I can't wait to have you all to myself." Mitch breathed into her ear as he pulled her close.

"Your sister says I'm too good for you."

"That's not what you say when we're steaming up the windows in the back of my car." He tickled the palm of her hand, sending shivers all through her.

She blushed and whispered back, "You know I have to wait until my mother is asleep. Just park in the alley around midnight, like always."

"Aahh," Mitch whisper-groaned as she pressed herself against him. "You're driving me crazy."

She laughed, pressed again. "That's the general idea."

Mitch held her so tightly against him that he lifted her clear off the ground and the room whirled. "Just don't make me wait too long, sweetheart."

She clung to him for balance, feeling how easy it would be to yield. "You know the rules," she said faintly, relieved when the music stopped and another boy invited her to dance.

WHEN OLENA flipped the sign to OPEN on Saturday morning at nine sharp, Mrs. Logan and Mrs. McTeer hustled into the store. "Imagine!" Mrs. Logan exclaimed. "All this time dead and rotting in that old slough. Do you think the Eyetie did it?"

"Very hot-blooded, those Eyeties." Mrs. McTeer's mouth puckered with distaste.

"Could just as easy be those Barkers," Olena cut in with a venom that startled May, and must have startled Olena too, because she immediately covered her mouth with her hand.

"Oh, I can't believe that," Mrs. Logan said. "Such longstanding citizens."

Yes, May thought, citizens you drove out of town with your gossip when we all thought Marie had run off with the Eyetie.

"Well, I did my civic duty." Mrs. McTeer's mouth unpuckered. "I told the constable that if the Eyetie didn't run off with Frenchie he probably went to Toronto, or maybe Montreal and I thought the Barkers had family in Minnesota somewhere. Or maybe Missouri. He was very appreciative, wrote it all down. Did that Frenchie say anything to you about where she might be going, Olena?"

"Not a vord." Olena's face twisted with what? Sadness? May didn't remember Olena caring all that much about Marie, not like June, who had practically worshipped her.

"Or maybe she said something to June?" Mrs. Logan prodded. "I always thought it strange Frenchie spent so much time with a little girl rather than making more suitable friends."

May winced, suspecting this was another of Mrs. Logan's digs. Marie wasn't the only one who'd had trouble making friends, but what could May have done? On the farm, where the sisters had been one another's only companions, May had been happy to have someone who would occasionally stop scolding or take her nose out of her book long enough to make paper dolls, or play down by the creek. But when the family moved to town May discovered what it was to have friends who, rather than tolerating her presence, sought her out, while the big sister she had looked up to was ridiculed, bullied. An outcast.

At first May had tried to protect her, but it had been a godsend when June became preoccupied with Marie, and May no longer had to feel the pull of divided loyalties. When June got so sick, May, guilty and terrified, tended her sister as often as she was allowed, feeding her like a baby, stroking her forehead and pleading, "Please don't die, please don't die."

She was glad June recovered from the fever, of course she was, but then, rather than return to normal, June started sleepwalking and forgetting things as simple as the times table, sometimes waking in the night screaming so loudly lights flickered all down the alley. May had thought nothing could be worse than the bullying June had endured, but then the kids at school stopped their jeering, leaving June utterly alone at one end of the playground at recess, as though the space was contaminated, treating her as if she truly was the ghost girl they called her. Invisible.

One day, May, finding her sister again in tears, grabbed her by the shoulders and shook her hard, trying to dislodge that distant look from her eyes. "You have to smarten up, June, you have to fit in, or you will be nothing." But June just stared at her mutely as Carrie Logan wandered up, flanked by her two best friends.

"Do you want to have lunch with us?" Carrie was in the grade above May. She wore nothing but store-bought clothes, and once for show and tell brought a china doll dressed in an evening gown of real royal blue velvet and a rhinestone necklace, with blue eyes that batted when you moved her head back and forth. May had never seen anything so beautiful. Carrie and her friends always ate lunch on the front steps, while May and the girls she played with had to be content with the yard.

"June?" May glanced at her sister, knowing the invitation did not extend to her.

With the same remote expression June answered, "You go. I'm all right."

"Shove over, Audrey. You can sit beside me, May." Carrie opened her factory-made lunch box with the picture of Snow White on the side. "We swap lunches sometimes." She unwrapped a wax paper package and peeled back the thin slice of white bread to reveal a pallid slice of meat. "Hmm. Turkey sandwich. Not bad. What have you got?"

May pried open her battered lard pail. Perogies stuffed with potato and cottage cheese, dotted with crisp-fried salt pork and onions and congealed butter, leftover from last night's supper. Her favourite. She was hungry, and hated the idea of sharing it, and Carrie's sandwich didn't look very tasty.

"Eww!" Carrie said. "What's *that?*" All the girls peered into the pail.

"Perogies," May stuttered.

"You eat that? They look like blobs of white poop with insects on them."

"My mother makes me. I don't really like them." May stood and dumped the contents of her pail into the trash can by the door.

"That's OK." Carrie offered half a sandwich. "You can have some of mine."

The sandwich had hardly any texture and even less flavour, and melted to pap in the mouth. As May was trying to make herself swallow, Carrie gave her a measured look over her own half sandwich, as though weighing something in her mind.

"Your sister," she said slowly. "You know we call her the ghost girl?"

May nodded.

"I mean, she's kind of... a freak, isn't she?"

May turned the same measured look on her sister, who was sitting by herself, staring into space, picking at her lips until they were raw. She looked back at Carrie, felt the pull of the top step, of the chance to touch, maybe even play with, that velvet-clad doll. Swallowed hard, and said, "Yes, I guess she is."

From then on June walked to and from school alone, and on the days when she woke with her throat swollen, clawing at her neck and crying, May was relieved that her sister would be staying home. Even relieved, mostly, when June was sent to the San, a reaction she was pretty sure her parents shared. And now June had been gone seven years. There had been the occasional superficial letter early on, but after June's relapse, nothing. She hardly seemed real to May anymore, stowed away as she was at the back of May's mind.

THREE WEEKS AFTER Constable Miller's first visit, May looked up from sorting change in the till to see he was back, this time with an older officer who introduced himself as Sergeant McIntyre. They had discovered that Mr. Antonio Bruni had moved back to Italy with his wife after the war, but the scoliosis that had kept him from serving in the war would have made it impossible for him to lift a body without help. The Barkers had been tracked down in Michigan, but they could not have transported a body to so remote a spot without a car, and Old Mr. Barker's car had been in the garage awaiting the delivery of a coil from Saskatoon, without which the car could not be moved. The investigation appeared to be at a dead end, but then Mr. McTeer suddenly remembered the little ghost girl, June, who had been out sleepwalking so often, always to be found staring up at the Barkers' landing, and he wasn't sure but maybe he remembered seeing her that night, the night they'd all thought the Eyetie and Frenchie had run off together. What if she'd witnessed something? Something that haunted her enough to send her out night after night in her sleep. She always had been a bit strange.

"So you see, Mrs. Zalesky," Sergeant McIntyre said gravely. "We need to ask your daughter what she knows about this matter."

"She is sick! Sick vith TB. She knows nattink and you could kill her vith your questions! This is just crazy gossip! I don't talk to you anymore."

"Ma'am. I don't need your permission. She is an adult. I am extending a courtesy. If you are concerned you may accompany us or hire a lawyer to represent her during questioning. Though that is hardly necessary. We only want to know if she remembers anything about that night."

"Do vhat you must." Olena's voice like a whip. "I vill not help to kill her. She vas just a child. A sick child. This is foolishness. She vas so sick she vas in bed for days, couldn't even be moved from my aunt's house. These people are talking empty talk."

"But Mom. Didn't Nurse Gillam write to say this new drug, streptomycin, was helping?"

"May! Don't speak of things you cannot understand. Helping, yes. Curing, no. She is still very sick. Ve'll see what your father has to say about this."

The sergeant put on his hat and signalled to Constable Miller to open the door. "We won't do anything to jeopardize her health, Mrs. Zalesky. You must see that if she is the witness to a crime I have no choice but to question her." He held out his hand but Olena turned her back on him.

That evening Taras came to the house, and Olena let him in, a circumstance May could not remember happening since she and her mother had moved in with Varvara, shortly after June was sent to Fort San.

"You run along to Carrie's," Olena ordered. "She probably has new records. You'll want to hear them, I know."

And May did want to hear them, but not as much as she wanted to hear what had drawn her parents to sit at the same table, with their heads so close together.

THE NEXT MORNING Olena woke May early and took her to the store hours before opening. Sergeant McIntyre and Constable Miller were waiting for them outside, faces sombre, and Taras was waiting inside, face grey.

"Good morning." Sergeant McIntyre removed his hat as he entered. Constable Miller did the same, but stayed by the door, twisting his hat round and round. "There's a car outside to drive you to the station, sir. We can take your statement there. Call you a lawyer."

"No lawyer." Taras's voice was firm. "But I vant to talk to my daughter before ve go."

"A lawyer? Dad, why do you need a lawyer?"

"All right, but I really do advise an attorney, sir."

"I tell you No. I know vhat I did. I vill plead guilty. No need to pay a lawyer to do that."

"What is going on? Mom?"

"Your father, he vill tell you." Olena's face unusually impassive, even for her.

"May," Taras spoke rapidly in Ukrainian. "I wanted to tell you what happened myself. It will be all over town soon. We had to use the party line, and that LeAnn, you know how she loves to listen in."

"Tell me *what?*" But a part of May already knew. That scrap of carpet. How had she not seen the significance? She saw herself years ago, crouching on the rug in the parlour, tracing its paisley patterns to create designs for her paper dolls. Wondering where it had gone, then forgetting all about it.

"May, I'm very sorry to tell you, but I am the one who killed Marie."

Constable Miller's ears were bright red and his Adam's apple was wobbling wildly even though he was not speaking.

"Mr. Zalesky..." Sergeant McIntyre tried to interject but Taras waved him down.

"It was an accident. She and I, we... well, she was threatening to tell your mother so we argued and I hit her and she fell and that was that. I didn't mean to..." His tone as matter of fact as if he were discussing how to price the latest shipment from Saskatoon.

Constable Miller was staring at her with pity, even though he surely couldn't follow the Ukrainian. Briefly, May closed her eyes, trying not to be sick. "But she was barely older than June!" Barely older than May was now. "How could you!"

"You wouldn't understand," Taras said.

"Oh, wouldn't I?" May jeered. "For years, all those rumours. My God, what will people say now?" Mitch, she thought. Mrs. Logan. Nausea swept through her again.

"May..."

"You've ruined everything!" May rounded on her mother. "Why are you just standing there? Say something!"

"What is there to say? What's done is done."

"This will kill June."

"We are not going to tell her." Olena's voice preternaturally calm. "This is why your father has come forward, to stop her being pestered when she is still so very ill. I called the San and spoke to Nurse Gillam. They will do their best to keep it from her."

"But the radio, the newspapers. Everyone will know once it goes to trial!"

"I am pleading guilty," Taras said. "No trial."

"But don't you think she would want to know? Has a right to know? She loved Marie, and you . . ." May pounded her thighs with clenched fists to stop the tears that threatened to break through. "She should know."

"So suddenly you care so much about your sister?" For the first time Taras lost his careful calm, leaning in close, his whisper spraying her face. "You think I didn't see all the times she came home crying while you were off with your friends? You leave this alone."

"Now, sir, please, you must speak English." Sergeant McIntyre placed a hand on Taras's shoulder. "I think it's time we left. They'll be allowed to see you in Saskatoon."

"No." Taras reined himself in. "I vant to see no one. I vant it finished. May . . ." He reached for her.

May thrust both hands behind her back, but Olena took his hands briefly in hers. "Go with God."

And then he was gone.

THE NEXT DAYS felt as though they were a turntable running at double speed. May hardly slept, haunted by images of her father's raised fist, Marie's cry as she fell, of cold earth filling her eyes, ears, mouth. May stuffed her pillow against her own ears to stifle the voices inside her head, against her mouth to muffle her moans when the horror threatened to overwhelm her. But the worst moments were when distant memories surfaced, of her father walking home across the fields, of May and June running to meet him, ransacking his pockets for treats, of being swung to his shoulder and carried home. Those were the only images that could force her to press her pillow, hard, against her eyes.

TARAS PLED GUILTY in the Saskatoon court and the newspapers predicted a lengthy stay in prison. But at the sentencing the prosecutor and judge had other ideas, pointing out that the coroner had found no marks on the skull as one would expect from a fall causing death, but had found a deep nick on one of the neck vertebrae, which most likely was caused by a knife. On searching Taras's car the police had discovered that though it had been carefully cleaned, there was dried blood in the seams of the wheel well and the far corner of the trunk, which implied far more blood flow than would be found after a simple fall. The defendant had clearly lied about the circumstances in an attempt to mitigate his punishment. This was not a crime of passion as the prisoner claimed, but a deeply depraved and cynical murder. The fact was that after a lifetime of adultery the murderer had taken advantage of a much younger woman, young enough to be his daughter, possibly even granddaughter, and when she threatened to ruin him, he had killed her in cold blood. A life for a life, the judge said, and condemned him to be hanged by the neck until dead, one month from sentencing.

OLENA WENT THROUGH IT ALL with a face carved out of stone, even when, as increasingly happened, customers came not to buy, but to gawk. May had refused to go back to school, hoping to bury herself in Varvara's house, away from those prying eyes and venomous whispers, but all her mother had said was, "You don't go to school, you work the store." No escape.

"Why don't we just leave?" May wailed.

"I won't let anyone push me out of something I have built. Or into something I don't want. Not ever. Why should I sell up at a loss like the Barkers did for such vultures? You'll see. People have short memories. They will stop circling." And then she started grimly shovelling dried lima beans from a burlap sack into a glass case.

But how could they forget when Olena was doing everything to rub their noses in it? Right after the sentencing, she'd made arrangements for Taras to be buried in the Eldergrove cemetery. May could just imagine the awfulness of being the only two people in the church, at the gravesite, the tongues that would be rattling like locust wings. The fodder it would give the town for months. And now, the day before Taras's execution, Olena was actually going to Saskatoon, spending money on a motel room with a kitchenette so she could take him his last meal.

"Why?" May gripped her hands tight together to keep herself from shaking her mother, slapping some sense into her as she wrapped bread, salt pork, a jar of sauerkraut in towels and tucked them into a wooden crate. "You haven't lived together for years! And it's not like Marie was even the first. I heard the rumours, I remember that night in the wagon when you had to shame him into coming home." She fell back before the fury in Olena's eyes.

"This is none of your business. If you want this town to stop talking, stop behaving like a spoiled child. What's done is done. There is nothing left but to face it." She hefted the crate from the table and headed for the door, saying over her shoulder, "Keep an eye on Varvara."

BUT INSTEAD OF staying to tend to Varvara May put on a clinging pink angora sweater and flared black skirt cinched with a thin patent leather belt, an outfit ordered from Eaton's that had taken every penny of her saved wages. She scraped her hair into an updo and applied makeup meticulously, hand shaking a little at the memory that she had learned the art of putting on a face from Marie, watching her apply rouge and lipstick in the storeroom, then smear them off with cold cream just before the arrival of the dark cloud that was Old Man Barker.

May straightened the seams of her stockings, slid into her two-toned dancing shoes and appraised herself in the mirror. Ready for battle. Carrie hadn't invited her to one social since Taras had been arrested, but it wasn't Carrie May needed to see, or be seen by.

Carrie's face was a frozen mask of surprise when she opened the door, but at least she didn't shut it in May's face, which was something, May supposed. Until she found herself sitting alone at one end of the living room, while Carrie danced every dance, not once glancing her way, not even to throw a look of triumph. When May went to the food table, with its usual spread of punch and sandwiches and aspic, people floated away with full plates and cups, without one word. Face burning and gorge rising at the thought of food, she wandered to the record player, where the same circle of lonely space surrounded her while she flipped through Carrie's records, trying not to see Mitch dancing with Audrey, who was not even good-looking, with her straggly hair and an overbite that grinned mockingly at May every time she whirled past. If Albert had been there he might have joined her, at least warmed her with his smile, but Albert was nowhere to be seen.

"Um, May?"

She looked up with relief only to find Gordon, a fat boy with dreadful acne, shuffling his feet before her, smiling shyly.

"Care to dance?"

Her humiliation was complete. He would never have dared to ask her if she hadn't been lowered to his level by these people she'd thought were her friends. His kindness did what their cruelty could not: she fled.

As she was putting on her hat with shaking fingers in the vestibule she heard Mitch telling a joke: Why does a Uker-ainian carry a piece of shit in his pocket?

Identification.

THE ONLY PLACE she could think to go was the store. She crouched in the waning light behind the till where no one could see her, like a rabbit run to ground, crunching her fists into her eyes to force them dry, remembering all the times she had found June in the same position, and had felt so superior. May was always the one who knew how to get along. She had tamed her accent, tweezed those rebellious eyebrows, studied the fashion magazines for the right clothes, hairstyles, made the right friends.

She shivered, and, not wanting to draw attention to the store by lighting the kerosene lamp, fumbled in the drawer beneath the till for a candle, matches and a saucer, more for the illusion of warmth than the light. Dribbled wax into the saucer, pressed the candle into the puddle of wax and set the makeshift candlestick on the counter. The flame flickered its reflection on the designs of the tin ceiling overhead and the round brass keys of the till.

She had to get away. But all her money had been gambled on the ridiculous outfit that was now wrinkled and dusty from cowering on the floor. There was next to nothing in the cash drawer, and even if there had been a hundred dollars, where could she go? She'd only ever known this horrible little town. Her efforts to fit in hadn't extended to excelling at school. She'd had no ambition other than to seduce Mitch Logan, who wasn't worth the gum she would scrape off the sole of her shoe, into marriage. She writhed under the shame of it.

There was a tap at the door and the bell tinkled as Albert limped in, leaning on his cane and ensuring the CLOSED sign was still up as he shut the door behind him. An image ignited her brain: Tom Barker, with his cane and his beautiful bride, that first time they came to the store. Rage coursed through her.

"What are you doing here?" she asked belligerently.

"I saw the candle." He remained standing just inside the door as though he recognized that she was a cornered animal. Dangerous. Unpredictable. "I heard what happened at Carrie's. Thought I'd ask how you're doing. Stopped by the house but all the lights were out so I came by the store just in case."

"Why?"

Albert remarked, more to the floor than to May. "You know, when I was serving overseas I saw a lot of strange stuff, the stress, you know. One in ten planes didn't come back, so people developed odd superstitions, even really good people. Anyway, there was this stray dog, probably lost his family in one of the blitzes, and he'd hang around begging for scraps, for a scratch behind the ears. He was a border collie, bright and cute and one of the crews sort of adopted him. And when they didn't come back, another crew felt sorry for him and they fed him for a while. But when they didn't come back, no one wanted anything to do with the dog. It was like he had a curse on him. He'd crawl up on his belly, begging, and the guys'd throw stones at him until he crawled away again. But still he'd hover at the edge of the camp, whimpering, so when I could I'd go out after dark, take him some food." He looked mildly shamefaced. "But I didn't try to take him back to my crew."

"Are you saying I'm a whimpering dog?"

"No, just making conversation. Just saying I don't follow the herd."

May drew a long breath, looked into eyes that she saw for the first time were grey, flecked with golden brown. She was probably crazy. Certainly she was desperate. "I need to get out of this town. Will you take me?"

"I'm headed for Toronto. Would that suit?" Albert's tone as casual as if she'd asked for a lift to the Eldergrove bus station.

"We'd have to get married."

"I didn't assume anything different." He sounded almost amused. "It will take a few days to get the license, but that will give your mother time to . . ."

"No. I want to leave now. Tonight. We can hold off on marrying until we get to Toronto. But . . ." She stopped, suddenly unsure.

"It's all right, I understand." Albert smiled. "Separate bedrooms until then."

"Yes. Thank you." But that had been only part of her unspoken question.

"Shall we seal the bargain?" He took her hand and led her out from behind the counter, bent down to kiss her, paused, the amusement leaving his voice. "You don't have to worry. I won't press you to do anything you don't want to."

May held herself still. She had made up her mind, but what if her body rebelled? She had never been close enough to Albert even to catch his scent.

Just before their lips met she inhaled. Only the faintest hint of soap and none of the heavily scented aftershave Mitch favoured. The kiss had none of Mitch's urgency, but a gentle insistence that calmed her, and if her body did not yet rise to him with the abandon Mitch had called out in her, it did not reject him. May breathed a sigh of relief against those lips, then pushed him away. It would do.

"I'll pack and you can pick me up in the alley behind the house in an hour. And then there's one stop I want to make on the way."

MAY CREPT INTO the dark house and listened at Varvara's door, relieved to hear nothing but snoring. Olena had taken the only suitcase to Saskatoon, so May stripped the sheet off her bed and started heaping essentials into it: underwear, her favourite dresses, stockings. As she scraped up a nightgown from a drawer her fingers bumped against a metal tube. Patriot Red. "It would be treason not to buy it, non?" That sparkling laugh. May's fingers shook so violently the lipstick skittered out of her grasp and across the floor, almost under the bed, before she stopped it with her foot. She had stolen the lipstick from the display case shortly after that first sighting of Marie, when she still thought such beauty meant power.

June had been devastated when Marie eloped with the Eyetie, but May had been glad to see her escape her brute of a father-in-law and weakling of a husband. It was unbearable now to realize that Marie, who had seemed so much more alive than anyone in this town, had been buried all these years. Dead at May's father's hand. Unthinkable, yet so it was.

And now here was May, doing what they'd all thought Marie had done years ago: running off with a man. May couldn't imagine Albert raising his hand to her, but she was not her mother's daughter for nothing. Into her handbag she tucked the can of hairspray that Carrie had brought back for her from Saskatoon when they were still friends. Just in case. If things got ugly she could spray it into his eyes, buy time to run.

She slung the makeshift sack over her shoulder. Still no sign or sound from Varvara. May eased open the ice box, took out what was left of a honey cake studded with raisins and currants, which Olena had made for Taras. She wrapped it carefully in a tea towel, then placed it in a small bag. June would appreciate a taste of home, something sweet before the bitter news May was bringing.

She moved her belongings to the back door, then picked up the piece of paper bearing the phone number of the motel where Olena was staying. However angry she was with her mother, her mother's stubbornness, May could not simply vanish as Marie had.

Picking up the handle of the telephone, she clicked until LeAnn, the operator, answered, then gave the number. No doubt LeAnn would listen in. Good. May would take added pleasure in listing all the reasons she was leaving this crummy little town.

But when she heard Olena's voice — "Is it Varvara?" — sharp with anxiety, May did not think of LeAnn at all, spoke as reassuringly as she could in Ukrainian.

"She's fine. Sleeping." A pause, almost as if Olena knew what was coming and wanted to stave it off for a few moments.

"I called to tell you I'm leaving. I'm getting married. To Albert McGrath." Still nothing. So May told her what had happened at Carrie's, including Mitch's joke. "I'm not like you, I can't stare them all down. I need to get out, get away. This is my chance."

Finally Olena spoke. "Where are you going?"

"Toronto. Tonight." May was startled to find herself almost crying. She had prepared herself for anger, recrimination, to hear that this was rash, she was too young, had her parents' disastrous marriage taught her nothing? But her mother never had been one to waste words on the obvious, or the inevitable. Her voice was calm, almost gentle.

"He will be good to you, this Albert?"

"I think so. He has kind eyes. And he stood by me when no one else did."

"And you care for him?"

Now the pause was May's. "I believe I will." Speaking again into her mother's silence. "I'd better go. Albert is waiting. I'll write." But of course, May had never learned to write in Ukrainian, and Olena could write only the most basic English.

There was a shaky sigh on the other end of the phone, then, "I wish you every happiness."

And now May really was crying, and placing the handle in the telephone's cradle as tenderly as if it were a living thing.

THEY DROVE THROUGH the night but just before sunup Albert pulled onto a patch of gravel at the entrance to a hay field. "It's too early for them to let us in and I can't keep my eyes open. Might as well have a nap." May curled up against the passenger door expecting sleep to elude her but was surprised to find that not only had she slept, in her sleep she had migrated to Albert's side, her cheek nestled against his shoulder. When she stirred he smiled down at her, eased his arm from under her and rubbed it briskly. "It fell asleep too. I didn't like to wake you."

AN HOUR OR SO later, Albert parked in front of Fort San's imposing sandstone, went around to open May's door. She smiled shyly up at him as he took her hand to help her out of the car. "Do you want me to go with you?"

"No, it's all right." May straightened her skirt, checked her seams, hid her mussed hair beneath her hat. "I won't be long."

She asked for Nurse Gillam at reception, giving her name. When the nurse arrived she took both May's hands in hers, beaming. "Oh, my dear, I'm so glad you're here. June has been improving a bit, physically, thanks to the streptomycin but her spirits are still very low. I'm sure it will perk her up to see you, though if you can get her to talk it's more than the rest of us can do." She led May outside onto a wooden walkway, her rubber soled shoes squeaking, May's heels clacking. Nurse Gillam kept up a steady flow of chatter and May was grateful that there didn't seem to be any need to respond. "I must say, though, I was never so thankful for how she keeps herself to herself as when your mother asked us to hide that dreadful news about your father." Well-kept garden beds lined the buildings, pansies and marigolds turning to the morning sun. "I asked the women to help and they were all very willing to try, they're sorry for her, lonely little thing." All those empty letters May had tossed off, impatient to get first to Carrie, later to Mitch. She glanced sharply at Nurse Gillam but the nurse's face was innocent as an egg. "And really it wasn't all that difficult. She never asks to read the newspapers, doesn't listen to the radio. Doesn't really talk to anyone. She just has no interest in the outside world. Or this one, I'm afraid." The nurse sighed and lowered her voice as they neared a balcony that looked out over spacious lawns, graceful stands of weeping birch. If it hadn't been for all the white uniforms and the faint smell of disinfectant that tainted even the open air, you could have mistaken this place for a fancy hotel. "This is the women's balcony. The local choir is here to entertain the patients and even though technically June no longer needs to chase the cure, we wheel her out for the music. Come, she's just over here."

For a moment May's courage failed her. Not only at the thought of telling June about their father, but at seeing her after all these years. She squared her shoulders, adjusted her hat, and strode up the stairs onto the veranda where all those bodies lay forced into rest.

Nurse Gillam led her to a gaunt young woman reclining in a half-raised hospital bed who lifted dull eyes when the nurse touched her arm. "June, dear, your sister is here. Isn't that lovely!" The same dull gaze turned to May.

"May?" Her voice croaking with disuse. "May," she said again as if it was the most beautiful word in the English language. In any language.

May stumbled forward, bending awkwardly to give her sister a cautious hug. She looked so frail. It was as though they had switched places, the older sister now the smaller, weaker of the two, the younger one filling out into womanhood, leaving June behind.

Still beaming, Nurse Gillam placed a chair at June's bedside. "I'll leave you two to catch up."

When May moved to sit, June clutched her hands as though she feared May would vanish if she loosened her grip or closed the eyes staring hungrily, unblinkingly into May's. Her face so thin, her cheeks so pale, her frown so much deeper than May remembered. She eased one hand out from June's, traced the frown with a gentle finger.

"Oh, June," May whispered. "We should not have left you alone so long." Unable to bear that searching gaze any longer, she buried her head in June's lap, her hat tumbling to the veranda.

June stroked May's hair, murmuring words May could not make out. She was the little sister again, listening to fairy tales told to distract her from grim realities just beyond their bedroom curtain, behind their parents' door. June giving May the last crust of bread in a wagon cold with moonlight and fear. June's straight back, shoulder blades straining her flour-sack dress, as she stared down a man with a gun yelling incomprehensible threats. June placing herself between May and danger.

May raised her head from June's lap, rescued her hat and put it on the bed, then opened her purse, took out the honey cake and carefully unwrapped it. "Look what I brought. I bet they don't bake anything like this here!"

She broke off the plummiest piece and pressed it into June's hand, set the rest of the cake carefully on the bed. Saw herself feeding June bits of egg and praying she wouldn't die. June looked almost as ill now as she had then, and May felt just as helpless. Perhaps her parents had been right, that coming here was just a selfish attempt to assuage an unassuageable guilt, and worse, a threat to June's precarious recovery. "Go on June, eat." Her sister obediently took a bite, chewed.

Down past the trimmed green lawn and shimmering poplars, above the deep blue of the lake, pelicans wheeled, blinding white against the sky. In the pavilion in the middle of the lawn a young boy blew a wobbly note on a recorder and the choir launched into their first song. They ranged in age from the very young to the very old, with the quavering notes of the ancients punctuated by the breaking voices of the young. May, accustomed to the sinuous harmonies of the Andrews Sisters, barely repressed a shudder, though June didn't appear to notice.

I am a poor, wayfaring stranger,
A-travelling through this world of woe

There was nothing May wanted more than to hold her hands over June's ears, to shield her from what their father had done, to whisper any story other than the one she had come to tell. Longing for just one minute more before she changed June's life forever, she said with as much jollity as she could muster, "You'll never guess, June, I'm getting married!"

June appeared to be straining to understand the words.

"He's over there, by that big Buick. We are moving to Toronto and when you are well, you can visit. Maybe even live with us."

I'm going there to meet my father
I'm going there no more to roam.
I'm only going over Jordan
I'm only going over home.

Still no response and May realized June had asked not one question about Eldergrove.

"You see, things aren't the same at home. Oh! There's no way to do this but just to do it. I wish I didn't have to but — June, dear, Marie —" was that a glint of interest? "It turns out Marie didn't run off with Mr. Bruni as we all thought."

Painful, futile hope deepened the frown on June's forehead.

"No, dear. She didn't make it past Norfolk. I'm so sorry, June, but her remains were found in a dried-out slough not far from Eldergrove."

June gave a sharp cry, holding up one hand as though to keep May from speaking further.

Would that choir *never* stop singing that dirge? Pale, emaciated faces turned to watch the two sisters. A whole pavilion of ghost girls. Didn't they have enough to bear without an interminable hymn about dying? Something about a blood-washed band? Even if the ghosts didn't mind, it was too much for May. She had to do what she came to do and get out of here. "Marie was murdered, June," she blurted out, "and it was Dad who did it."

"No! That cannot be right. It must not be right. I don't believe you!"

"June, I was there when he confessed. He said they'd been having an affair and she threatened to tell Mom. It was an accident, he was angry, he hit her. She fell. It was done. But the judge didn't believe him . . ." May's voice fizzled at the expression of horror on June's face.

"Why are you telling me this? Why have you come here?" June hauled herself up from her reclining position, knocking the honey cake to the floor.

"Mom said not to tell you. She said you weren't strong enough yet, but I knew you would want to know."

"I have to see him."

I'm going there to see my mother
She said she'd meet me when I come . . .

God, it was excruciating. "You can't, June. He didn't want to see you. I told him you'd want to but . . ."

"You are lying, you must be lying." June was gasping for air.

"I wish I were, June, I wish . . ."

"He would never say such a thing. Why are you keeping me from him?"

A dreadful rattle from June's chest that May had not heard for seven years.

"June, there's nothing to be done," she stammered. "His funeral is next Saturday in Eldergrove . . ."

"Go away!" June rasped. "I don't know why you came. Go away go away *go away!*" Her cheeks flamed red against her chalk white face. A wave of coughing rose from the ghost girls on the veranda. Nurse Gillam ran up, face wiped clean of its smile, an intern on her heels.

"I'm sorry but you have to go," she said tersely. "We cannot have you upsetting her, them all, like this. What on earth did you say?" She turned her back on May. "Hush, June, hush. Breathe now, like me: one two threeeeee. Hand out those ice chips!" she snapped at the intern, then tenderly to June, "Try again: One two threeeeee." Over her shoulder, to May, "Please leave."

May scooped up her hat, whispered to the empty air, "I'm so sorry." Words too few and too small, but they were all she had.

JUNE WAKES to find Dale on the ward, astride one of the women on the veranda, the moon looking down at him, making bars across his back, but then the woman he is straddling turns to look at June and it is not a woman but her father and Dale's face blurs into a sad clown's and her father has his hands tangled in the clown's black hair, he is winding it around her throat, and the clown's red mouth opens wide and says "Keep quiet, you must keep quiet." Her words are bleeding down her chin and onto her white gown, onto the white floor and white locker that holds the secret book, a red haze that covers everything, stains the back of June's brain. Hands are pulling at her, trying to hold her down. She is running, running with Baba Yaga at her back. She wants to call out to her father, but the red is choking her throat, sealing her lips, she has to bite it off even though it was Marie who put it there. "Stop, June, you're hurting yourself. Stop now."

June wakes to find herself on the veranda, in only her nightdress and with bare feet, shivering under a moon that is silvering the grasses and turning the far lake into liquid metal. Someone has hold of her, and she screams, but when her vision clears it is only Nurse Gillam who is softly shaking her and calling her name. "You were sleepwalking, June," she says. "But don't be afraid. It was only a dream." The words echo inside June's skull. Her mouth is on fire. She raises her hands to her lips and touches something sticky. Her blood-tipped fingers look black in the moonlight.

"I need to go home."

SHE STOOD on the front steps of Fort San, waiting for her taxi, on her own two feet, even if they were a bit shaky. That morning Dr. Wilkes had tried to talk her out of leaving. "The streptomycin has beaten back the disease, but you are still not strong. I'd like to keep you at least another couple of months."

"Am I contagious?" June asked, the only point on which she could be forced to compromise.

"No," Dr. Wilkes said reluctantly, "but we don't know what might cause you to relapse at this early..."

"Fine." June rose and extended her hand. "I do thank you for all you've done, Doctor. I assure you I'll take excellent care of myself." Wondering if that were indeed true.

"Please sit." June sat. "Before you leave there are some things you need to know. You must never marry. Marriage leads to children and you have only three quarters of a functioning lung. All we have done is halt the disease. It will always be inside you. If you were to get pregnant you would have to abort."

"Isn't that illegal?"

"Yes, of course." Dr. Wilkes waved an impatient hand. "For normal people. *Your* body is just too dangerous for you and for a foetus. And another reason there must be no children. You will likely not live past forty." He overrode June's gasp. "Your heart has to do double duty because of your lack of lung power. It can last only so long. But if you eat a healthy diet and get some rest and some non-strenuous walking in every day, who can say? We have done our best for you."

June stood and held out her hand again and this time he took it. "I know. Thank you."

"Nurse Gillam phoned your mother as you asked. She'll be waiting for you at the depot."

Now as June shoved Mrs. Logan's hand-me-down suitcase into the trunk of the taxi, Nurse Gillam appeared at her elbow. "Were you going to leave without saying goodbye?" June was surprised to see her soft brown eyes filmed with moisture and felt a pang of loss. She had not realized until now that Nurse Gillam was her friend, and now she was saying goodbye. She'd been so buried in herself she hadn't even learned her friend's first name.

"Here, I brought salve for your lips." Nurse Gillam dabbed delicately at June's stinging mouth, pressed the jar into her hand. "I am so very glad you are going home, June dear, even if it is for such a dreadful reason." She took June's face in both her hands, gently but inexorably, not allowing her to look away. "Now you listen to me. Doctors don't know everything. Look at this experimental drug that has given you a new lease on life. Who could have predicted it? What did your father say when he left you here? Fight. Well, whatever else he may have done, that day he spoke the truth. You are stronger than you know. You should have been dead any time these last seven years, and now look at you." She released June's face, straightened her own, and planted a kiss on June's forehead. "Be well."

SEVERAL HOURS LATER June was staring out a window into the rain, trying to use the hypnotic rhythm of the huge bus windshield wipers to calm her mind. She was going home, but a home without her sister, her father. Without, if Dr. Wilkes was right, even much of a future. Going home to a town that had always felt like alien space and to a mother she hadn't seen in almost eight years. The wipers squeaked futilely. Waves of rain filled the windscreen as quickly as they were wiped away, blurring the flat fields stretching endlessly on all sides. June had chosen the bus because she wanted to avoid the memories of that long-ago train trip with her father, but the memories were not on the train, they were here in her chest, nestled in with the scars on her lungs, with the fear that was carving a hole deadlier than any tuberculosis scar and blacker than Baba Yaga's maw: the fear that what May had said about their father was true. And still the impossible conviction that it was all some terrible mistake, that he would be there to greet her at the station.

The rain pelted down even harder, pounding like hail against the metal sides of the bus. A torrent creating rivers in the grooves of the asphalt illuminated by the headlights. Panic ignited in her, with the familiar thinning of air that made her gasp and wheeze. She'd be dropped in the centre of town, and would have to walk several blocks to the store. She hadn't an umbrella, not even a decent rain coat.

Forcing herself to breathe slowly, deeply, her hand on her diaphragm, she told herself not to be ridiculous. Of course her mother would think to bring an umbrella. Besides, she didn't need to be afraid of wet hair anymore. She'd been having regular shampoos, even tub baths, for over a year. Water was no longer the enemy, and would be the least of what she had to face in Eldergrove. Almost as if through her force of will, by the time the bus stopped at Norfolk the rain was a light drizzle, and when they reached Eldergrove it had stopped, the clouds had cleared and the moon was high in the sky. June tried to think of it as a good omen.

At the bus station, her mother's strained face searched for June's in the row of windows. When June disembarked and she and her mother embraced stiffly, she realized she had no memory of her mother touching her, not in anger or affection, except that one night — "Don't leave me" — when her mother's hug had been so fierce it was the only thing capable of holding June back from the edge of that dark swirling world. Now Olena's brittle embrace hadn't even the power to anchor June in this moment, this place, as her mind skittered in all directions, running from questions she didn't want to ask, crashing against Olena's stony refusal to meet her eyes.

"You shouldn't have come." Her mother retrieved June's suitcase from the belly of the bus. "The car is over here." She spoke in English, as though her daughter was a stranger. Which, when she thought for a moment, June realized she was. To the Ukrainian language, which she hadn't spoken since she left, to Olena, to herself. Certainly to LeAnn, who was peering around the corner of the depot to ogle the new arrival. As she must have ogled Marie all those years ago.

"When did you learn to drive?" All the questions that had been crowding her mind and this was the best she could come up with.

"Long time now, maybe five years." Olena clutched the wheel, body tense and bending forward so she could squint through the windshield at the pools of light thrown by the head lamps. "You are not supposed to be here. Doctor say you are not vell enough yet."

"I need to say goodbye." June paused. "I need to understand."

"Vhat's to understand?" Her mother's voice was harsh and she kept her gaze fixed on the road that was inching by. "Vhat's done is done. No good dwelling."

"I need . . ." So long ago, those words on Olena's lips. A voice like a knife and the clinking of coins. June closed her eyes, faintly nauseated.

Olena braked hard in the middle of the street and June's eyes startled open. "Enough!" Her mother banged her hands on the steering wheel. "I cannot tell you vhat I do not know." She yanked the car into gear and they resumed their slow crawl. And what after all had June been expecting? Tears? Vulnerability? Who if not her mother had taught June to keep herself so deeply in check? "Vasilisa must give up a year of her life to Baba Yaga for every question she asks," Varvara had warned May. But it was June, who had always kept her mouth—and now, it appeared, her eyes—firmly shut, who had surrendered not only seven years, but most of her lungs, any claim to a future. And still June could not find the courage within herself to ask her mother any of the questions that had been tormenting her since May's visit, including the most pressing of all: If what May said is true, if he really did those things, why don't you hate him? Why have you brought him home?

They continued down Main Street, June sharply aware of all the eyes behind the lamplit windows. The tongues that would be wagging at the sight of the ghost girl who had been gone so long. What was her mother thinking to put her on parade like this? Shouldn't they be going down the alley? But they didn't stop at the store, just trundled along until they pulled up at Varvara's house.

"Oh, yes, you don't know." Olena rammed the car into Park. "Varvara, she get sick a few years back. Sick in the head. So I move in vith her. Your father, he never did get on vith her so he stayed in the apartment."

"That's funny. May didn't mention it."

"May shouldn't be telling you anyting at all."

Grabbing June's suitcase from the trunk, and waving off her attempts to help, Olena pushed open the creaking gate and led the way up the moonlit sidewalk, past blood-red poppies nodding in their beds. June's throat constricted.

She followed Olena into the kitchen, half expecting to see May playing the itsy-bitsy spider game at the worn wooden table, to see Varvara dipping her ladle into the depths of the black iron stove. Offering her a cup filled with hissing fire. Moonlight through the window cast bars of shadow along the wooden floor. June's hand rose to her throat, then to her eyes to rub away that familiar red haze.

Her mother, lighting a kerosene lamp, frowned at her. "You need to lie down. This is all too much for you."

"I'm fine. Don't fuss!" June shook her head as though to clear it.

"Varvara! We're back." In English Olena said, "She probably not recognize you. She got very strange these last years. Losing memory. Doctor say early oncoming demon... demmon..."

"Dementia," June murmured.

"Varvara!" Olena called again. "Here, June." She pulled a chair to the table. "Sit. I get you some tea. Ahnt Varvara, if she say strange tings it is just the sickness. Don't you pay her any mind."

"She say strange tings sometime," her father had said to the doctor who was to take out her tonsils, and the cup that smelled of death had descended.

From the back bedroom an ancient woman emerged. She was achingly thin, a stained shirt falling over a concave chest and a stained cardigan drawn over that, fastened in the wrong hole and falling askew. Her skirt barely clung to her skinny hips, threatening to slide to the floor at any moment. Varvara? Her mother, misreading June's expression, said defensively, "She don't let me help her dress, ahnt sometimes when I feed her she fight the spoon." Again June shook her head, barely recognizing the crone in front of her. Where was the nightmarish figure of June's memory and dreams?

"Hallo?" Varvara squinted at them, her face hard and brown and deeply scored. She still looked like a witch, her chin and nose hooking toward one another, the wart on her forehead. But a witch stripped of her power, and her expression wasn't evil, or stern, just blank. Not one hint that she recognized June, or even Olena.

"It's Olena, Varvara." Olena took the old woman's hand and stroked it. "You remember June. She's been in that hospital outside of Regina. I picked her up at the bus station. We talked about her coming two days ago." June struggled to keep up with the flow of Ukrainian.

"Oh — tak?" Varvara smiled vaguely, wandered to the iron stove, cranked open the door and shoved in a stick of wood from the pile of kindling on the floor, her looming shape thrown into eerie relief by the flames from the stove, her shadow huge against the wall. Varvara stretched out her hand toward June, one twisted finger pointing, advancing. "I know you. You're the one with the mark. Your mother put it there. We knew no good could come of it."

June's chair scraped the floor as she tried to back away from that pointing, gnarled hand. Fear flickered across Olena's face. "Hush now, Varvara. You don't know what you are saying."

"*She* knows," Varvara still advancing. "She knows but she mustn't say."

June fell back before them, the floor heaving beneath her, she could almost hear the scrabbling of chicken's feet, the lice whispering "Run." She raised one hand as though to ward off an evil spell. "No," she whispered. "No, you don't know me." And fled. "Don't!" she said as her mother moved to follow her. "Leave me alone."

She walked blindly, not caring where she went so long as it was away from that house, the world still teetering beneath her feet. Past the schoolyard, *baby bohunk*, past the fairgrounds, *Bang sploosh*, until she reached the edge of town. The graveyard. She entered and walked until she found a simple wooden cross by a gaping, freshly dug hole. Kneeling by the cross, she traced with her finger:

Taras Zalesky 1896–1949

Taras Zalesky, hanged by the neck until dead for the murder of Marie Barker. She could not believe it. She had to believe it.

June stared into the dark hole that tomorrow would contain her father. Felt as though she was staring into herself, an emptiness there, a darkness, a nameless dread. Years ago he had told her, tapping his chest with her hand, "Who you are is kept safe in here," then tapping her chest, "and here. You cannot get lost if you always look in those two places." But she had buried herself too deep, hidden herself too well. And now he was gone. No way for him to explain himself to her, no way for him to lead her back to herself. She sat down at the edge of the grave, dangled her legs into the abyss.

NEED

I need a mouth as wide as the sky

...language

as large as longing.

Rumi, "The Fragile Vial" trans. Coleman Barks

‹ 1940 ›

Fair Night

MARIE SHIVERS IN HER light dress, but is reluctant to fish in her suitcase for something warmer in case someone drives by and she misses the chance to stick out her thumb. Her feet ache in the open-toed high heels she hasn't worn since Tom bought them for her. Tom, whom she married because he seemed to offer the chance at a new life, only it ended up life here amounted only to different people making the same tired assumptions about who she is. As an infant she'd been dropped off at an orphanage run by nuns in Montréal. A foundling. No note or distinctive piece of clothing to give any clue to her parentage. "I think it's best for you to say you have Italian blood, or maybe Greek," the nicest nun had mentioned when it turned out Marie's skin wasn't going to get any lighter than its olive hue. "People aren't always kind, and the good thing about not knowing who your parents are," said with a bright smile, "is that you can be anyone. It's up to you." But early on, when people called her squaw or half-breed or nigger or kike, when men's eyes flickered over her like the projector in the Eldergrove theatre flickering its images over the blank screen, Marie had realized that the flip side of being anyone was being no one. No solid ground to stand on, no home to retreat to where your wounds could be tended, no people to know you for who you were and pull you close anyway. To be anyone was to be at the mercy of how others saw you. While the white girls were trained for office positions, Marie was told that with her quick mind and good ear for English she would make an excellent domestique. Which had led to her job at the hospital, and to Tom.

When he proposed to her, she saw a way to escape not just the place but the person she was in. She convinced him to say she was from the south of France to account for her skin tone, that she'd escaped at the outset of the war, a poor orphan. It wasn't straying far from the truth, not like the lie she kept for him. She wore her makeup and styled hair like armour, and at first it appeared the nun had been right: people took her for who she claimed to be. And for a while she thought that would be enough. But then a little girl with a funny frown had gazed at her, brown eyes ablaze with devotion. Marie had never encountered such a gaze in her whole life. June, so quiet, hiding not only in the storeroom but inside herself. As lonely and adrift in her way as Marie. Of course she knew the girl didn't see her as she was, was grasping at the twigs of affection Marie offered as though they were oaken branches, but for whole minutes at a time Marie could pretend she was the person June saw; that was when the armour she'd created began to itch, to weigh upon her like an iron hand.

So it was almost a relief when that horrible salesman showed up, blowing apart their lives, practically spitting with resentment not only because he'd been injured by Tom's stupidity, but because once he'd tried to shove his hand up Marie's skirt and got only a smack upside the head for his pains. No matter what the town gossips thought, Tom was the only man Marie had been with, and not until her wedding night. If Tom had only stood up for her, they might have been able to brazen it out, but of course he didn't. The malicious whispers from the town were bad enough, but it was unbearable to see June still faithfully staring up at the landing, and Marie, hiding behind the curtain because she didn't want to see disappointment, or worse, deepen that frown.

Impatiently Marie swipes at the moisture on her cheeks. Today at the fair, shivering on her perch, she looked at June and saw not devotion but rage, and she thought, good, be angry, hate me, feel anything for me but the contempt these people feel, and she put all her will into sending the message with her eyes: leave me, go now. And when June was gone, and once again Tom didn't defend his wife but did his father's bidding and threw the ball at the tank, there was nothing left to hold her. Right then she shrivelled him like a raisin, or a dried flower, till he was nothing but papery dry skin, dry brain, and she could crumple him up and throw him to the bottom of her mind. Right then she was gone.

FROM HER PURSE she pulls out her compact mirror and tube of Patriot Red, applies the lipstick as best she can with only moonlight to aid her, then eases one foot out of a shoe, teeters on the other as she rubs at the blisters on her heel and toes. Both lipstick and shoes are gestures of defiance, the shoes a foolish one, since in order to escape the town's prying eyes she had to walk five miles to the highway junction before daring to hitchhike. She was limping after the first mile. Lighting a cigarette she blows a defiant Damn You smoke ring through pursed lips in the direction of the town. She has never sworn in her life, just as she'd never had a drink, even on her wedding night; this is what they have driven her to. The cool breeze plays with her still-damp hair. After she was finally released from the dunk tank Old Man Barker marched her and Tom back home and ordered them to go to bed, even though it was only nine o'clock, as though they were children.

"I'm sick of the sight of you. Here," he threw a towel at Marie. "Wipe that muck off your face, dry yourself off and then mop up the floor. You're dripping all over it."

"And 'ose fault..."

"Be quiet, Marie!" Tom hissed. "Why don't you go to the beer tent, Dad," he said in his best conciliatory manner. "You know you always..."

"Yes," the old man spat, whipping himself into more heights of rage. "Yes, I did. I may not hold with drinking as a rule," he laughed bitterly in Marie's direction, "but I've always made an exception on fair night. Now you've ruined that for me too. You've made me a laughingstock. I don't know how I'll hold my head up again. All those lies you told. I don't expect any more from a half-breed, but you Tom! How could you?"

Marie laughed. "'ow could he not, you old ogre?"

Tom's hand snaked out and smacked her mouth. "Don't talk to my father like that."

"Don't do me any favours." Old Man Barker stomped off to

his bedroom, Marie and Tom to theirs. Tom put a tentative hand on her shoulder but she shrugged him off with as little thought as if he'd been a fly, wiped the remnants of makeup from her face, climbed into her nightgown and then into bed, her hair still leaking into the pillow. When Tom climbed in beside her she turned her face away, and waited.

Once she heard Old Man Barker's snores and Tom's heavy sleep breathing she slid out of bed and dressed in darkness, eased the suitcase from the top of the bureau. She packed by touch only, not knowing what she would find in the suitcase when she finally got where she was going, wherever that was. Just not here. That's all she knows. She twists the wedding ring on her finger. She did not take any money, knowing they would say she had stolen it, but the ring is hers. Old Man Barker doesn't think so, of course, and keeping it is a delicious slap in his face. She is almost sorry not to see that face when he discovers the loss, wishes he could know she plans to pawn it as soon as she's found a place far, far from here.

Headlights loom on the highway. She sticks out her thumb.

TARAS PUSHES DOWN harder on the accelerator, until his speed almost outstrips the light thrown by his headlights. Not long now to the Eldergrove turnoff. He is a day earlier than he told Olena he'd be. A couple of days ago he overheard her ask Varvara to take the children not just for the evening of the fair, but the whole night, and he knew something was up. The fair would be a perfect cover. All those snooping noses at the barbecue and dance, her husband and children away all night. Well, he will throw a wrench into her plans. Even now he hopes he is wrong, that he will merely surprise her out of sleep alone in their bed, inventory done, papers neatly stacked, sheets and pillows on his side of the bed uncreased. But the pit of his stomach tells him otherwise. She has been too compliant, smiling absently when he tries to start a fight. In the bedroom, not herself at all. From the earliest days of his marriage making love to Olena has been a battle to make her betray herself and surrender to him at least her body. Her rocking beneath him, her breath exploding on his shoulder, the cries dragged from her gave him pleasure deeply twisted with pain. But at least it was something. These last few weeks, even when he has been deep inside her, she has lain still, giving him not one word or cry, unreachable. His worst fears are telling him that by the time he gets home, she will have vanished, her body as well as her soul, which has been gone for some time. The old engine groans its protest as his foot presses even harder, and just as he eases up on the gas he sees a figure, a woman, by the side of the road. She is teetering on high heels, peering into the darkness, a shabby suitcase beside her lit up by his headlights. The orange flame of a deep inhale on her cigarette throws her face into eerie relief. Marie.

He stops the car, rolls down the window as she grinds out her cigarette, then picks her way across the road, the disappointment palpable on her face when she realizes who he is.

"Marie," he says. "Vhat you doing out here at this hour?"

She glances down at her suitcase, no point in lying. "I am leaving."

"But hitchhiking? That is not vise. Vhy not take a bus? A train?" and her lip starts to tremble.

"I have no money, not of my own. I would not give them the satisfaction of saying I am a thief. I cannot wait one more minute. *Non, non, non.*"

"Come," he says. "Get in. Ve sort this out. You tell me vhat is so bad you need to go." He leans across to open the passenger door and when she still hesitates, asks, "How long you been here already vithout a car going by?" Her shoulders slump and she slides into the passenger seat, tucking the suitcase beneath her feet.

"Now you tell me vhat happen." Probably something like an argument with Tom. Nothing that hasn't happened before, nothing that doesn't happen in all marriages. But when she tells him about the salesman, about Old Man Barker's fury at Tom's lies that he has somehow managed to blame on Marie, about the dunk tank, rage and pity rise in him like bile.

"I tell you vhat," he says. "I take you to the store. Ve go the back way, no one vill see you. I give you money for fare, drive you to Norfolk to catch the bus, but this, vhat you doing here, is not the vay."

She turns to him as he starts the car. "You are so kind, Mr. Zalesky." Her hair is a dark cloud, he half expects to see stars come out in it, something stirs deep within him and he reaches to touch that cloud, soft as night. She pulls back, he has startled her he thinks, she has misread his intent, but her eyes widen with a question as she takes his hand, presses it to her cheek, then his palm to her lips, and when he draws her against him, her mouth is as hungry as his, and it is all he can do not to drive right off the road.

JUNE WAKES with a cry that is like swallowing knives. She cannot see and cries out again but realizes it is only that her hair has fallen over her eyes. She has lost her red ribbons, or no, she gave them to the thorny bush but can't remember why. The kitchen is dark, the witch is gone. She must escape before the hag comes back with her evil potions. Sliding from the bed, she shivers, wraps the blanket around her for warmth. There was a little girl here before, wasn't there? She has run off and left June to face the witch alone, or perhaps Baba Yaga has taken her. June's head aches, has swollen to twice its size, and something buzzes incoherently at the back of it. "Take them Baba Yaga, they are yours." The huge black stove is cold and dead. She will have no fire to carry home but surely her father will forgive her. Easing the latch on the door, she prays no creak will betray her, and for once her prayer is answered. She slips out of the witch's house into the night, the poppies that lead away from the house bright red blotches in the moonlight.

The moon throws huge and menacing shadows, but she claws through the cloud of fear and danger and keeps moving, blanket trailing behind her, gravel stinging her bare feet, ears achingly tuned for the whisk of Baba Yaga following in her mortar and pestle, silent, deadly. Wishing she had the guidance of the flaming skull.

MARIE STUMBLES behind Taras as he leads her up the back stairs to the apartment above the store, still smouldering from the powder keg of rage and shame and desire their lips ignited in the car, and if Olena were home, but she isn't home, and the fire has to find someplace to go, so she lets it consume her, burn its way deep into her body, lead her into a pleasure she has never known with Tom, always so afraid of his father hearing them, always stopping her cries with his hand, why not with his tongue as Taras does, his moans fuelling, becoming hers. He holds her face away from his and gazes at her for one still moment. A tear trickles a tortuous wrinkled path from his eye to his cheek, "Olena," he whispers, and she knows what this is, how little it has to do with her, once again she has become the blank space for someone else's desires, but this time she welcomes it. She has seen the raw hunger for his wife in Taras's gaze when Olena doesn't notice him watching, has seen that same hunger when Olena looks at Tonio. Has felt it in the emptiness born of betrayal that yawns between herself and Tom. This lovemaking with Taras is pain meeting pain, and beneath the tumult of their bodies it is suddenly the most tender thing she has ever known.

WAIT, he says, I want to watch you, and marvels at how this old, worn out line, used so many times as to become parody, is suddenly true. He wants to watch his every movement play across her face, ripple through her torso. He wants to hold her so close inside him she will always be part of him, even when their bodies separate, he will hold her within this moment forever. Her lipstick has smudged under the urgency of their kisses. He has never seen anything so beautiful. She bends down to kiss him again, and he tastes the salt taste of her. "Olena," he murmurs and she cries out, shudders against him, eyes wide with surprise, and suddenly she *is* Olena, as young and beautiful as Olena when he first saw her, but something Olena has never been. Open and giving and utterly his.

JUNE CLIMBS the stairs to the landing, shaking violently with cold and heat and fear. Someone is missing, in danger. But who? Her feet are freezing but her head is on fire and she leans her forehead against the door to cool it, hears a woman's voice. Hope flares when she thinks her mother must have decided not to give them away after all. Then she hears her father's voice and is flooded with relief. He will know how to save them from Baba Yaga. June opens the door a crack. Moonlight spills through the parlour window, the same moonlight that has silvered her way home, blurring the worn boards and siding of the town with ominous shadow, but it's colder here, making everything unnaturally white. Her father's legs, which are bare, and a woman's naked back. A woman sitting astride him with black hair that spills over his open shirt like ink and lips that leave a trail of red splotches across his bare chest.

"Oh," she says to him, almost like she is sobbing. "Oh."

June's father's face is stretched like he is in pain, but he doesn't move her off him, instead twines his hand in that coiling black hair to pull her closer while she presses that red mouth onto his, as though she wants to swallow him whole.

June has never seen kisses like these, that seem to be inflicting, and inhaling, pain. Something is wrong. The woman gives a sharp cry, her body arching and her father whispers into that red mouth, his voice breaking, "Olena."

OLENA MOVES silently through the quiet and dark Eldergrove streets, her thighs slick with Tonio's saliva and sperm, her breasts tingling with his lips, teeth, tongue. Their meeting was supposed to have been brief, just long enough to make sure all was on for tonight, but once they darkened the lights and drew the curtains in the restaurant, their plans sparked a passion and lovemaking that should have blown the old wooden structure to smithereens. It is all set. Tonio put his wife on the train a few weeks before with a ticket back to Toronto and a lie that he would join her there as soon as he wrapped up the sale of the hotel. She was pregnant, she told him, clinging to him and crying, as though she knew how unlikely he was to keep his promise and was trying to hold him any way she could. When he told Olena this, she felt fiercely happy: he too would be making a sacrifice to their new life. She will meet him on the highway out of town and they will leave tonight, driving in the opposite direction of the train, headed west to the places he has drawn on her belly. She'll have money from the till, he from the sale. And in the end, she doesn't care how far they go, how long they stay together. She will waltz out the door, she who for years has known only the heavy one-two of the slap in her face, the oompah beat of the universal NO, waltz out of this town and into her lover's arms. She has waited years for this moment, reined in her desire, trampled it down, but never once did she forget it. She has fed it and her bitterness together, like a falcon dropping bits of bloody flesh into the gaping mouths of its young, all the time waiting until she could make good her escape. It is not a complete escape, she leaves behind fifteen years as ransom. The world does not open before her as it did when she was young. But she will find the openings that are still there. She will pour herself into Tonio's mouth, suck him up whole and carry him inside her, his body throbbing inside hers like a heartbeat. He will burrow in her darkest places while she travels a tunnel of forgetfulness and every thrust he makes will ease the fist around her heart, guide her back to the woman she never had the chance to be. Young, childless, eyes taking in an open sky. Any time she feels the slightest waver she touches herself between her legs and shivers herself back into resolve. June and May are with Varvara, Taras on an overnight buying trip. By the time they get home she'll be gone. She rounds the corner to the apartment and stops short. What is the car doing in the alley?

"OLENA," he says with a lonely tenderness that sounds like love. "Yes," she says, "yes" and as she leans into his kiss a liquid fire burns through her wave after wave and there is no town, no Tom, not even herself, everything incinerated but her body and this pleasure and once the waves recede he pulls her to his chest and his wildly beating heart. They lie like that a moment, then he rises from the couch, wraps her tenderly in the afghan throw that has been beneath them all this time, as though she were a child on a cold night. He looks oddly shaken, his face naked and raw, and she hopes he is not regretting what they have done. Olena need never know. As he leaves the room she wants to call after him, reassure him, tell him she needs nothing from him, nothing more than this. He has returned her to herself, a rare and precious gift. It is more than enough. She stretches luxuriously, as far as the sofa allows, her head falling back over the edge.

Into her upside-down vision walks a young girl.

AND NOW the red haze consumes her. The world is bucking beneath her feet as though she is standing in Baba Yaga's hut with the chicken legs pitching it up and down. She cannot catch her breath, get her balance. This is what comes of invoking the witch. "Take them, Baba Yaga, they are yours." The witch is here, not following June down the alley as she'd feared, but here before her, the hideous hag hidden in the beautiful young woman, just as the skull warned she would be, doing unspeakable things to her father, and when she is done, June's father's bones will join the skull's. And June will be left alone. When her father leaves the room, June steps into the wreckage that was once her home.

SITTING ON the edge of the bed Taras touches the bit of moisture still in the corner of his eye and wonders what Marie thinks has just happened. He would like to know himself. After all the women he has bedded this is the first time he has felt shame, and not just for his foolish fantasy that one day Olena would walk through the door to find him deep inside someone who doesn't hold him in contempt. Shame because he has dragged this innocent girl, a girl for whom he feels honest affection, into his folly. Yet for all that, he would not trade the sweetness of those moments with her for a clearer conscience.

He has to get her out of here. It is still dark. There is time for him to drive her to Norfolk, put her on a bus to wherever she wants to go. Hope she will accept whatever money he can scrape up to see her safely there.

The apartment door clicks, footsteps enter the parlour. Shoulders sagging, eyes closed as though to shut out what is happening, he prays that Marie will have dressed and be sitting on the couch ready to pretend nothing has happened. He hears a cry from the living room. "Oh my God, my God." Opens his eyes, straightens his spine and walks out of the bedroom. Nothing for it but to face the consequences of a long list of mistakes.

In the living room Olena stands with hands at her mouth, her purse dropped to the floor, staring at June. (June? his staggered brain thinks.) June, standing in a pool of something dark, holding the knife they use for carving up rabbit and chicken and it glints silver in the moonlight but is dull and dark along one edge. Marie's lips are frozen in an "oh" of surprise. Along her neck, a deep gash, and from it, blood is slowing to a sluggish flow, feeding the pool that licks at June's feet.

"Jesus," he breathes, instinctively searching for one of his peasant mother's useless prayers. "Jesus." June is staring at the upside-down face, her own face white and remote.

Olena inches forward. "Give me the knife now, June." Eyes vacant, June hands the knife to her mother. "Go to your father now, Junie." Olena propels June towards Taras, who blindly holds out his hands to his daughter. As soon as June has turned her back, Olena digs inside her dress, finds a handkerchief and places it on Marie's face, sucking in a tremulous breath. Then she slips from the room and is back in what seems an instant with a bucket of water and some rags, and another nightdress.

"June." Olena kneels in front of her, strips off the blood-spattered nightgown. "Junie, did you tell Aunt Varvara you were coming home?" June turns a stunned face toward her, muttering something that sounds like "Baba Yaga," and Olena slaps repeatedly until June's eyes focus, and she starts to cry. "Not now, Junie. Now you have to tell me, did anyone see you leave Aunt Varvara's?"

June shakes her head no and Olena says, "Good. Now Junie, you listen very carefully. You didn't come home tonight. Do you understand? You were never here. You didn't see anyone because *you were never here*. Tell me, Junie, say it back to me."

All the while Olena is scrubbing hard at June's face and hands and feet, dipping and wringing the rag into the pail beside her.

"I was never here." June's voice a painful croak, her face twisting against the words and the harshness of the rag, eyes fixed on the pink streams of water flowing into the pail.

"Good, now go — back to Aunt Varvara's, and don't let anyone see you." Olena pulls the fresh nightgown over June's head and arms and pushes her out the door.

Taras starts to move with creaking old man's joints. He will never feel his real age again. Only forty-four and his life has come to an abrupt halt. He turns to Olena, but she is wrapping one of the rags around Marie's neck. Was that a glint of bone beneath the red? He gags.

"For God's sake," Olena flips aside his shirt and flicks his shrivelled penis with a contemptuous finger, "put some pants on." He realizes he has been standing naked from the waist down the whole time, and moves his hands helplessly to cover himself. She turns her back on him and drops a rag into the puddle at her feet, then kneels heavily to start mopping.

"Jesus, you are cold, Olena," he starts to say, but stops when he sees how her hands shake as she tries to wring the bloody rag into the bucket.

He kneels in front of her, tries to take her hands. His elbow bumps Marie's dead thigh. It is still pliant and faintly warm, and he is sure that in a moment she will get up off the couch. He gags again. Olena pushes his hands away. "How could you. Of all women, this—child." She whispers, but her voice carries the weight and cut of an axe blade. "And what in God's name were you thinking to bring her here!" The venom in her voice and words thickens until it rattles like phlegm in her throat. She practically chokes when she says, "For God's sake get dressed. I can't stand to look at you."

Knees so weak he has to sit on the bed, he pulls on his pants. By the time he gets back to the living room Olena has drawn herself back into tight control.

"Would anyone know she was here?"

"No." His voice rusty, out of use. "No one. She was hitchhiking, outside of town. Trying to get away."

"Well, she certainly is now. The poor child." Her voice wavers, but she yanks it back. "You're sure no one saw you."

"No. We came in the back way. She snuck out when Tom and Barker were asleep, and their bedrooms face the street, not the alley."

Olena nods. If she and Taras keep quiet, they have a good chance of sneaking out without being seen. And they are quiet as death as they shuffle the body, rolled in the blood-stained afghan and carpet, out the door into the pitch-black night, the moon mercifully behind thick cloud as they roll their gruesome burden into the trunk of the car.

JUNE STAGGERS ALONG the alley, her mother's voice thudding in her brain, Stay in the shadows! The ache in her throat expands into her chest and swallows everything, the street, the houses, all in that red haze. She is no longer Vasilisa but the skull aflame, her world flaring in ashes around her. In the heart of the haze she finally finds Varvara's house, lurches crazily through the gate and up the path, making sudden departures into the flower beds on either side. Varvara will be cross, June thinks, as she pitches forward into the flower bed, crushing the poppies and unable to do more than wonder why she can't find her feet, can't even feel them, though for a while their coldness was a pleasant contrast to the throbbing fever of her upper body. Varvara materializes out of the haze, miraculously not cross at all, but murmuring with an odd gentleness. She leads June to her own still-warm bed, glances sharply at her feet, then fetches a pot of water from the stove's reservoir and silently and thoroughly bathes them, rubbing them to painful life so that now they burn too and June becomes a huge red fireball, then just as suddenly a clump of ice.

Varvara holds her through the rest of the long night, while the fever makes her cry and moan so violently Varvara can barely keep the blankets around her.

The next morning Varvara moves June into the kitchen bed, and orders May to keep an eye on her until Varvara's return. She is back in a short while, grim faced, to rummage through her chest of herbs, selecting several with large pinches of her twisted hands, grinding them to powder in her ancient mortar and pestle, then mixing them with warm water.

"This will make you sleep," she says, forcing a spoonful of it between June's chattering teeth.

And it does. For days, but not a kind of sleep June has ever known. Inside her slumbering body her mind and her mouth are running from terror to terror, and she can hear herself as though from a great distance, now whimpering, now shrieking as she tries to save herself from the claw-like hands of Baba Yaga whose slit throat yawns open and pulls her toward its pulsing centre. Through it all either Varvara or Olena stays by her, stroking her forehead, holding her down when she starts up screaming, murmuring to her helplessly but constantly, "It's just a dream, little one, only a dream."

Eventually the dream leaves her and Baba Yaga becomes Varvara, but a Varvara whose crooked hands, when June clutches them, anchor her and bring her back to the reality of a bed and a fire in the wood stove and eventually a soft-boiled egg that May feeds to her by the spoonful.

COUNTLESS DAYS Olena and Taras wait for an officer who never arrives. Too afraid of what June might say in her delirium to send for a doctor, Olena prays for the first time since her marriage, and could swear her atheist husband is praying too: that Varvara's skills will be adequate to the task of keeping their daughter alive, and burying any memory of what she's done. The rumour that Frenchie and the Eyetie have run off together is a godsend for her daughter and Olena does what she can to fan the flames, steeling her heart against her own loss.

"Good riddance to both of them," Mrs. Logan says to Mrs. McTeer, whispering just loudly enough that Olena can hear, while Mrs. Logan can pretend she can't. "What can you expect? Eyeties and half-breeds. No more morals between them than a cat. But I must say," her voice rising infinitesimally, "I did think his attentions were directed another way."

Mrs. McTeer titters, "Yes. She seems to be bearing it very stoically though."

Olena wraps another band of iron around her heart. Let them gloat.

WHEN VARVARA finally takes June home the world is still off-kilter. Olena bends down to brush June's hair from her eyes, plants a tender kiss on her forehead. Taras, looking older and greyer, holds Varvara's hand briefly in both his own. June blinks in astonishment, but when her father takes her in his arms, they are as strong and warm as ever, and her body unclenches.

THE FIRST DAY Olena feels June is well enough to be left on her own, she walks to the butte that rises suddenly from the flat land all around. As she climbs, bushes snag at her sleeve, slap at her scissoring legs. The way is steep, her breathing laboured, the dust she raises chokes her, but there is no way around that. When she reaches the top, she pulls out of her pocket the stone she and Tonio passed between their mouths that day on the butte, when for the first time she knew the joy of emptiness to be filled, thirst to be slaked, the stone so tight in her fist she'd thought surely she would crush it to powder. Now she turns it over in her hand and weeps herself empty. Weeps for Tonio, perhaps waiting for her in Calgary at the hotel he told her about, hoping she has only been delayed; more likely angry at what he imagines is her betrayal, already returning to Toronto to the wife he packed off thinking never to see again. Weeps for June, feverish and raving for days, and thank goodness for that if it means she will never have to know what she did, and to whom. Weeps above all for Marie, the poor child who wanted only to escape, who like Olena wanted simply to get out and away, and paid for that transgression with her life. Perhaps if Olena had been braver, more generous, she could have found a way to help. But those are vain wishes now. What did June's fairy tale book often say? "In the days when wishing helped." Long ago indeed. Even though she doesn't believe it is possible she makes a kind of bargain with Marie: my life for yours. Keep my child safe and I will do anything. And just when she thinks there are no tears left, she weeps for having glimpsed so briefly another life, only to have it snatched from her, and to be driven from those heights to the flatland of a marriage made even more intolerable. Made imperative if they are to keep June's secret. Yet perhaps she was wrong about her ability to sever all those ties to her children. In the worst of her fever, June grabbed Olena's hand and pleaded, "Don't give us away, promise me. Promise you won't leave." Olena, swept by a tenderness so powerful it drove her to her knees by the bed, clasped June's head between her palms and cradled it to her breast, kissing the fever-matted hair and saying, "I will never leave. Never." And meant it with every fibre of the same body that had been so sure it could abandon everything for Tonio. When June has one of her frequent nightmares, waking to find herself in the darkened living room or even in the alley, Olena fetches her, takes her back to bed, and sits by her for as long as it takes to coax her back to sleep.

AFTERMATH

Sleep; and if life was bitter to thee, pardon,

If sweet, give thanks; thou hast no more to live;

And to give thanks is good, and to forgive.

Algernon Charles Swinburne, "Ave Atque Vale"

‹1949›

THE IRON DOOR clanged behind Olena and she hesitated in the doorway, adjusting her eyes. All was shrouded in gloom, the concrete walls painted grey, a few dust motes struggling in feeble rays from a small window carved into the wall, rays that could barely reach the narrow metal bed with its rough, grey wool blankets, its tenant clad in grey stripes. Taras rose to his feet, eyes bleary, grey face gaunt and raw.

"You came," he said. "I didn't think you would."

Olena lifted the tea towel off the wooden box she was carrying, placed it and then the box on the little table by the prison cot, and began removing dishes. "They told me I could bring your last meal. I have a small kitchen at the motel."

"Olena." Voice cracking, he grasped her wrist as she laid down on the small metal table a plate of perogies, redolent of butter and browned onion, scattered with dark brown nuggets of fried salt pork. A bowl of borscht heady with dill and lemon juice. Another of freshly baked bread. A slab of honey cake. "I am so sorry."

She took his hands in both her own and spoke in a tone so gentle he barely recognized it as hers. "Sorry? Why? This is . . . I am so grateful . . . what you are doing for June . . . God forgive me, when she went to that San I almost wished her to die there so she need never know . . ." Her voice sank into silence.

"Not sorry for this." He raised her hands, her willing hands, to his lips. "For all of it *but* this."

She released herself from his hold, but gently still, and busied herself with setting out cutlery. "Too late for that. Whatever we did, we did together, and it is good June will not pay for it. Here. Eat while it still has heat."

He pulled up the rickety metal chair, leaned in to smell the last good smells of home.

"Still, I am sorry not to be able to see her. What will she think, why we never visited, barely wrote? I would like her to know . . ."

"No. We agreed. We could not risk her remembering. Any of it. And we were right. You don't need to worry. I will keep her safe. I will do my best to give her a life. Perhaps send her to school in Saskatoon when she is well enough. It will be best if she doesn't come back to Eldergrove."

"And May?"

Olena winced. "She phoned me at the motel to say she is leaving. Going to Toronto, getting married to Albert McGrath. It is for the best, for her to get away." Out and away, May had said, and Olena had been pierced by the memory of her long walks as a girl not that much younger than May. Out and away was what she'd wanted, had thought she'd found with Antonio. She shook herself into the present moment. Let May have her chance, and at least this man was her choice. Pray God history won't repeat itself. Hardly something she could say to Taras now. "At least it's not that Mitch Logan."

Taras nodded, lifted a piece of bread to his lips, put it back on the plate, eyes lowered. "Will you be there tomorrow?"

"If you wish it. Now eat."

THE NEXT DAY he stood on the scaffold, refusing the blindfold offered, scanning the small group of spectators until he found her eyes. And they held him until the plank banged beneath him.

EPILOGUE

> You can live in that hunger as home.
> *Dennis Lee, "Poetry and Unknowing"*

A STOCKY WOMAN with greying hair and iron will signs the form at the morgue that allows her to claim your bones, staring down the man who tells her they can be placed for free in a pauper's grave; why go to all this trouble and expense, especially for someone who is not a blood relative? But she will not have you placed in the ground; you have spent enough time there. When she fills out the forms for the funeral home, she gives only the name Marie, not knowing your maiden name and refusing to surrender you even in this small detail to the Barkers. Nor will she surrender you to Eldergrove.

At the funeral home in Norfolk, she places a hand on the cardboard coffin that holds you. The mortician tells her that he has done as she requested, taken the jumble of bones in the box sent by the morgue — femur jutting against clavicle, fibula sprouting skeletal fingers, pelvis impaled on an ulna, skull nestled in a triangle of ribs — and arranged you in your proper order. Beyond you yawns a huge oven, waves of heat lick hungrily at your coffin's walls. The woman nods. She has said her goodbyes. One great shove and you are engulfed in flames, a conflagration so hot it feeds even on fleshless bones. There is an old tale of bones singing the true story of their death, but yours do not sing so much as sigh one last gust of release as the metal door bangs on the crematory and the fire claims you for its own. The stocky woman watches to the end. Until the last of your crumbled remains have cooled and been pounded to ash and placed in a simple urn. Then she takes you to the car where a gaunt young woman is waiting, weeping silently. Together they drive along a gravel road until there are no signs of civilization, no outbuildings, houses, nothing for miles but prairie sky and open air, and there, they release you to the wind.

ACKNOWLEDGEMENTS

Excerpts from Taras Shevchenko, "Testament," and "I Am Not Unwell," translated by John Wier, and "The Maiden's Nights," translated by C.H. Andrusyshen and Watson Kirkconnell. In *Kobzar: Poetry of Taras Shevchenko in Ukrainian, English and French*. Toronto: Taras Shevchenko Museum, 2014. Introduction by Andrew Gregorovich. Reprinted by permission.

Excerpt from "Poetry and Unknowing" by Dennis Lee, from *Poetry and Knowing*. Kingston: Quarry Press, 1995. Ed. Tim Lilburn. Reprinted by permission.

Excerpt from "At the Justice Department, November 15, 1969" By Denise Levertov, from POEMS 1968–1972, copyright © by Denise Levertov. Reprinted by permission of New Directions Publishing Corp.

Excerpt from "Ode to Salt" from *Selected Odes of Pablo Neruda* by Pablo Neruda. Berkeley: University of California Press, 2011. Translated by Margaret Sayers Peden. Reprinted by permission.

Excerpt from "22" from IF NOT, WINTER: FRAGMENTS OF SAPPHO by Sappho, translated by Anne Carson, copyright © 2002 by Anne Carson. Used by permission of Alfred A. Knopf, an imprint of the Knopf Doubleday Publishing Group, a division of Penguin Random House LLC. All rights reserved.

Excerpt from "Ave Atque Vale: In Memory of Charles Baudelaire" by Algernon Charles Swinburne. In *Victorian Poetry and Poetics*, 2nd Edition. Eds. Walter E. Houghton and G. Robert Stange. Boston: Houghton Mifflin Company, 1968.

Ezekiel 18:2 King James Version Bible.

Excerpts from "Where Are We?" and "The Fragile Vial" from *The Essential Rumi: New Expanded Edition: Translations by Coleman Barks*. San Francisco: HarperSanFrancisco, 2004. Used by permission.

NOTES

Although Baba Yaga and Vasilisa are usually assumed to belong to Russian folklore, one of my early introductions to Baba Yaga was in "St. John's Eve," by Nikolai Gogol, a story told to him by his Ukrainian mother. It is hard to pin down folk tales that began as early as the 1700s to any one nation, so I have done what many of the early tellers did, which is to take a story and make it my own, for my own purposes.

I am a fiction writer, not an historian. For anyone wanting an excellent examination of Ukrainian history, I cannot recommend too highly Orest Subtelny's *Ukraine: A History*, 2nd ed. Toronto: University of Toronto Press in association with the Canadian Institute of Ukrainian Studies, 1994.

THANK YOU

My sincere thanks to Deborah Willis. I couldn't have asked for a better editor and advocate for the book. Thanks also to Kelsey Attard for all other matters and her unfailing good humour when dealing with them. I am so lucky to have been able to work with two people for whom I feel not only great respect, but also deep affection. Thanks to Freehand for believing in the book and to Natalie Olsen of Kisscut Design for the stunning cover.

D.M. Thomas, Edna Alford, and Janice Kulyk Keefer gave early and invaluable encouragement. It saddens me beyond expressing that two writers who were so generous with support, Robert Kroetsch and Alistair MacLeod, cannot see that I did indeed finish this book, or know how much their words meant to me.

Jane Baird Warren and Susan Ouriou were generous and judicious readers from the beginning, never refusing to look at 'just one more draft.' Rosemary Nixon showed me how it all could hang together when I had given up hope it ever could. Betty Hersberger and Marty Sherman were outstanding readers when I was at a low ebb. The Bitchin' Banff Babes offered wine, lunches, lively discussion, and laughter when most needed. Everyone should be so lucky as to have friends like these in their corner.

Thanks to Tom Erdman for details of surveying. To Brenda and Tony Rustemeier for overcoming their reticence to give many of the details about killing a rabbit. To Gord Masiuk for his help with the Ukrainian accents. Barb Clarke did me the enormous favour of reading the manuscript when I needed fresh eyes and had run out of friends who hadn't read at least some version of this book. Carolynn Hoy gave the wondrous gift of many visits to Willowbend, where I tussled with so many of the early drafts.

Thanks to the Canada Council for the Arts and the Alberta Foundation for the Arts. Thanks also to the many fine artist retreats and programs in my part of the country: the Banff Centre and Leighton Studios, the Sage Hill Writing Experience, and the Markin-Flanagan Distinguished Writers Program (now called the Calgary Distinguished Writers Program). And at the other end of the country: Blueroof Farm. My chortling thanks to Kim Ondaatje for the incredible opportunity of working on a novel that begins in a chicken coop *in* an actual chicken coop.

Above all, gratitude and love to Keith: words fail.

BARBARA JOAN SCOTT's first book, *The Quick,* won the City of Calgary W.O. Mitchell Book Prize and the Howard O'Hagan Award for Best Collection of Short Fiction, and was shortlisted for the Henry Kreisel Award for Best First Book. In 2015 she received the Lois Hole Award for Editorial Excellence. *The Taste of Hunger* is her debut novel. She lives in Calgary.